LINKED IN HISTORY

NIGHTWOOD CLAN SERIES, BOOK 5

HARPER DAKOTA

Cover Design by: Jay Aheer

Editing by: Lori Parks

Warning:

This book contains mature themes and is intended to be read by ages 18+. Contains sex, some curse words, paranormal and magical themes, fated mates, and some secondary characters are a male/male couple.

Trademark Acknowledgements:

The author acknowledges the following trademarks and trademark status of these items mentioned in the book, including:

Library Lion by Michelle Knudsen

The Absent-minded Professor

Happy Camper

ZiplockCorn Palace

Zephyr by Riverside Casino

Yeti

Corelle

DawnPayDay

Calgon

X-Chock

Custer State Park

Amazon

Wall Drug

Mount Rushmore

Yellowstone National Park

Deadpool

weBoost

Thank you to my husband; you've always believed in and encouraged me. You are the best husband and friend I could ask for.

Thank you to my kids. While I hope you never read my books because you reading steamy scenes I wrote would be awkward, thank you for your patience for every time I've called out "you can't come in here, I'm writing something you can't see".

I love you all.

LINKED IN HISTORY

Merri loves her job as a librarian in her hometown but, lately, her magic has been restless, pushing her to leave. Uncertain what is causing it, she takes a leap of faith and visits her sister in Rockfort. When she's given a mating dream about a man with brunet hair with a white streak, she recognizes what was pulling her to the town.

Gawain, a peregrine falcon shifter, is an archeologist specializing in paranormal history. He finds joy in discovering lost things and helping preserve the past. A friend's call for help leads him to Rockfort, where he discovers information about shifters believed extinct.

As Merri and Gawain set off on an adventure to find the long-lost shifter settlement, will they unearth a world-changing discovery? Or will digging for the truth put their lives at risk?

PRE-NOTE FROM THE AUTHOR

Thank you for choosing my book to read! I hope you enjoy it.

If this is your first time reading one of my books, or it has been a while in between reads, here are some helpful things so you don't feel lost.

There is a character list in the back of the book.

Mates and members of the Clan can speak telepathically to each other. This type of communication is indicated with a single apostrophe and the words are in italics.
Example: *'I can't wait to see you,'* Gawain said.

Text messages are indicated with a name in capital letters and are in bold with a colon.
Example:
MERRI: I'll be there soon.
GAWAIN: Drive safely.

Nightwood Clan members and their respective mates:

- Rolf - Shaye
- Sam - Tess
- Doc (Albert) – Emma
- Ian - Berkley
- Gawain - Merri (Meredith)

PROLOGUE

Gawain grabbed another scroll, trying to find something he knew he had seen just a few minutes ago. He had scrolls and papers strewn about his room. Rolf had even brought in an extra desk for him to have more space to lay everything out. He had use of the library too, but he rather liked his room. The large window provided a lot of natural light that his bird side was happy to have. To think that just a couple of months ago he was combing through some dusty old bookstores and living out of his RV. He and Betsy, his Airstream, had been through a lot of adventures together and she had been his home for many years. He had never settled in one place, always moving to a new job site, scouting out potential digs, or finding research in random places.

It was crazy how much his friendship with Rolf had recently changed his trajectory and brought new people into his life. He had been friends with Rolf for… well, he couldn't remember exactly when they met, but it was at least sixty-five years ago. Rolf had already been friends with Sam and Berkley, but they had welcomed him in. Rolf had owned the land here and had been in the process of building onto it. Sam, Berkley, and Rolf all chose to live there permanently, although they left to travel, sometimes for months or years. At least one of them usually stayed back to keep an eye on things. Gawain had stopped in over the years to catch up, making an effort to come and celebrate the big things like when Sam first opened the brewery and when Berkley opened his pottery shop.

He had been ecstatic for his friend when he got a call from Rolf saying he had met his mate. Gawain had been introduced to her over a video call, and she seemed perfect for his friend. Shaye had been human when she and Rolf met. It wasn't exactly a meet-cute story, as she had found him being tortured by Vlad, his father. Vlad had run off when Shaye arrived, although Gawain wasn't entirely sure why, since a human wasn't really much of a physical threat to him. Shaye had used her healing gift on Rolf, saving his life. She had had no clue paranormals had even existed until that day. When Vlad tried to kill Rolf a second time, Rolf sent out a call to his friends to help make a stand against his father. Vlad had been evil; convinced vampires were superior, he often killed others in his path to grab more power. Sometimes he killed just because they were a different species. Gawain had been happy to come help, wanting to help make it safer for his friends, not to mention everyone else.

When he arrived, he had met all sorts of new people. People that made him feel welcomed and like part of their found family. First, he had met Tess, Shaye's witch friend and who also ended up being Sam's mate. Shaye had called her friend Ian, who apparently had been a vampire the entire time she had known him, although she hadn't known that until about a month before the battle. Ian was a kickass blacksmith and leathersmith and had brought some gear and weapons with him when he arrived. He had turned out to be Berkley's mate. Gawain was thrilled the Fae finally found his mate. They suited each other so well.

He was also able to finally meet Emma, Rolf's mom, in

person. Rolf had always called her fairly frequently, and if Gawain was in town visiting, Rolf would include him in on the calls. She was just as charming and sweet as she had been over the phone. She had met her mate in Doc. Gawain didn't know him very well, but he seemed nice. He was the town's doctor and a shifter of some sort. He and Emma were taking their mating slow, letting Emma grow to trust him and be comfortable around him.

After they had defeated Vlad, Rolf had offered for them all to stay at his house and Gawain had taken him up on it, eager to keep the feeling of being part of a family.

He shook his head, focusing back on hunting down that darn paper. He wasn't sure why he felt this driving need to research unicorns at the moment, but normally when he was this fixated on something it ended up being important. He had a feeling that when this journey was over, he would find something huge.

There was a knock on his door.

"Come in," he shouted.

"Hey, Gawain," Tess said, poking her head in. "Just wanted to remind you that everyone is here for dinner tonight. We're doing a make-your-own-pizza night."

"Sounds good. I'll be there," he said absently, still flipping through his desk. Aha! Found it! He didn't look back up even as he heard the door shut. It wasn't until his stomach grumbled loud enough to startle him, that he realized just how late it had gotten. He grabbed his tablet, wanting to finish writing a few last notes, but not wanting to be even later. If he was lucky, he might still be able to catch the end of dinner.

"Sorry, sorry. I got caught up. There was this really interesting rumor that I'm hunting down about a unicorn tribe. There is a claim that they settled in Montana. Did I miss dinner?" he asked, still looking down at his tablet.

"We went ahead and made your pizza so it would be ready," Tess said. "Gawain have you met my sister?"

Gawain racked his brain, trying to remember if he had met anyone new recently. "Um, I don't think so?" he said with a slight question in his voice. Hopefully not, he would hate to be rude to Tess's family. He looked up as he heard footsteps, his nostrils flaring as he caught the scent of his mate. He vaguely registered that Tess was introducing them, but he was caught in the beautiful hazel eyes of his mate. She had a family resemblance to Tess, although she was a little taller. Her blond hair was longer, hitting between her shoulder blades, with a slight wave to it. She was slightly curvy, with an adorable button nose. She was beautiful.

Merri stood there, struck speechless it would seem. The man in front of her was her mate, there was no mistaking the brown hair with the white stripe through it. She had seen him in her dreams just the day before. His eyes were kind, a striking amber color. His hair was on the shaggy side, a little unkempt looking as if he had been running his fingers through it. He was taller than she was, probably about five foot eleven inches or so. He had some very lean muscle, but overall was rather on the thin side. His face was handsome with a sharp nose and a little scruff. He was staring at her rather intently as his nostrils flared, taking in her scent. She had not been expecting this when she volunteered to help her sister bring Sam, her injured mate home.

Her sister Tess spoke up. "Merri, this is Gawain. He is our resident historian slash archeologist. Gawain, this is my sister Merri. She is a librarian and excels at research."

"Mate? Are you okay?" Gawain asked, concerned. He didn't think she had blinked once since they saw each other. He put his tablet down in case she needed him.

Tess rolled her eyes and gave her sister a tiny shove. "She can be a little shy. Why don't you grab your pizza and show her what you have been working on?" Tess suggested to Gawain, knowing that would help break the ice.

When he walked into the kitchen to grab his food, Tess looked at Merri. "Hello? What was that? Wasn't that the person you dreamed of?" Tess asked to clarify, a little confused. She had literally jumped on her mate Sam the moment she had met him.

"He is so handsome!" Merri whispered. "Why would he want me as his mate?"

"Are you saying I'm ugly?" Tess shot back, amused.

"What? No, of course not," Merri responded, confused. Who had told Tess she was ugly? She would yell...smack... okay send them a strongly worded letter or email. Her sister was beautiful.

"We look a lot alike. So, if you think I am cute, pretty, or even only acceptable looking, then so are you. You are beautiful, sister. Why wouldn't he want someone as nice as you?" Tess asked gently.

"Merri, I grabbed you a glass of wine," Gawain said, handing Merri a glass as he came back in the room. "Would you like to see what I've been working on? I'm trying to track down this legend of a unicorn tribe. I just found a rumor that they were seen in the Montana area in the 1000s, AD of course. The Vikings came to North America around 1020 AD, and I found one reference to unicorns. I'm not sure if it's the same type of unicorn though."

"There are different types of unicorns?" Merri asked incredulously.

"Well, no," Gawain admitted. "But the Vikings used to sell narwhal horns to the Europeans, claiming they were unicorn horns. They sold for quite a lot too; Queen Elizabeth paid ten thousand pounds for one. King Frederick III of Denmark made a coronation throne out of narwhal horns. So right now, my problem is trying to figure out if there were real unicorns in North America, or if it's just a note from a long-ago prank or a well-run con. Montana is a long way from the ocean, so I am trying to find any corroborating evidence that might point me to an actual tribe of unicorns existing," Gawain explained as he grabbed his tablet and led them to the dining room.

Merri looked through his research notes as he ate his pizza. This was fascinating. She had always assumed that unicorns had either long since died out or were an actual myth in both paranormal and human legends. To think that they could be real was amazing. She had felt a little intimidated when she had met her mate, knowing that as an archeologist he had probably traveled all over the world, and she hadn't even traveled to much of the United States. However, this was something she could help and connect to him with. She loved research and had quite a knack for it. She couldn't wait to help him on his journey.

Tess stood up and Sam gave an exaggerated yawn. "I think we're going to head to bed," Sam said, giving them a wink.

Ian laughed but pulled Berkley off the couch. "We're off to bed as weel."

Shaye gave her a smile and followed Rolf up the stairs.

"Night," Emma said softly, Doc chuckling as he followed her out.

"That's not awkward at all," Gawain said dryly.

Merri laughed, but she had to agree. At least their family was supportive and happy for them, she thought.

"I'll leave it up to you, mate," Gawain said. "I'm happy to wait until you're comfortable, or I'd love to escort you upstairs. Either way, I'm happy."

Merri took a good look at her mate, his amber eyes sincere, his handsome face looking down at her. Tess had told her about how she had leapt into Sam's arms when they first met. Merri decided to take a play from her sister's book and be daring. Standing on her tiptoes, she pressed a kiss to his lips. "Take me upstairs, mate."

She let out a small scream as he scooped her over his shoulder and ran up the stairs. Merri gripped the waistband of his pants, holding on tightly. He opened the bedroom door, kicking it shut behind him. Walking to the bed, he gently laid her down on the rumpled covers. Gawain looked at her, a question in his eyes as he touched the front of her shirt.

"Yes, mate. Touch me. Make me yours," Merri said. She reached up and pulled his shirt up, slowly revealing his body. He was lean, but he had defined muscles, a nice V at his hips. He didn't have a lot of hair, though there was a faint happy trail leading into his pants. Pulling the shirt all the way off, she took in the defined abs and pecs, his biceps.

"You're gorgeous," she said as she ran her hands over his chest.

Gawain slowly unbuttoned her shirt, revealing her black lacy bra. She was glad she had worn her pretty underwear today. This particular bra was even a frontal clasp. She had the matching panties on, and she loved hearing his breath catch as he pulled her pants down. Gawain eased her clothes all the way off her legs, tossing them somewhere behind him. He gently ran a finger along her cheekbone, down her neck, over the swell of her breasts, past her stomach, to gently rest on top of her mons. He gripped her thighs, easing them open, his face coming down to nose her mons through the fabric. Her breath sped up, her heart beating faster as he hooked a thumb through either side of her underwear and slid them off. Gawain took a deep breath, scenting her, before his tongue came out to lick her seam, his fingers spreading her lips. She moaned as his tongue gently applied pressure to her clit, rubbing it. She loved feeling the rasp of his tongue, he played with her clit, his tongue swirling all around, finding different pressures and motions to make her squirm.

"That, just like that," Merri demanded as his tongue hit the perfect spot. Oh god, she wanted to come so desperately, her body hot. Merri's hands flew toward his head, grabbing his hair as he licked and nibbled.

"Up, here, please," Merri pleaded. "I want to come with you inside me."

Gawain stood back, shucking his pants and underwear off. He loved watching her eyes widen, her pupils blowing wide as she looked at his dick. He thought it was a decent penis, he was cut, a good six inches, but he was wide. He leaned down, kissing his mate deeply, their tongues twirling together. Gawain reached down, gently sliding a finger into her body, slowly thrusting a few times before adding a second finger. He wanted to stretch her opening, not wanting to cause her any discomfort later.

"Do you know how bird shifters mate?" Gawain asked, his hand moving to cup her breast, his thumb flicking against her nipple.

"N-no," she gasped, her back arching as he bent to gently bite it.

"During sex, we exchange the vow, and then at climax, I mark you. I change one of my fingers into a talon and I'll mark you right where your shoulder meets your neck and collarbone area."

"I just need to say the vows," Merri said as she pulled him closer, wrapping her legs around his waist.

Gawain gave her a kiss before kissing his way back down her body, each nipple getting a lick, the top of her mons, her clit, and then he finally plunged his tongue into her entrance, lapping at her juices. One finger rested on her clit, slowly rubbing, barely touching it. It was so good, but it wasn't enough.

"I need you. Now. We can go slower later," Merri demanded, desperate to feel his body inside her.

Gawain stood, climbing up the bed to cover her body. She spread her legs, making room for him, his arms on either side of her, his hard length stretching toward her body, precum dripping from the tip. Merri's breath caught as he started to ease into her. She could feel his hot hard length stretching her, almost to the point of pain but it never crossed that line. He waited a moment, letting her adjust to him, bending down to kiss her. She tangled her fingers in his hair, playing with the white stripe in the front. Merri loved the stripe, it was so different. She wrapped her legs around him, her feet resting on the small of his back, pulling him in.

Gawain's hips started moving, slow small thrusts at first. When he saw she wasn't in pain, he sped up, his cock sliding along her channel. She could feel him everywhere, he was resting down on his elbows, his breath brushing her face, his lips touching hers. She could smell his scent, see the passion and lust in his eyes. Those gorgeous eyes watched her, and he smiled down at her.

"You feel amazing," he breathed out.

"So do you," Merri gasped, as she tilted her hips and his cock hit her G-spot.

"There," she panted. "I'm almost there."

Gawain leaned back, moving to sit on his heels, pulling her body with him, so she now rested with her hips tilted up, his hands holding her in place, his own hips pounding into her. She let out a small scream as he pulled almost all the way out and thrust in hard hitting all the nerve endings perfectly.

'I take you, Gawain, as my Mate. To love and cherish forevermore,' Merri said telepathically.

'I take you, Merri, as my Mate. To love and cherish forevermore,' Gawain said, letting go of her hips. He pressed down on her clit with one hand, feeling her inner muscles begin to tighten, her wet heat grasping him even tighter as she cried out in her orgasm. Gawain quickly changed a finger into his bird's talon and slashed a mark in her skin. As he saw the blood weep from the cut, he felt the mate connection form, connecting them for all time as his climax barreled through him. He wanted to stay buried in his mate forever.

Merri pulled him close, taking a kiss from him.

'Mm, that was amazing,' Merri told him, trying out their new telepathic link.

'It was, thank you, mate,' he said, kissing her on the forehead. *'Let me get a bandage for that. I'll be right back.'* Gawain hurried to the bathroom, grabbing a bandage and a wet cloth to clean her up. Merri smiled drowsily at him as he took care of her, rolling over to be the little spoon as he climbed in bed. Gawain pulled the covers up, snuggling against his mate as they both fell asleep.

Merri looked in the mirror. She took in the blonde hair, a little longer than shoulder length, with a slight wave to it but not enough to be considered curly. Her hazel eyes were tired, but happy. To be fair, she hadn't gotten a lot of sleep last night. She pulled her shirt collar to the side, looking at the still healing claw mark. It was both something that made her wince as her clothes brushed against it and made her smile as she thought of her mating last night. Today though she wished she had the faster healing of a shifter. Of course, she loved being a witch but in cases like this, the increased healing would be helpful. She put on the salve that Tess had given her and covered it with a gauze pad.

Walking out of their bedroom, she saw Shaye waiting for her.

"Hey, Merri. I, uh, well, now that you're mated to Gawain, I can sense how you're feeling. Not all the time, just when it's strong," Shaye rushed to reassure her. "I think you must have been cleaning the mating mark or jarred it, because I felt it cause you some pain. Would it be okay if I healed it?" Shaye asked, a little nervously. She didn't know Merri very well and didn't want to seem like she was intruding. Merri had always been so quiet when they had met before.

"I would appreciate that, truly. It's just in such an awkward spot, the shirt keeps rubbing against it, even with the gauze covering it."

Shaye came over and held a hand over the wound. Merri felt a bit of warmth flow through her, a calming sensation following soon after.

"There, that should do it," Shaye said. "Do you mind if I ask you a question?"

Merri shook her head. "No, of course not."

"Why didn't you heal right away? I know I did from Rolf because vampires can lick the bites and their saliva heals it. Tess stayed at the brewery for a couple of days, and it was healed by the time she came back to the main house, so I'm not sure how long hers took to heal."

Merri wasn't sure how much Shaye knew about paranormal matings and decided to explain it like she didn't know anything. "Humans can choose to not form a mate bond and live as a human, or form a mate bond and get the longer lifespan, or turn/change into whatever their paranormal mate's species is. Normally that's done by a bite. Interspecies paranormal matings work a little differently. We cannot change our species like a human can. However, once mated, the lifespan will match whichever species has the longest. If we were both witches, not much would change. Since Gawain is a falcon shifter, my lifespan went from about two hundred years to a thousand. We get a mate bond and the telepathic link, but witches don't inherit any other traits from our mates," Merri tried to explain.

"So other than living longer, you're still essentially a witch. You don't have any of the increased sight or healing," Shaye said.

"Right. Tess gave me a healing salve, so it probably would have been healed up in the next day or two. That's what she would have used when she mated with Sam. Werewolves don't have the same healing properties in their saliva that vampires do. But I am very relieved not to have that rubbing anymore," Merri said, peeling off the gauze pad. She took out her phone and put it in selfie mode, using it to look at the now-healed mark.

"Oh! It's not a bite mark," Shaye exclaimed. Her face turned red. "Sorry! That was inappropriate. I'm just going to shut up now. Do you know if there's a reference book on paranormals? I keep telling Rolf that he forgets just how much there is to learn. He tries to tell me things, but he doesn't realize how much he takes for granted, things he's 'always' known. I'd love to not stick my foot in it," she muttered.

Merri laughed. "It's fine. It's a claw mark; bird shifters partially shift to form a mate mark. Only a finger or two turns into their bird's talon, so it's not a large shift but it's still weird to see.

"I can't imagine having to learn everything from scratch. You were human not that long ago, right?"

"A little over a month, I think," Shaye admitted. "It was the very beginning of November, so yeah, almost a month and a half."

"I don't think there's anything like an official paranormal handbook. It's a lot to learn, and it's going to be easier and faster if you ask us questions. We're a safe space," Merri told her. "There are still things I'm learning along the way as well. I have a notebook where I write down new things. Maybe you can start your own?" Merri suggested.

"That's a good idea," Shaye replied. She had a book in her room that she had been saving for something. This was as good as anything else to use it for. She could make a page or so per species and add to it as she went. Maybe have species, any weaknesses or strengths, lifespan, mate marks and how they knew their mate. It could be really helpful, especially if they ever got another human in the Clan. "Thank you for not getting upset with me putting my nose where it doesn't belong," Shaye said, giving Merri a quick hug before running off to her room.

Merri smiled after her. She thought they could be good friends. Shaye was quieter and they both loved books. This was a good house to live in, with a good group of people. They had welcomed her even before she had met Gawain and realized they were mates. It was an interesting mix of people. There was Rolf, the vampire who owned the house and did quite well with investments, and Shaye, his mate who was a nurse. Tess, Merri's sister, was a witch and a nurse, her mate Sam was a werewolf and the Black Wolf Brewery owner. Ian, another vampire and one who Merri knew at least through the stories Tess told about their friendship, was mated to Berkley, a Fae who owned a pottery store in town. Emma, who was a vampire, and Doc, her shifter mate who was also the town's doctor.

She could see herself really feeling at home here. Tess had taken her to explore the town and there was pretty much everything she could want. If there wasn't, there were other larger cities not too far away, and of course two-day online shopping. The town contained a city park, had a delicious bakery, a bookstore with a café, a library to drool over, a large outdoor market area, and was butted up to the National Park. Then there were the daily conveniences like Doc's clinic, the mechanic's shop, town hall, sheriff's office, grocery store, a fire department, and the hospital. She had already met Marge, the town librarian, and had been offered a job. Everything was lining up and falling into place. Now she just had to tell her mother.

1

G awain and Doc were holed up in the house's library, the documents that Ian and Berkley brought home spread out over the old mahogany table. It was a good thing the table was large enough to seat the whole family, as the documents took up a major portion of the tabletop. They each had their own notepads, not wanting to write on the originals.

Gawain had been poring over these for days, and his hair was a tangled mess from running his hands through it. These documents were nothing short of amazing. There were secrets galore on them and he had never been more thankful that his friends had enough magic to keep them safe. Something like this in the hands of the hunters could cause irreparable damage. There were species of shifters mentioned that he had never heard of. Although, he supposed it did make sense that Nessie was a shifter. He had always wondered but had never spent enough time in Scotland to really explore it. Maybe he should encourage Ian and Shaye's idea of taking a Clan vacation. It could be fun, and he would have an excuse to try to find Nessie. Or whatever the shifter's name might be.

Doc gasped from the other end of the table.

"Gawain! Look at this," he said excitedly.

Gawain jumped up and rushed over, peering over Doc's shoulder to see what he had found. Doc was wearing cotton gloves to keep any oils or residues from his skin from getting on the parchment. He pointed to a section about midway down the page. It looked like it might be in Latin...no... maybe Greek? The handwriting was horrible. He stared at it longer, trying to make sense of it. He read many languages, but damned if this one wasn't making sense to him.

"I can't make it out, Doc. What language is that?"

Doc looked up at him funny. "What do you mean? It's in Greek."

"Doc, I can read Greek. That is not Greek. I can't make out any of the words," Gawain told him, squinting and tilting his head, trying to make sense of the scribbles.

"Really?"

Gawain nodded. Nope, nothing.

"Merri, come look at this!" Gawain shouted.

A minute later, his mate walked in. "You rang?" she asked, exasperation in her voice. She had been enjoying a nice cup of tea and a book in the living room.

"Can you read this?"

Merri walked over to the table, looking over Doc's other shoulder. "No. No, I cannot. Are those even words?"

Doc looked at both of them, frustration on his face. "Are you putting me on?"

Merri shook her head. "Honest, I can't make out a single word. You can read it?"

He nodded. "It's about rare shifters, the one-offs. It goes on to say they can claim their families, share their life gift, and that their immortality is true immortality. I need to go through the rest of these documents and see if there is anything to back this up."

Gawain nodded. "I'll set aside any documents that don't make sense to me and see if you can read them. Maybe we should have Tess or Berkley see if there is a spell, because I'm not sure why we wouldn't be able to read it otherwise."

"That's a good idea," Doc replied. He grabbed his phone and sent off a quick text. Berkley came in a few minutes later, holding a cup of tea.

"You wanted me to look at something?" he asked. "Tess is…um…upstairs…with Sam. So, it's just me for now."

Doc bit his lip to keep from smiling at Berkley, whose face was a nice shade of red. "Can you read this?" he asked, pointing at the document.

Berkley leaned over, his hair falling forward before he leaned back and grabbed a tie out of his pocket to pull it into a ponytail. "I cannot," he replied. "Hmm, well that's interesting," he said, looking at the paper. He held a hand over the top of it, concentrating. "I didn't sense this when we brought the packet home. There's definitely a spell over this, almost like a type of concealment spell from what I can sense. Can anyone read it?"

"Merri and I couldn't, but Doc could," Gawain replied.

"Have you come across any others?" Berkley asked.

They shook their heads no.

"What does it say?" Berkley questioned, looking at Doc.

"It was talking about rare shifters, forming a bond, sharing immortality. It seemed like it was a true immortality, not the immortality we normally associate with paranormals where they can still be killed in some way."

"Like the Fae," Berkley responded. His species was immortal so long as someone didn't do anything too drastic like lose a head or destroy their heart. They were much harder to kill, but there were still ways to do it. Other paranormals had a natural lifespan where they would stop aging for a while. When it got closer to the end of their life, they would begin to age again. The Fae simply stopped aging, living forever unless mortally wounded.

"Yes," Doc said. "I'm hoping I can find something else in

here to help collaborate it. It would be nice knowing how protected you all are now that we performed the ceremony which should have shared my lifespan."

Gawain started zoning out, finding a new document to read through. He would let them talk about spells and whatnot until they came up with an answer. Merri was probably still listening too, but there was something more in this pile calling out to him. It was just like when he was on a dig. If there was something to discover, he had a knack for finding it. The antiques buried in the ground occasionally called to him. He had a feeling that there was something that would help him with the dig he was planning for Doc's old tribe's home. Doc had marked on a map the different places the tribe had lived. The first site they were going to was the one Doc had lived at the longest, the settlement that he had been kicked out of when he reached adulthood. Gawain just couldn't understand how someone could kick out such an amazing person, not to mention Doc's shifter side. Seriously, who got rid of an alicorn?

They had plans to travel in the late spring or early summer to scout out the area and Merri had already let Marge know she would be taking a break from the library. Gawain couldn't wait to get his hands in the dirt again.

Merri glanced over at her mate, realizing he had zoned out. She shook her head. He was on a mission for something on this table. "Berkley, are you positive you didn't notice anything weird about the documents when you got them?"

He shook his head. "Honestly, it was a bit of a whirlwind. The woman gave them to us, Ian hid them under his sweater, we walked down the aisle to give her time to pack up, and then we were attacked in the parking lot. When we got to Ian's parents' house, I put them in my luggage with an invisibility and protection spell. I was so distracted with getting Ian better, that I didn't really pay much attention to them. Nothing stood out, not even when I gave them to you."

"Do you still have the bag, Doc?" Merri asked.

Doc nodded, handing it over. Merri skimmed it with her magic. "I don't sense anything on the bag either. Do you?" she asked Berkley.

Berkley looked at it, flipping it inside out. "No, nothing. I can't even be sure if she cast the spell over these to keep them from the hunters before giving them to us, or if the spell is much older than that."

Gawain looked up, holding another document. "I found another one!" He passed it over to Doc.

Berkley moved down to the other side of the table, running his hands over the papers there. Nothing. Nothing at all. There was no magic, no spell, nothing his senses could pick up. It was bizarre. He picked up a few of the papers, skimming them. Nothing jumped out, nothing changed until he reached an older piece of parchment. As soon as he looked at it, he felt a spell activate, the words becoming garbled. "I found one as well," he said. "I didn't sense any spells when I came over, but as soon as I looked at this one, something activated and now I cannot read it." He passed it down to Doc.

"The more sensitive documents must be spelled," Merri mused. "And since neither of us picked up on it, it must be a sleeper spell."

"That only activates when a regular paranormal, and probably a human, look at it? My guess would be that it was to keep the documents safe, keep them to be viewed by only rare paranormals. It's intriguing. I haven't heard or come across anything like this before. Have you?" Berkley asked Gawain.

Gawain shook his head. He had never witnessed anything like this, much less heard about it. Their community wasn't that large, someone would have said something, and the gossip would have spread like wildfire. It was a mystery and the scientific part of his brain wanted to experiment to see how far the spell extended.

"Doc, what happens when you write down what is on the document? Try taking the shortest paper and copying it in your notebook," Gawain suggested.

Doc looked at him curiously but did as he asked. They waited until he was finished writing before looking over his shoulder. "Can you read it now?" Doc asked.

"Nope," Gawain stated.

"What if you wrote in code? Use Doc or RP instead of 'rare paranormal,' and instead of the words use an ampersand for the word and, the at symbol, and abbreviations like b/w for between?" Merri suggested.

Doc tried again, using modern language and abbreviations. It got a little better, but they still ended up only being able to read the abbreviations, not the entire document.

"What about taking a picture?" Merri asked.

Berkley took a picture with his phone and Doc took one with his. Both screens looked blurry to everyone but Doc.

"I wonder if Emma could read it, since she's your mate?" Berkley asked. "Even though we have the Clan and tribe bond, we still can't understand what's written. It must be a way to keep you safe, even though I can't imagine a tribe turning on someone," Berkley said, before turning red when he remembered that Doc's tribe had done just that when he shifted for the first time and wasn't a unicorn like the rest of them.

"It would have been easier and faster to cast a general spell, only allowing rare paranormals to read the documents. They probably didn't have time to create every conceivable exception, like ours where I found you guys much later in life and created a new tribe," Doc replied. "Imagine a child or young adult in their birth tribe or pack and when they changed for the first time, they ended up being a rare paranormal. Now if it was a case like mine, their tribe would have tried to kill them or kick them out; but before they were officially removed from the tribe, they were still technically members so everyone else would have been able to read it. That wouldn't be in the best interest of any rare paranormal."

"That's true," Berkley said.

The library door opened again as Emma walked in.

"Hello, my dear," Doc said as she came over, giving her a light kiss. "We've found some interesting things. Can you read this?" he asked, showing her the original document.

She shook her head.

"How about this?" he asked, handing her the copied down versions. As she shook her head again, he handed her his phone.

"No, nothing. What is it?" Emma asked.

"Spelled documents," Berkley replied. "No one but Doc seems to be able to read them."

"What if someone else wrote them out? Albert dictates and one of us tries writing it down," Emma suggested.

"That's a good idea," Gawain replied.

Emma took the pen and Doc's notebook, sitting down to write.

"'Whereas, you, the unique paranormal, are truly immortal, others are not. There are those that may claim to be immortal species, but they can still perish. The bonds that created you cannot be destroyed. Neither fire, nor blade, nor spell, nor anything in between shall harm you. You may incur an injury, but death shall not befall you. You shall eventually heal and overcome. If you should find a new family, one you wish to claim as yours forevermore, you may of course share this gift with them. Then they too shall become truly immortal,'" Doc read.

"At least we know the answer to that question now," Merri said quietly.

Emma looked down at her paper. "What in the world?" she exclaimed.

It looked like she had drawn scribbles over the sheet, even

though they had all watched her neatly write everything down.

Berkley shook his head. "I'm at a loss," he admitted. "I've never come across something like this."

Shaye pushed open the door, bringing a plate of cookies. "I figured you guys could use a snack by now," she said. "How's it going?"

Merri spoke up. "The documents are fascinating, at least the ones we can read."

"Are they in another language?" Shaye asked. Between Berkley, Gawain, and Doc, she would have thought that they could read almost anything. She knew they each spoke multiple languages.

"No. Well, yes, some of them are but we can read those. These have been spelled so that only Doc, or I'm assuming other rare paranormals, can read it. We've tried having Doc write it down, Doc dictating it, taking a picture. It ends up blurry or illegible every time," Merri said.

"What about an audio recording?" Shaye suggested.

Doc shrugged, grabbing his phone. "Might as well try it."

That too didn't succeed. All they heard was static, not even a whisper of Doc's voice.

"If it's to protect Doc, why did the spell let him read it to you then?" Shaye asked suddenly. "Have you tried projecting an image of the paper through the Clan or tribe link?"

"No, I haven't," Doc replied. She was right, it didn't make sense that he would be able to read it to them and have them understand, but nothing physical had worked so far. He stared at the parchment, focusing on the bond with his family. He figured focusing on the tribe link would work better as it was directly run through his animal side, which was what gave him his rare shifter status.

Gawain sat still, concentrating on Doc.

'Sorry to interrupt, everyone. We're trying an experiment in the library and I thought it would be better if I used the tribe link to do

it,' Doc thought at everyone. He looked down at the paper, imagining it in his mind, reading the words over the link. He thought it was going through, but he wasn't going to look up until he was done with this section.

Gawain waited, hearing Doc's voice in his head. He suddenly could see the image of the document as well. It finally worked! It looked like Doc had picked a new spot to read to them, which made sense if he thought about it. They wanted to make sure they could hear and see what Doc was projecting, that they could remember it, so picking a new portion was smart.

'Your immortality, whether you keep it as yours alone or you share with your grouping, will be passed on to the next generation. Your tribe/pack/etc. is now immortal in their blood, and that gift will be passed on to any of their offspring. No need for another ceremony unless you are adopting more people into your group.' Doc finished reading the passage. *'Please let me know if you heard me clearly. Wait about a half hour or more, and then come tell me what you heard.'* He wanted to make sure it wasn't a short-term memory type of thing. He would ask them again tomorrow and a few more times in the future.

Gawain was extremely excited. He loved discovering new things, the stranger the better. This was quite the puzzle to solve.

2

Checking the weather app on her phone, it looked like they might have a warmish day. It was still February, but it was supposed to get close to sixty degrees today. Marge, the head librarian, had asked her to come in early today and Merri thought it would be a good day to walk. Marge had been amazing to work for so far and Merri was loving her job. She still had a few things to learn, but she was beyond happy working there. They had a wonderfully wide selection of materials. She had fallen in love with the older two-story stone building as soon as she had seen it. It held so much character. The front of the building had columns and stone steps. When you opened the heavy, intricately carved wooden front doors, you entered into a large open space, the stained-glass windows casting colorful patterns around the room. The help desk sat in the middle of the library. The interior's second floor only existed in a U-shape that covered the right and left sides of the building and along the back wall, leaving the middle of the building open all the way to the ceiling. The bookshelves were old; huge and made of wood. It was a gorgeous, welcoming building. The smell of books and paper made her happy every time she entered.

There was one part of the library that she had not worked in yet. The back room was a separate wing encasing the entire back wall. From the main space of the library, it certainly didn't look remarkable, just a large solid wood door that was locked. However, on the other side of that door were untold treasures. Paranormal history books and books written about paranormal myths and legends were back there. Not the human versions, but actual paranormal lore and history. Only paranormals, or humans who were part of paranormal families, were allowed in this room. Some of the books were very old. None of the items located in the back room were allowed to be checked out or even leave the room. She wanted Gawain to come and explore the space with her. She just knew he would love it. Maybe when he was done going over the new documents Ian and Berkley had brought home. They hadn't finished reading them all, but they were making headway at least. Doc had his own pile to go through, the ones that no one else could read due to the magic.

Merri walked down the driveway, pulling her coat closed when the wind picked up. She should have grabbed a tea before leaving, but this gave her an excuse to make a stop on the way to work. Opening the bakery's door, she drew in a deep breath, the smell of baking bread and sugar filling her nostrils, making her smile. The little bell gave a cheerful jingle.

"Morning, Merri!" Mary greeted her from behind the counter. "How are you this morning?"

"I'm good. I forgot to bring a tea with me for work, so I figured that was the perfect excuse to stop in." Merri grinned.

Mary smiled back. "What kind do you want today? The chai might be nice with that chill this morning."

"It is a little chilly," Merri agreed. "I'm hoping it warms up like they claimed it would. The chai sounds great. Can I get two almond croissants and a caramel macchiato as well? Marge could probably use a pick-me-up."

"Bill just pulled a new batch out of the oven a minute or so ago. Would you like a hot one? It should still be warm by the time you get to work," Mary offered.

"That sounds delicious! That would be great, thank you," Merri replied, her mouth watering at the thought of warm almond croissants.

"Bill, pack up two warm croissants, please," Mary shouted through the doorway to the kitchen.

Merri stood by the glass cases, looking over all the goodies. She'd stop back later and grab some of the cookies for dessert for tonight.

Bill stuck his head through the door, holding two small boxes. "Hiya Merri. Are these for you?"

She nodded. "I'm sharing with Marge."

"Was there anything else you wanted?" Mary asked, finishing up the coffee and tea.

Merri shook her head. "Not right now. I'll probably stop on the way home and get some cookies for dessert."

"I'm making lemon cookies this afternoon. I know Doc and Emma would love those. If there are any others you want, tell me and I'll set some aside for you. I have some of the oatmeal orange cranberry ones you love in the oven now. Oh! And since you're here, we're closing the bakery for a week or two around May. Our daughter is having her first baby and once they're born, we're going to head down to visit."

"That's exciting. I'm sure you must be thrilled. Do you need someone to keep an eye on the bakery while you're gone?"

Mary shook her head. "It's just the two of us now since the kids have all moved out. None of them are interested in taking over. It will be easier to close it while we're gone. I'm letting the Sheriff's office know so they can keep an eye on it. Thank you though. I thought I'd give you guys a heads-up; it seems like at least one of you stops in daily. Ian especially has quite the sweet tooth. Although Shaye and Tess seem to stop in for at least coffee a couple times during the week too."

"We'll have to place a big order before you leave and freeze it to tide us over," Merri joked. Well, now that she thought about it, it was a pretty good idea. They were frequent customers and although they could all cook and bake enough to feed themselves, there was just something about buying the delicious treats instead of waiting an hour or more to make them at home.

"Just let us know when you're going. We can help close it up, keep an eye on it, whatever you might need," Merri offered.

"Thank you. You guys are the best," Mary said, giving her a hug before handing over the drinks in a carrier and the croissants in a bag.

Merri walked down the street, grateful the breeze seemed to have died off. She was looking forward to warmer weather when the park's fountain would be turned back on. There was a tree that looked perfect for sitting under and reading a book. Rolf's house was nice, and she loved the library and the backyard, but that tree was calling her name. Passing the Black Wolf Brewery, she could see the lights on in the kitchen area and figured that Sam was there getting things ready for the lunch rush. She waved, seeing Berkley and Ian working to change out the window display of the Winged Potter across the street. It was amazing to have so many friends working this close. She always felt safe, knowing they were nearby. The fact that there were several spots in town with magic wards helped too. The clinic was just far enough down the street that she couldn't tell if they were in the office yet. She would guess at least Doc was there, and since it was Wednesday, Tess should be at the clinic to work on insurance stuff, while Shaye would be working as Doc's nurse for the day.

Pulling out her keys, Merri unlocked the back door of the library. "Marge? Are you in yet," she called out, seeing a light on in the office. She didn't want to startle the cat shifter, although she had probably heard Merri come in. "I have coffee and breakfast!"

A rumbling purr sounded right before Merri had the sense that a predator was nearby. Turning toward the office door, she gasped as she watched the large cat prowl into the room. "Marge?" she squeaked.

The cat nodded its head, pulling its body into a long stretch before jumping to sit on one of the chairs. Merri hurriedly put down the drink carrier and bag from the bakery. "You're gorgeous. Can I come closer?" she asked, wanting to get a better look, but not wanting to invade Marge's space. She knew in her animal form, the need for a personal space could get a lot stronger.

When Marge nodded, she took a few steps closer, looking at the gorgeous coloring of her fur. When Marge nudged her hand, Merri laughed. "Okay, okay," she said, laughing before running her hand over the large head. Looking closer she could make out the faint pattern in the fur. She hummed before leaning closer. "Jaguar?" she asked, thinking she saw rosettes in the pattern.

Marge nodded again.

"Whenever you're ready, I have an almond croissant and a caramel macchiato for you," Merri told her.

Marge gave her a final head nudge and went through to the office door, reaching up to grab it with her teeth to pull it closed.

A black jaguar. Wow. Merri had not seen that one coming. She thought maybe a house cat, or something smaller. Although she did wonder why Marge was shifted in the library. She thought of that kids' book *Library Lion*, and laughed at the fact that they had their own library jaguar.

"Thanks for breakfast," Marge said as she came back

through the door, carrying her jacket. She looked like her regular self, her sleek dark hair pulled into a bun, her green eyes twinkling, her five-nine, medium-build body clad in her normal pair of dark jeans, black biker boots, and royal blue camisole. Merri knew that soon enough Marge would be wearing the black blazer she was carrying. Once the library opened, any breeze from outside would sweep right in when someone opened the door. It could make for some chilly gusts since the reception desk was right in the middle of the room.

"No problem. Thanks for sharing your animal side. You're gorgeous," Merri told her.

"Thank you." Marge smiled. "I like to have at least one morning a week in the library in my cat form. I like to sniff around to make sure we don't have any mice trying to make a home here. My cat likes to take care of them if we have any and I think the scent of my cat keeps them mostly away."

"I was just wondering; is the *Library Lion* your favorite book?" Merri teasingly asked.

Marge laughed. "I do like it. Maybe I should write my own version."

"I'd read it," Merri replied. She really would too. She thought it would be awesome to have a book written by one of their own in the library.

Marge gently bumped her shoulder against Merri's as she moved to sit at the table. "I was thinking I would show you around the back section a little more this morning. We open later today, so it would give us some more time back there, if you'd like."

"I'd love to! I've been eager to explore it," Merri replied, excited. She sat, taking a sip of her tea before trying a bite of the croissant. It was still warm, flaky, the almonds on top providing a nice crunch, and the almond filling lending a sweet taste. It was delicious and she wondered if she should have bought more than two.

Marge finished her coffee, tipping her head back to get the

last drops. "Thank you for breakfast. It was great. I'll have to stop in to grab something soon. I keep forgetting that they're open earlier than we are. Are you ready?" she asked, making sure to wait until Merri finished her pastry. At Merri's nod, she stood up, throwing out her trash. "Let's wash our hands before we go back. There are protection spells on everything, but I always like to be careful with the documents. A lot of them are one of a kind."

Merri threw her trash out and washed her hands. She would hate for any of the buttery goodness from the croissant to end up on a hundred-or-more-year-old document. She followed Marge to the back, where her boss pulled a key from her pocket and opened the door. The smell of old paper and books wafted out and Merri took a deep breath. She loved the smell of books, she thought as she walked through the door. There was a brief tingly sensation as she passed through the ward surrounding the room.

Looking around, she was a little surprised to see that it looked very similar to the front of the library. There were a couple of tables with chairs around them directly across the door in front of them. Bookcases lined both sides of the walls, making two rows coming toward them. Near the seating area, two large wooden-framed, glass-topped display cases took up a fair amount of room. Walking closer, she looked down at the display cases, stunned to see some extremely old parchments on display. There was plenty of lighting to see them, and even a magnifying device to hold over the glass.

"The glass is spelled, so there won't be any harmful UV or other light damage to the papers," Marge told her. "These are some of the oldest parchments we have in the collection, so we don't take them out anymore. We do have a photograph copy if someone needs a closer look, and the magnifier isn't working well for them. Our desk is over here, behind the door. If you are searching for an item on the front computer and *'archives, back'* comes up, then you know the item is back here."

"This is amazing," Merri said. She couldn't wait to spend a day digging into all the reference materials. Maybe on her next day off she could come visit. "I normally get a sense if someone is a paranormal, but how do I know for sure? Like if I don't pick up on them being a paranormal or if they're a human mate. Is there some way to know if they're allowed in here?"

"There are a few different ways. This whole room is spelled for protection and is created so that only paranormals or their human mates can enter. There's also a spell to keep ill-intentions out. Many of these are one-of-a-kind documents and we have them protected so that they cannot be destroyed. Even if the library collapsed or burned down, the contents of this room would be safe. I know you all had problems not that long ago with other paranormals, so if anything pops up while you're in town, this is another safe place to go.

"If a patron comes up to the desk and you cannot tell if they're paranormal or a human who's allowed back here, there is a way to verify that. The front desk has a form that everyone must fill out to gain access to this room. Once they fill it out, it uploads to the computer system. The computer lets you know if they can go back, if they're human, or if they're banned."

"Banned?" Merri interrupted.

"Yup. Some people just don't know how to behave. Take someone like Vlad for instance. He would have loved to have been able to enter and destroy a bunch of the documents. We can put an alert in the system when someone is banned. There are other paranormal libraries and the alert travels to all of them. Just because the papers are protected, doesn't mean they couldn't still disrupt the library and put us in danger, or even try to circumvent the protections. Each librarian sets up their own system, and I had a lot of great help with mine. Not everyone is so lucky, so their protections might have loopholes or gaps."

"If they change their name or write down a fake name, wouldn't the system not work then?"

"Ah, that's the beauty of the magic on this form. The moment they touch it, their identity is recorded, not by their name, but by their essence. I'll show you how it works when we go back out front and explain a little more. Let me finish showing you around here first. I wanted to keep everything similar to up front; there's no reason to have to learn two different filing systems. Now, once again, it's left up to each librarian, so it may be different at another location," Marge explained as she walked around and showed her where the different areas were.

"You have a children's section?" Merri exclaimed. That would be amazing when or if any of them had kids.

"It's not as large as I would like, but there aren't a lot of children's books written for paranormals."

"See, you should write your own version of *Library Lion*… maybe *Cat in the Card Catalog*. Or *Jaguar*…well, the only J word I can think of in a library is Journal, but I don't think that works that well in a children's book title. I think that would be amazing to have actual paranormal fairy-tale books. I know each species seems to have their own myths and folklore. It would be nice to have local kids learn about each other's heritage," Merri said.

"That would be nice," Marge said wistfully. She could have story time in the back room, help the new generation learn about each other so they weren't so segregated going forward. The jaguar species, like their wild counterpart, was pretty insular and solitary. Once she was old enough to fend for herself on her own, her mother had taken off. She had never known her father, although she would recognize him by scent as a family member. If she had that type of community growing up, she would have had more friends to rely on when her mom left and wouldn't have been left feeling so stranded.

"Okay, let's head to the front and I'll show you how the form works," Marge said, shaking off her melancholy. Locking the door behind them, she led the way to the front desk.

"There is only one physical copy of the form, and it stays here," Marge said, pointing out the thin drawer the form lived in.

"That would be bad to lose," Merri replied. She didn't think that sort of thing would have a backup lying around and she was a little nervous to be responsible for the only copy. She didn't want to be the one to lose it.

"It can't be lost." Marge smiled at her. "It's spelled to stay here for just that reason. Now, it doesn't matter what pen or pencil they use to fill it out," she started to explain as she pulled out the form. "It's pretty simple: name, phone number, address, what book or document they were looking for, a signature and date line confirming they were asking for the book. We really only need people to touch it, so that the form's magic can scan them, but humans are so used to having to fill out their name and other information, that we made it in the likeness of other forms they fill out so that it seems normal. Once they write their information down, it is automatically sent to the computer's database. If they are new, it will create a new file for them. If they're a paranormal that has been to any other library, it will grab their file and create an updated log of their name and contact information, as well as which library they had visited. Once the database has their information, the screen is going to have a small pop-up. If it's green, they can go back; it means they're a para-normal or a mate and haven't been banned from any libraries. If it turns orange, they're a regular human and are not allowed access. If it's red, you need to be careful because they have been banned from all paranormal libraries. Now, if they went back there anyway and tried to force their way in, our wards would keep them out."

Merri nodded, glad there was a secondary protection, but was questioning why they needed the form at all, other than to alert other libraries. "If our wards will keep them out, why have the form at all? I'm not criticizing, just trying to understand."

"Our wards are amazing, and I had lots of help setting them up and getting them to a level I was comfortable with. Not all libraries have that option. A Warden will stop in a paranormal library when they are first set up and put up the basic protections. Some will do more, but because there are not a lot of Wardens, they can be extremely busy and only have the time to put up the bare necessities, maybe planning to come back to do more, maybe hoping the librarian will get more added on. Sometimes the libraries are in an almost all-human location, or there are not magic users in the area, and they don't have the option to add more to the wards. The computer system is magic-run, so even in towns that don't have great power stability or internet they will be able to use the forms. If they have a tablet or iPad instead of a computer, it updates there. If they are very remote, or in areas where computers may not be a common thing, their form acts as the computer and the person's signature will briefly change colors when the librarian is holding the form. Luckily, smart phones are almost everywhere it seems, so we have been able to convert a lot of locations over to phones. For those places, the Wardens will bring solar chargers or place a spell over the battery to keep it alive. Some people aren't comfortable with technology either, so the physical form works best for them.

"Now, the librarian who is assigned as the library's protector keeps hold of the key to the back room. You'll have your own key to the main parts of the library, but as the guardian, I hold the only key to the back room. I'm here most of the time and actually live in an apartment in the basement, so it would be rare that you would need to open or close, but you'll have the main key just in case," Marge told her.

"Don't you ever go visit family or take a vacation?" Merri asked, concerned. It wasn't healthy for her to be tied to the library all the time without a break.

"Jaguars are solitary creatures, even in the shifter world," Marge replied, smiling sadly. "My parents aren't around any longer. I never met my dad, mom left as soon as I was considered old enough. I used to spend a lot of time at the library that was nearby. The old librarian there was a paranormal and had her own room to guard. She took me under her wing and taught me. When the position opened here, she helped me get it. I've been here fifty-ish years now. It's my home. The woods are close enough when my cat wants to explore."

"Well, if you ever need a break, please call me. Our family is great at helping and any one of them would be willing to watch the library for you if you need to shift or anything. I know Rolf has Clan runs every once in a while, and I'm sure he would be more than willing to let you run on the estate grounds too. It's a little more protected than the park's woods are right now," Merri offered.

"I remember hearing that he let shifters use his property. I just always went to the woods, but with the things I've been hearing about the hunters, I may talk to Rolf," Marge replied thoughtfully.

"What have you been hearing?" Merri asked curiously. They had heard a bit from Gage, but it seemed like he hadn't been too successful yet. He was getting frustrated.

"Gage stopped by and filled me in. I've known him for a long time. I know he was sent here to help enhance some of the spells on the library when it first opened. He was assigned as a Warden to this area maybe thirty or forty years ago? Something like that; I can't remember the exact year. He decided to make this town his home base. It helps that he can hold the position of Sheriff; having most of the town aware that there are paranormals here, and that we work to protect them, means he gets to keep his position much longer than he could if he had to pose as human. The man will go out of his way to help, but he's a bit of a loner like I am. I still don't know what type of paranormal he is. He comes over to keep me updated on any potential trouble so I can keep a closer eye on the library. He helps with keeping the wards strong as well."

Merri looked over at Marge. She hadn't picked up on any relationship vibes from either one of them, but it sounded like Gage visited the library more than any other place besides the brewery and his work.

"Are you two..." Merri suggested.

"No! Definitely not. He's more like a—not a brother since I wouldn't say we were that close, but maybe like a distant relative that you get along with and who checks in on you from time to time. It's nice to hang out with someone when you get lonely, but who also realizes when it's getting to be too much peopling. I don't know why, but work is different, not as draining as regular social situations," Marge confessed.

"I think you would get along just fine with everyone in the Clan," Merri told her. "We should have a grill-out when it gets a little warmer. The guys tend to grab the hammocks and relax until it's grilling time. I did hear Rolf say he was going to add another hammock pavilion so more people could use them. Shaye and I prefer curling up in a chair though. There's a couch, some chairs, picnic table, the hammocks. The woods are great to run in, although there are quite a few of us non-runners who stay back and have a tea or coffee and read. We have a nice mix of introverts and extroverts, but the extroverts have been around us introverts long enough to realize when to give us our space. Well, most of the time."

"That's quite the sales pitch," Marge said with a small laugh.

Merri felt her cheeks get hot. She didn't want to come on strong, but something told her that Marge needed a group of her own. She might be biased, but Merri thought her Clan was pretty amazing. "Sorry. I just want you to know you're not alone. You can come knock on the door or text if you need something. We all know how to introvert together." She laughed. It was true though. Many times, she, Shaye, Emma, and Tess would all be in the library reading. Together, but doing their own thing quietly. The guys had their hammocking and Inebriated Inconsistencies, an old tradition that they had created many years ago where they turned watching historical documentaries into a drinking game every time the show got something wrong. Although the girls had started participating in the game and Berkley had started hanging out with them reading.

Marge nodded at her. "Thanks," she said softly. "I may come over if you get that grill out. Gage was bragging about what good food he had, including a leftovers bag to bring home, when he went over last time."

"Emma likes to feed people. It's how she shows she cares. It still takes her a while to be comfortable and talkative around new people but feeding them is something she can do and show she's thinking about them," Merri said.

"I've noticed she's been coming into town more. Doc's been good for her," Marge agreed.

"Fate knew what she was doing. After all the problems with Vlad, she needed someone who had patience and would show her that she was special. Doc did that. They work great together. Although I still look around for someone else when she calls him Albert." Merri laughed.

"It is funny," Marge agreed. "I didn't even know what his real name was, everyone just called him Doc. It's like a cute nickname that's just hers, even though it's his actual first name."

A sharp beep sounded, startling them both. Marge

reached into her pocket and pulled out her phone to silence the alarm.

"Ready to start the day?" she asked.

Merri nodded. She loved unlocking the doors to the library and watching the first patrons of the day come in.

3

G awain touched his ear, looking for his pencil so he could make a note on the map. He had been trying to narrow down the location of Doc's old tribe's location. He looked at the notes Doc gave him, along with a few other documents he had, working on narrowing down the spot. Not finding it in his ear, he reached out, his hand searching across the desk as he read. Ow! What the heck? He looked over, seeing the fork that he had just smacked his hand into. The fork was resting on top of a plate with scrambled eggs. He vaguely remembered Merri kissing the top of his head and dropping the plate of eggs off before she left for work. His stomach growled, reminding him that he hadn't eaten them yet. Grabbing the fork, he absently took a bite while reading through a few of the other documents and trying to figure out where it might be on the map. As soon as the eggs touched his tongue, he spat them out.

"Gross," he muttered. He must have been working for longer than he thought, because the eggs had turned cold and had a weird texture from sitting out. Eating cold eggs was nasty, so he was going to need to grab new food. There was always something quick to eat in the kitchen. Grabbing his tablet, phone, and the plate of eggs, he left his room. Reaching the bottom of the stairs, he could hear Rolf talking excitedly in his office. There was a pause, but Gawain couldn't hear anyone else, so Rolf must be on the phone. Gawain shrugged and turned to the left, intent on grabbing some food.

"Gawain? Is that you in the kitchen?" Rolf called out a minute later, just as he finished making a sandwich.

Grabbing his food, Gawain walked over to Rolf's office. "Hey. I was just grabbing lunch. What's up?"

"Do you have time later today? I have something to show you but need to pick something up first. I was thinking after dinner?" Rolf asked.

"That should work. I'm just waiting on hearing from one of my colleagues. They were looking into something for me." Gawain was curious now. He wondered what Rolf had to show him.

"I don't actually know how your job works," Rolf admitted. "Do you often have help when you're looking into a new location?"

He hummed. "Sometimes. It really depends on the dig and who I might need help from. Not everyone is trustworthy with sensitive information. I know a few people who will hear things and have useful tips, but they deal a lot in stolen goods on the black market. I make sure to never give any hint of where a site might be because they'll sneak in and steal anything that might be valuable. Then I have some other contacts that I've worked with on other digs, ones that I would trust with information or locations. Doc's background makes it a little tricky. I have a couple of guys that I would trust with my life; but I'm not willing to risk Doc or the Clan. I have never heard of anyone seeing an alicorn and I'm not going to be the one who accidentally outs Doc's shifter side. I'm finding workarounds to try to get the information I need.

"This guy, Rob, is really into early Nordic settlements and has spent years researching around the time Leif Erikson came here. I reached out to see if he had any other informa-tion on the unicorn horn trade out of North America. Specifi-cally, if all the 'unicorn' horns were simply narwhal horns, or if there were some actual shifter horns mixed in as well, and where they might have gotten them. If he has any info on real horns being used and can pinpoint where they were found, I can look for other settlements besides Doc's. One, because I'm interested and would love to compare locations. Mostly though, I don't want to do anything that will draw attention to why I'm focusing on that one particular site. I don't want to make it easier to trace back to Doc. If I'm looking at a few different areas, it makes it seem like I haven't hit paydirt yet and it won't get much notice. If I only stop at one place, only ask about one location, then someone might pay more atten-tion and start asking questions, trying to get in on the action. It would be bad if anyone from Doc's old tribe was still alive or there were descendants who passed down the story of the weird shifter that got kicked out of the tribe and told other people. The last thing we need is my work catching some-one's attention and bringing them into town to confront me about it," Gawain said, knocking on the wood of Rolf's desk. Seriously, with the attacks on Rolf and then Sam and Tess, followed by the threat of hunters being nearby, and then the attack in Scotland on Ian and Berkley, they needed the town to remain quiet and safe. Gawain knew that Rolf, Sam, and Berkley had adopted this town many, many years ago and worked at keeping it protected. It was one of the reasons why it had been safe for them all to live here: Rolf helped the people in the town, the people in the town accepted that they might not be human and kept their secrets.

"No doubt. I've kept this town safe for a hundred years. I don't want to let them down now. I keep them safe, they keep us safe. It's been our unspoken agreement for decades. I do think we need to seriously sit down with Gage, Tess, and Berkley and come up with a way to put protection over the town. I'd imagine it will take some time to get the spell just right, so if we start now, it will hopefully be ready when we need it," Rolf said.

Gawain nodded. "Merri and I will start researching as well. I know I read something about a 'magical dome' keeping a village safe somewhere. I just need to remember where. Merri can ask Marge if there's anything in the library's back room too. There's bound to be something we can use at least as a starting point."

Gawain's phone started ringing. Looking down, he saw it was his friend. "I need to get this. I'll try to be down for dinner, but come get me if I get distracted," he told Rolf. Depending on this phone call, he could see getting distracted in a new trail of research. "Hey Rob. How are you?" he asked, hitting the answer button. He ran up the stairs to his office. His falcon loved being at the top of the house, looking over the grounds. There was a window he could open and fly out of when he needed to stretch his wings. Luckily, he was somewhat common looking and could blend in easily with the local wildlife when he flew.

"Heya. I'm alright. I saw your voicemail about the unicorn horns. It's hard to really find anything. Any settlements at that time were made of wood, so it's like trying to find a needle in a haystack. I've worked on a few sites that folks claim to be unicorn settlements; if you wanted to see them, I can send you the information. Most of them were duds though. I'm in South Dakota right now on a site, also rumored to have unicorns nearby, if you want to come visit. I'd love to get your opinion on a few things. What's with the interest in unicorns?" Rob asked curiously.

"I'd love to. I'm actually taking a road trip with my new mate soon. I'm still planning it out, maybe spring/early summer time frame. How long will you be there?" Gawain asked.

"I'll still be here. I have this site, plus a few potential satellite locations nearby. I'm guessing we might have enough to be here for maybe another year. Congrats on the mating," Rob responded.

"That's amazing. I'm glad you found something. I came across some unicorn documents at another site, and it piqued my interest. I've never ever met one in real life but was curious to see if I could find any information if they were still around or if they had died out. What their lives were like, where they lived, what they did, how they died out if they're extinct…you know the usual." Gawain laughed. Rob would get it, he also dug into a project to find out everything he could. "Have you found anything?"

"Hm, maybe. I have a paranormal scientist looking at a horn I found. It wasn't with a body, so I can't say for sure it would be unicorn, but it doesn't look quite like any of the narwhal horns I've seen so far. There is a settlement here for sure, just still trying to determine if it was shifter or human. I'm waiting on the horn results to see if I need to alert the Wardens that I have a confirmed paranormal site. I can send you some images of a few documents I found about unicorn shifters. It looks like a decent-sized tribe escaped from Greece. They had human and paranormal hunters on their tail, at least according to a couple of letters I found. It looks like they were headed toward North America, a 'vast and largely unexplored land.' I'm hoping that this site might be one of their settlements or a homestead. I haven't come across anything to suggest that they might still be around or even died out. It's crazy just how little information there is. I found stories in the paranormal histories, a few letters, and my great-great-grandad always claimed he knew a unicorn shifter but there was never anything to back up his stories," Rob complained.

"Same here. I found a few documents, but they were in pretty rough shape. Everyone seems to agree they did exist, but I don't have any confirmed recent sightings." Gawain figured that the last time Doc saw his old tribe didn't count as recent. He wanted to avoid lying to his friend as much as possible. He hated not being able to share such cool news, but Doc's alicorn was just too important to tell anyone outside of the family about. Even if Doc was truly immortal, that didn't mean that someone couldn't take him and torment him in the name of profit or 'science.' Gawain knew that he was hard to get along with sometimes, he got lost in his work, fixated on a project. But these people had accepted him for who he was; they were his family, and he would protect them.

"Can you send me pictures of them? I'll send you what I have as well. Let me know if or when you might come over so I can give you directions. We're on private property and it's not well marked. It'd be nice to see you again, it's been a while," Rob replied.

"It has. About three years now?" Gawain mused. "I definitely want to stop in. Let me finalize the trip plans and I'll let you know when we'll be there. I'm thinking May or June."

Gawain disconnected the call before sending his friend the pictures of the documents. They had been ones he had discovered on a previous dig, not something that had been in the stack of items Ian and Berkley had brought back with them. He was simultaneously eager to see what documents Rob had found in his search for answers but was also worried that the letters Rob mentioned were referencing Doc's old tribe. Maybe there were others that had been escaping hunters from Greece and just so happened to also come to North America. But that was a pretty big coincidence. He would have to keep alert for any reference to Doc's animal side. It could be something so small that unless you knew what Doc was, you would miss it. However, he knew there were too many people out there that hunted through old papers and other documents to find clues to hunt down paranormals. Gawain wondered how he could find a way to get those documents and keep them safe. He'd just have to cross that bridge when he got to it.

His tablet dinged, alerting him to a new email. Walking over to the library, he settled on one of the couches on the main floor. He eagerly opened the documents, frowning as he started reading through the letters. Based on what he knew now, these had to be about Doc's tribe. It seemed like a woman had written the majority of them, sending them to a man. He couldn't tell if this was a friend, relative, or lover. She spoke of being tired of always looking over her shoulder, wanting to be able to enjoy her later years in peace. The man offered her a home, but she spoke of a vision that told her that she needed to go with the tribe to this new land. That she had a job to do there, something that Fate said she needed to do. She wasn't sure what it was or how long it would take. She would miss him, but she had to go. Something teased the edge of his mind as he read. What was the name of the lady who had quasi-adopted Doc? The healer lady…Talc, no that was baby powder stuff…Thea…Thalia. That was it. He skimmed the documents, looking for a signature. Surely, she signed off on a letter at least once. He could tell there were two authors based on the handwriting and the language, so if he could find a name, he would know half of the people involved. Seriously, who doesn't sign their name? Although, if they were worried about hunters, they probably would have kept any identifying information vague. He flipped through a few more, finally finding an earlier letter that had a signature. 'With love, Thalia.' There can't have been that many people named Thalia. Well, okay there probably were, but not that many who were talking about moving across the ocean to escape hunters around the same time frame. He'd have to show these to Doc, see if he could confirm it was the same Thalia that trained him.

Gawain looked up at the knock on the door. Rolf was standing there and based on the light in the room, Gawain had been in here awhile.

"Hey. You worked through dinner. Are you still able to come out tonight?" Rolf asked.

"Yeah, just lost track of time. I have some stuff to show Doc, but it can wait," Gawain replied. He wondered what Rolf had to show him. He looked excited and nervous at the same time.

"Do you want to grab some dinner before we leave?"

Gawain shook his head. "I'll just throw together a sandwich and eat it on the way."

As they walked out of the library, he noticed Merri was waiting for them, coat in hand. Shaye was there too, smiling. Huh. Was he the last to know about whatever this was?

"He's just going to grab a quick sandwich, and then we'll head out," Rolf said.

Gawain made a quick turkey and cheese sandwich, grabbing a bottle of water out of the fridge before heading toward the front door.

'Do you know what's going on?' he asked Merri over their telepathic link.

'No. Shaye seems really excited though,' she responded.

Gawain opened the door for Merri, walking around the car to climb in. He ate his sandwich as they drove into town, turning down a side street. Hmm, he hadn't been down here before. Of course, he hadn't been in town much, sticking close to the house and his research. It seemed nice, the concrete sidewalks wide and even, streetlamps at good intervals. There were concrete planter boxes placed in between the lines of the street acting as a median. The planters were empty now, but he imagined they would be full of flowers in the spring and summer. Rolf pulled over, parking in an on-street spot.

"We're here," Rolf said, before getting out of the car.

Climbing out, Gawain looked around, it was a nice area, but he wasn't sure what he was supposed to be looking at. There weren't any shops that were open, so they clearly weren't going shopping. There wasn't a coffee shop here either, so they weren't getting a drink.

"What exactly is here?" he asked, confused.

Rolf pointed to a building across the street. It was a two-story brick building; solid, but it was odd-looking, nothing really seeming to match or go together. Gawain studied it, his eyes working their way down. The roof line had a castle type of façade, but it seemed like that was the only castle-inspired decoration. The second floor held three windows; a large bay window sat in the middle, a rectangular window with a rounded top on either side. The main floor had a single wooden door, solid except for a set of windows at the very top. A window sat on either side of the door, in line with the matching rectangular windows on the second story. There were two different colors of brick making up this building: a reddish color-brick covered most of it, with a multitone, more brownish brick making up the middle section. Four decorative brick pillars, one on either side of the door and on either end of the building, were also in the brownish multicolored brick. The front of the building looked bumpy though, like the bricks weren't completely flat.

Merri gasped. "Is that clinker brick? I love buildings like that! I think they look so cool." It had been a while since she had seen a building using clinkers in the design, and she adored how quirky it made the building look.

Shaye looked over at her. "Clinker bricks?"

"They're bricks that were too close to the heat when they were baked. It turns them a different color, and can change the texture to where sometimes they look like glass or volcanic rock, they're often misshapen, sometimes they fuse together. Supposedly they get their name from the sound they make when they hit together. They used to be thrown out, but in the early 1900s architects started using them because they were so different. They're a little heavier and denser than regular bricks. I love how unique it makes everything look. I didn't know this was even back here."

"It's a weird-looking building and off the main street. It's been for sale for a long time, but I had a feeling it was meant to be yours," Rolf added, holding out a set of keys.

Gawain stared at Rolf, but Merri took the keys. "What do you mean?" she asked.

"I bought it back around Christmas. I just knew it would be great for you guys. I thought you could maybe create a paranormal museum? We would ward the heck out of the building. Gawain, I know you have a lot of neat things in your storage bins and have lots of cool stories to share. We could market it as an oddity museum or something else quirky for regular humans, but for those in the paranormal world, they would know it was an actual paranormal history museum. The library has some great resources, but you need to know that the back room is there, which not a lot of people do. The museum could have some sort of materials for those new to the paranormal community. Shaye has complained a few times that I forget to tell her things because it's something that I just view as common knowledge—which it may be to the older paranormals, but not to newly turned or changed humans or human mates."

Merri nodded. "Shaye asked me a question recently about why I hadn't healed the next morning from the mate mark. She didn't know how everyone's matings worked, especially with matings where both were paranormals but were different species. I'm betting she's not the only one who would have these questions. We should have a self-help section, maybe pamphlets or something for when people come."

Shaye jumped in. "It would be helpful, kind of a how-to, or paranormals-for-dummies type of thing. We'd want it spelled so that only paranormals or mated humans could read it. Kind of like with Doc's garbled documents. Merri also recommended keeping a notebook of things I learned when I asked if there was a handbook around. If we could make a Paranormal Handbook, keep it in the store, a back room or upstairs maybe, and have it heavily spelled, I think it would be really useful. We could have sections for each paranormal species, and then subspecies."

"Like shifter, and then the different types," Merri mused. It was a good idea. She had told Shaye to start a notebook, but it had to be hard to know where to even begin when you had always been human and hadn't known the paranormal even existed.

"Yes! I know the species we've discussed, but I know there's more out there that I don't even know to ask about. It could have things like their abilities and weaknesses, if they're immortal, mating information, food issues. Everyone could add notes to it. I'm worried that I'm going to run into a paranormal I don't know and accidentally say the wrong thing. I know Merri told me you all are a safe space, and you are, but it's still a little awkward asking why her mating mark hadn't healed yet. And then making it even more awkward by blurting out that it wasn't a bite mark."

Gawain tried to smother his laughter with a cough. He was glad he missed that scene. Poor Shaye's face was bright red even now just remembering it. "Nope. Flying shifters do a claw mark, or sometimes there's multiple claw marks."

"But see, that's my point. Coming in as a human who had no idea this existed, this stuff all seems like common knowledge to you, but it's not to me. If something like this existed for human mates or those newly turned, it could help a lot. I thought we could get Marge and maybe Gage to help with the wards and getting ideas on what might be good to keep here."

Rolf joined in. "Even among the paranormals, we tend to keep some things to ourselves. Not sure why, just how it's always been done. Most of the time it's not even something that could harm anyone; for example, the history and the myths aren't really shared amongst each other anymore. I can see keeping major weaknesses from the general populace, but I know very little about certain paranormals."

Gawain nodded. "I've run into a few humans who have been changed or turned and then left to their own devices. Gives the rest of us a bad name; if you change someone's species, you should at least train them. Something like this would be helpful for them as well. Especially vamps. Good lord, I met one guy who thought he had to drain someone when he ate because the only information he had came from the movies. Whoever created him left after he turned, and the only thing they told him was that he was now a vampire. The Warden who caught up to him at least realized he wasn't being malicious, but they brought in a TruthSpeaker to make sure." That memory still made Gawain shiver. He knew they had their place, but watching the TruthSpeaker be able to know if someone were lying or telling the truth by simply being near them was a little creepy. He had heard rumors that they could force someone to tell the truth as well, like a truth serum, but by only using their presence and voice. "Luckily for him, they took the time and realized he wasn't evil, just misinformed. I mean the man broke down into tears when they told him he could take just a few sips and seal the bites, or even use blood bags to drink from. He had been waiting until he was starving, and his instincts took over because he didn't want to kill people. He had been trying to feed from only people he knew were bad, but he still didn't want to hurt anyone."

"Wait a minute. Can every paranormal turn or change someone?" Shaye asked.

Rolf looked confused. "Some paranormals can, but not everyone. Didn't we talk about this?"

"No," Shaye said as she lightly smacked his arm. "Not really. We talked about turning or not turning as an option in mating, that you have to intentionally will them to become a vampire when you bite someone, it won't happen from a simple bite while drinking. I knew you had been turned by Vlad, Ian by his uncle, and you turned Emma. Everyone else we know was already a paranormal when I met them, and I didn't think about how they got that way. I guess I assumed they were all born that way. It wasn't on my radar that someone could or would go around willy-nilly turning people," Shaye finished.

Rolf gathered her in a hug. "We have had a lot recently, and I didn't explain it well. Witches cannot change a human into a witch, not even their mate. Vampires, werewolves, and some shifters can make a human change their species, even if they're not mates. Not all shifters can though. For example, Gawain can't change someone. I don't think a rare shifter like Doc would be able to, otherwise there would be more of them. I know werewolves and cat shifters, at least the ones I've met, can change a human. You know, the book is a good idea. I'm assuming all cat shifters have the ability based on the ones I know, but I don't know if that's true. We would need to ward the book against copying, removal, pictures, stealing, anything to keep it from getting in the wrong hands. Gage and Marge would be good references for those types of spells."

Merri nodded. She had experienced firsthand how strong the wards were at the library and the Sheriff's station. They could figure this out. She had no doubt that this was something that the Clan was meant to do. Just think of all the fun things they could showcase in the museum.

"And I want to clarify that there is absolutely no pressure if you hate the idea. Having additional buildings as the Clan grows can only be beneficial and financially speaking, having real estate can be a good decision. If you aren't interested, I'll keep it in case someone else wants to use it down the road. It was just a thought, and I didn't want to miss out on the prop-erty," Rolf told them.

"Let's go check it out. Is the electric on?" Gage asked, taking Merri's hand.

"Yes, I have the heat, electric, and water all turned on. I thought you might want to have the contractors come take a look if you wanted to change the layout inside," Rolf said.

Gawain was strangely excited. He normally didn't like anything that would tie him down to one place, preferring to travel and find new dig sites. However, he knew Merri, although willing to travel and explore with him, was more of a homebody. She might be willing to travel, but he knew that she would prefer to have a home base. She was really enjoying the library job too. Gawain thought this would be a good compromise for between digs. He could have a second office upstairs for when he wanted to get out of the house. The library was down the street, making it convenient to Merri's work and their home. He thought he would enjoy teaching and helping other paranormals learn about them-selves and their history. It would give him a place to display some of his collections. A few of the dig sites only wanted to keep some of the artifacts, so he gave a home to the others. Some he had found on his own time as he traveled, some he had saved from construction sites, some he had even saved from oddity museums and traveling shows. He tried to keep the artifacts from being exploited, especially if they were paranormal in nature; for example, there was one time he bought a skeleton because the showman was allowing people to chip off bone pieces to keep for a fee. As an archeologist there were times when he dug up bones, but he always tried to do it respectfully. He had skeletons of ancient shifters that no longer existed (to his knowledge), pages from a witch's spell book, historical documents and myths that delved into paranormal history. There was enough that they would have a good start to the museum. He thought he had a few colleagues that would want to donate or let him borrow some items as well. For example, if he could get a narwhal horn, it would be a fun myth exhibit for the humans, but also to point out to paranormals the dangers of hunters and that unicorns did actually exist at one point. Tess and Merri could help out with some witch type of exhibits, maybe about crystals or something.

"I just had the locks changed," Rolf told them as they got to the door. "There's another set for you guys at the house, as well as a backup key in case you are out of town and want us to check in on it."

Gawain unlocked the door and the deadbolt before walking in and letting his eyes get used to the lower light. The windows must be covered, he thought. There wasn't a lot of light coming in from the street. His eyes saw well in the dark though and he quickly found the light switch. He felt a grin come over his face after his eyes adjusted to the sudden brightness. Oh, this would do nicely, he thought as he looked around. It must have been a warehouse of some kind, with high ceilings, large old wood plank flooring, exposed wooden ceiling beams. The interior walls were mostly bare, the exposed brick a plus in his mind. There were support beams scattered about, huge thick wood square pillars. He may have to make sure those were strong enough to support anything he wanted to keep upstairs. It was one huge open room, other than a small closed-in corner to the left of the door. He would guess that would be the bathroom. There were windows along the side walls, placed high on the ceiling, so while they would let in light, you wouldn't be able to look out of them. Unless you were climbing up the metal spiral staircase that was in the center of the building.

Merri took one look at it, her eyes lighting up before looking at Shaye and nodding toward the stairs. The girls took off running, Gawain and Rolf grinning at how excited they were.

"I love these types of staircases. It's amazing upstairs. It's all open, but if we closed part of it off, I think you could make a fun office slash sitting area for you guys. I was envisioning in the front, where the bay window is, so you would have bright light and a great view. I think we could bring the plumbing up that wall and create an upstairs bathroom in the office space as well," Shaye said.

"That sounds good. I'd like to have a lot of light in the office if we're going to be spending time there. I can spell the glass so the sun doesn't damage any documents or artifacts as well. Maybe have a conference area and then the paranormal-only area in the back?" Merri's voice trailed off as they walked up the stairs.

"This is amazing Rolf. Thank you," Gawain said, looking at his friend.

Rolf grinned. "I'm so glad you like it. It's close enough to town that Merri could walk, there's a roof hatch if you wanted to fly. It can get foot traffic from town, but it's not so close to the main street that paranormals would be hesitant to come. I know you get bored between projects, so I was hoping this would sound like a fun project. I already have my construction guys on standby. Once you get a layout designed, they can start putting in another bathroom or updating electrical or putting in walls. Whatever you need. They're going to start on Doc's treatment room and the theater room in the house next week, but they said they could split the crews if you wanted to get started right away."

"Hmm," Gawain hummed. "I'll have to talk to Merri, see what she wants. I know Berkley and Ian wanted to get started on their workshop now that they finally have it designed." It was a good location; Merri would still be able to see their family members often. She probably saw them more than he did since she worked in town and was able to meet up with some of them for lunch sometimes. Wednesdays were usually a get-lunch-out day, since Shaye, Tess, and Emma were in the clinic. Sometimes they went to the brewery for lunch, sometimes they ate in the clinic's breakroom, if they had enough time they would go to the bookstore's café. Merri was especially happy on bookstore days when she brought home a new book or two.

"There are enough people on the crew and they're always looking for extra work in the colder months, although we're almost to spring. The theater room can wait, it's just for fun. Doc's shouldn't take that much time; he wanted a bathroom and some additional electrical added. I'm having them add some built-in bookshelves as well. I think they said maybe one to two weeks for Doc's."

"Maybe we can have them work while we're on our road trip," Gawain said. He thought he could get a layout sketched up, take some notes with Merri, and have construction going while they were gone. He trusted Rolf and the rest of the family to know what he and Merri would want if anything came up. Then when they came back, they would have someplace to put all their treasures. It would be exciting to have something fun to come back to. The prospect of having all his finds laid out in cases was intriguing. He had quite a few books that would go well in a reference area as well, or at least to use for information in the paranormal handouts that Merri mentioned. His mind was whirling with ideas, already creating informational display cards and fun things such as 'truth versus myth' signs. Like vampires and sunlight, werewolves and silver, witches and wands. Humans might get a kick out of it, and it might cause new paranormals to start a conversation with them.

"Definitely. If you meet with the construction crew before you leave and give them the plans and walk them through what you're thinking, we can keep an eye on things while you're gone," Rolf agreed.

Gawain walked around the room, loving how open it was. He could see waist-high display cases, something that would allow people to see the items, but not high enough that it would close in the room. As much as he dug into his research, if he was sitting in a room and not working, he needed tall ceilings and a feeling of openness, or his bird got anxious and felt caged in.

"I'm thinking maybe a combination of reception desk and gift shop area here," Gawain pointed to the open area to the right of the door. "I really want to keep the large open feeling. The tall ceilings are great for my bird. Maybe add a half wall to act as a stopping point, a barrier to enter the museum exhibits, but one that doesn't interfere with the airiness. Coat hooks on the other side of the bathroom wall for fall and winter when people will be wearing coats. I'd like low-sitting display cases, waist-high. Maybe some hanging displays on the walls," Gawain added.

"I like that idea," Merri said as she came down the steps. "Shaye and I have the upstairs laid out as well. There's a ladder that leads up to the roof. It's pretty cool. I could see putting some chairs up there to hang out, assuming the roof is sturdy enough for us to be on it. It looked okay when I peeked up, but we probably want to have someone look at it to make sure. I think Shaye's idea of the office in front will be great, there's so much light. I think maybe run the pipes for the bathroom down a little bit further. Have it on that side of the building still, but outside of the office so it can act as a guest bathroom when there are people upstairs. Conference room in the middle, secure area for paranormal-only documents in the back," Merri recommended. "There would be some open space to the right of the stairs that I'm not sure what we would use it for. Maybe some benches or just artwork on the walls? I don't know yet."

"Let me run up and see it. We could draw it out when we get home, talk to the contractors, and see what they think, make sure the roof could support additional weight and that the support beams down here are strong enough to support storage on the second floor. It looks sturdy to me, but I'm not a structural expert," Gawain said. He was eager to see what the top floor and the roof looked like. It would be great to have a way to fly into work. If the roof could support furniture on it, they could add a couch or chairs, a privacy screen so he could change forms without being seen, maybe even some plants. Hm, if he flew in, he wondered if others would come in their shifted form as well.

"Rolf, is there a backyard, or a separate parking lot for the building?" Gawain asked.

"No parking area at the moment. You do have enough land on the right of the building to put in a driveway. There is a smaller backyard. If you paved the whole thing, you could fit maybe six to eight cars? I'm just guessing based on the last time I was here, but I wasn't thinking of the space in terms of parking because of the on-street option. Why?"

"I was just thinking that I don't know how other paras might come to the museum. I started with planning a privacy screen of some sort on the roof so I could fly to work some days and not be seen shifting, and that led to wondering if others would come in their animal forms. I think having a dedicated parking lot would be a plus, maybe adding a privacy area in the back as well, somewhere they could shift and not be in the open," Gawain said as he walked up the stairs.

"That's a good idea. I didn't even think of that," Rolf admitted. He had been thinking of everyone coming in human forms, but there could be ones that came by paw or wing.

Gawain reached the top of the stairs and looked around. It was just as open as the main floor, and he could see the exposed brick in most places, although there were a few spots it looked like someone had tried to plaster over it. The front windows would let in a lot of light, and he could see why Shaye and Merri thought it would be great for an office. Some of his paranormal-only documents needed to avoid the sun's UV rays to help preserve them. They could use magic to protect them, but sometimes the simpler way of just not having them in the sunlight worked best. They could, and would, still add protections, but the passive protection of shade would be helpful.

Merri came to stand by him, sliding her hand into his. Gawain was happy when he felt her excitement through their bond. She walked him around the space, pointing out where she thought the rooms should go and he could see the logic of her choices. He was also stumped by what would be an empty area to the right of the steps. It was like a landing for the stairs, and his bird was not eager to have all of the area closed in with walls. He liked the idea of just having a seating area, maybe like a waiting area if they had paranormals coming to see the specialty documents. He would imagine they would have some sort of screening process before allowing them to go in the back room, so people could wait here while they got set up, finished with other guests, or worked through clearing each person.

"I like it. I think this is a great idea," he told everyone. "It could be fun sharing my knowledge and finds with other people. I'm sure at some point Merri will get sick of hearing my stories and I'll have new people to torment, I mean inform and teach." Gawain winked at his mate. He thought this would be good for both of them. The library only had a part-time position available for Merri, and he knew she got bored sometimes as she was used to working full-time. She had been hesitant to find another part-time job with their trip coming up. The museum would be a great thing to fill in the times they were home, and she wasn't at the library. They could work out of the upstairs office, and she could still help with research when she wanted to, and the museum was slow or empty. The museum would also be a great use of her research and library skills to help keep things organized. He was looking forward to seeing his treasures displayed instead of packed away in boxes.

They didn't really need the income, as he previously had minimal expenses and had saved a lot. Rolf had helped him invest as well. Gawain pulled a salary from local governments, the US government, and the Convocation when he worked for them. He also had published many articles and books over the years and had the royalties going into a trust that he could access. He had also guest lectured and acted as an expert when needed. Maybe they could make the entrance fee low or by donation to make it more accessible for everyone.

4

The silence was sudden and jarring, but so very welcome. The construction crew had been working on the theater room this past week, having already finished Doc's medical room inside the house. Merri was hoping they would never need it though. Seriously, this Clan had only been official since Thanksgiving, having formed right after they had defeated Vlad, Rolf's father. Merri hadn't been there for that one, but she had a front row seat to when Tess and Sam had been attacked in December. That was when she had driven them back to Tennessee to the Clan house to have Shaye attempt her healing on Sam when witch magic failed. It had worked and he was back to normal within a day or so. Merri had met Gawain during that visit, and she was so happy Fate had given her a mate that shared her love of learning. Then Ian and Berkley went to Scotland in February, where Ian was gravely injured. If Doc hadn't shared his alicorn's immortality with them before they left, he would have died.

Everyone had been home since then and while they kept an ear out, it had been quiet. Rolf was taking advantage of the slow time for his normal construction crew, trying to get a bunch of projects done before summer. Doc had loved how his in-house clinic turned out and was busy setting up all his supplies. Rolf had ordered theater chairs, and she thought the construction crew had helped move them in today after finishing the final touches. She was eager to have their first movie night. Rolf had even bought an old-fashioned popcorn maker. It was ridiculously cute how excited a two-hundred-year-old vampire was about popcorn bags.

Luckily, the rest of the construction was going to be outside, so hopefully it would be a little quieter. Rolf was putting in a second hammock pavilion, he was building a garage of some sort to help store Gawain's RV and Ian's work trailer. Ian and Berkley's workshop was also going to be built, although they had to clear a bit more land and run electric and plumbing out to the site first.

The best thing of all, is that a lot of it was going to take place while they were gone. Gawain had finalized their trip details and ironed out their visit date with Rob. Merri let him plan most of it, since he had the most experience with road trips. However, she did tell him some of the sights along the way that she wanted to see. She had already downloaded a bunch of books to her phone and had to refrain from reading them too early. There were spots along the way where they wouldn't have internet and probably even cell phone reception.

"The theater room is ready to use," Gawain said as he came into their bedroom. "We got all the chairs moved in and set up. They were heavy."

Merri looked up from the window where she had been looking outside to the sunset. Her mate was sweating, his hair a little wet, sticking to his head. Gawain pulled his shirt off, his toned muscles bunching as he threw it toward the hamper. She loved seeing his body; he was taller than her but not super tall like some of the guys. Merri adored his brown hair with the white streak that was off center. It was long enough for her to grab onto, but it wasn't too long, just enough to get messy. His abs moved as he shimmied out of his gym shorts, her breath catching as the V at his hips became fully visible as his underwear joined the pile of dirty laundry.

"I'm going to grab a quick shower. I think Rolf was going to set up a movie and Ian ran to the store to get snacks. Emma has a roast in the oven for dinner and it's smelling so good," Gawain said as he turned to walk to their bathroom.

Merri watched his butt cheeks flex as he walked away. He didn't have a bubble butt per se, but he wasn't flat either. It was a subtly rounded butt, solid muscle that made her want to dig her fingers in. Glancing at her watch, she thought they had time to have some fun before the movie. She sent a quick text to Tess, just to make sure they wouldn't be interrupted.

MERRI: Taking a quick nap. Will be downstairs in an hour or so.

That should do it. It was pretty common for someone in the house to be taking a nap at some point during the weekend.

TESS: Okay. Have a good *nap*.

Merri was just going to pretend that Tess knew nothing. She locked their bedroom door and walked to the bathroom. She could hear Gawain humming as he climbed into the shower. Quickly shedding her own clothes, she watched as he lathered up his hair, his biceps flexing, the water running down his body.

"Mind if I join you?" she asked.

Gawain shoved the door open so fast, she thought he was going to break the door.

"No. Ouch! Shit." Gawain shouted as he shoved his face back under the water.

Merri was a tad confused as to what had just happened.

"I got soap in my eye," Gawain said, his face still under

the stream of water, holding out a hand. "Come in and make it better?"

Merri grinned, stepping into the oversized shower and dropping to her knees.

"Mer? Where'd you go—" Gawain broke off on a moan as she ran her tongue around his balls. She gripped his hips, watching as his cock quickly filled. Giving his balls one last kiss, she took his shaft in her mouth, twirling her tongue around the base, licking as she sucked and moved her head up and down. She knew the best way to drive him nuts was to have her tongue stroking against his shaft, her fingers teasing his balls, and her head maintaining a steady rhythm. Tilting her head slightly, she carefully moved his dick to the side of her mouth, making sure not to scrape him with her teeth, her tongue sticking out to lap at his balls at the same time.

"Oh, god. I love it when you do that," Gawain groaned, his hands coming up to hold her head. He never pressed or held her in place, just simply touched her.

Merri held her mouth open, her tongue teasing his testicles, her mouth keeping his cock warm. She moved back to the head, tongue playing with the slit before plunging her mouth down to the base. His slightly salty taste was proof that he had been working hard today. As his balls drew up tighter against his body, she knew it wouldn't be long before he came. He leaned over her, keeping the water from splashing in her face, one hand gently cupping her cheek.

'Love you, Mer. God that feels so good. Yeah, lick like that, a little tighter. Oh shit!' Gawain shouted as she wrapped her fingers around the base of his cock, her hand stroking at a slightly faster speed than her mouth bobbing up and down. Her other hand cupped his balls, lightly playing with them.

Salty bitterness washed over her tongue as he climaxed. His hand coming to rest on the shower wall to hold him up.

Merri kept him in her mouth until he tapped her shoulder, their signal that it was getting too sensitive.

"What did I do to deserve that surprise?" he asked a minute later, helping her up.

"You looked all sexy coming in the room today," Merri said.

"Hmm, yay me. But I believe I could use a snack." Gawain smirked, picking her up to hold her against the wall.

Thank god for high ceilings, she thought as her head leaned against the wall. Gawain was strong, lifting her high enough to place her legs over his shoulders, her back pressed against the shower wall, her most private area right in front of his face. She grabbed his hair with both hands as he leaned his head in and took a deep breath.

"I love how you smell," Gawain said, eyes closing as he breathed her in, his hands gripping her ass to hold her in place.

Merri groaned as his tongue teased her lips, licking along the seam. Gawain looked up at her, those amber eyes mischievous as he only gave her light pressure, not pushing inside her.

'Gawain...please,' Merri begged. She wanted something, his dick, his tongue, she'd take his fingers, something. She needed more, needed to feel full.

She gasped as he buried his face in her, his tongue spearing to lick inside her as far as it would go, his teeth teasing against her clit, not hurting, just giving a barely there pressure. He kept changing the rhythm, alternating between light licks, and gentle thrusts of his tongue, even gently sucking on her clitoris. She was so wet, she knew that his chin was going to be covered in her juices, but at this point she just didn't care. She wanted to come desperately.

'Gawain, please, I need—'

Merri let out a shriek as he dropped her, only to catch her and gently slid his dick into her heat. She threw her head back and her body clenched, trying to keep him inside her. That was what she needed, the stretch from his dick, the sensation of being full. Gawain pressed her against the wall as he pounded into her, his eyes watching as her breasts bounced with each thrust. She cupped her breasts, lifting them up to offer him as taste. Ah god, she thought.

'Yes, there, just like that, don't stop, almost there, you feel so good...' she babbled as his hips pistoned into her. She loved how hungry and ferocious he got during sex. He was so laid-back and mild mannered any other time. But when it was like this, she had all of his attention and it made her wild. *'Please, mate. One little bite and I'll go.'* She screamed as he bit down on her nipple, her climax rushing through her. She felt the heat of his release seconds later.

Resting her head on his shoulder, she breathed in his clean scent, happy to stay there for a little longer. All too soon, his shaft slid out of her, and he let her down. Gawain grabbed her loofa and soaped it up, gently washing her body and hair before shutting off the water and drying her off. He led her over to the bed and they snuggled together, taking a quick nap before heading downstairs to the movie.

Tess gave her a knowing smirk as they walked in but didn't say anything. It looked like everyone was already here; Emma placing something on the back tables, Doc getting bags of popcorn, Ian snuggling against Berkley, Sam leaning over Tess to say something to Shaye.

"Looks like you had a good nap," Tess said. Never mind, of course her sister wouldn't let it go.

"I did," Merri said, giving her a smug look in return.

"Good for you," Tess smiled.

"There's dinner and popcorn and drinks along the back wall." Shaye pointed out the buffet-style setup.

"Go sit, I'll grab you a plate," Gawain said, giving her a quick kiss.

"What are we watching?"

"Sam drew the lucky straw, so we're watching Deadpool. Again." Rolf rolled his eyes.

"It's a good movie!" Sam protested.

"It is, but we've seen it before," Rolf said.

"Yeah, but there's a love interest, action, humor. Plus, Ryan Reynolds is hot," Shaye spoke up, giggling when Rolf glared at her.

Sam handed Shaye a candy bar.

"Did you bribe my mate to say that?" Rolf asked suspiciously.

"I'll never tell," Sam replied, miming zipping his lips and throwing away the key.

Shaye just laughed, but she bit into the candy bar with a huge grin on her face.

Merri loved this family.

5

"Merri! Have you seen my notebook?" Gawain asked, his head under the bed. He had no idea where it could have gone, but he really needed it. It had his notes and some observations that he had made for this trip.

"Have you checked your desk?" Merri asked, coming to stand in the doorway.

"Yeah. It wasn't there, wasn't under the bed, wasn't in the nightstand. I can't go without it! It had some good notes in it."

Merri shook her head. He had just had it this morning, writing down some last-minute ideas that he wanted to check out and/or verify the sources.

"Where did you write in it last?" she asked. Sometimes he got so caught up in a stream of thought that he didn't pay attention to where he put things. Merri made sure he attended Sunday dinners with the whole family, and she knew he had it last night when he was conferring with Doc.

She really did want to bring Marge into the fold. Marge worked at the library, lived at the library, and most times even ate at the library. With just the two of them, it wasn't possible to bring her along to lunch, since someone had to keep the library open. But if she introduced Marge to the others and they became friends, then she could meet them for lunch as well while Merri stayed at the library. The town wasn't huge, so if someone came in wanting to use the back room, Merri could start the process with the form and if they were cleared, she could call Marge to let them in. Just like Gawain, Marge needed to find a life outside of work. No matter how much you loved your job, you still needed to find other hobbies or people to interact with. The paranormal history museum would give Gawain another social outlet once it was up and running. Maybe Marge would be interested in helping there too, or at least with helping them with some of the knowledge for the brochures and information guides.

"Uh, I was writing here at my desk, then wanted to take a look at the map in the library again, so I went down there. I set the notebook down to trace out the route Doc thought the tribe had taken to that last village he had lived in. I wanted to see if it passed close to my friend's dig in South Dakota. Then I rushed upstairs to verify something in the notes Rob sent over. Ah. I may have left it in the library. Thanks," he said, giving her a quick kiss on the way out the door.

Merri smiled and shook her head, turning back to her own packing. She grabbed her extra phone cord, making sure her earbuds, laptop, charging cord, and mouse were packed in her backpack. She had already made a small first aid kit and magic kit to keep in the back of the SUV. Her backpack was more of a day pack, so she only kept a few supplies in it. The majority would be kept in the RV in her box.

A knock on the doorframe had her looking up. Her sister stood there, holding something in her hands.

"Hey, you almost ready to go?" Tess asked.

"Just about. Gawain is hunting down his notebook and I'm finishing getting my electronics together. I want to go through the RV one more time to make sure we have everything. We cleaned and stocked it yesterday. Gawain went through his checklist of things he looks at before a trip. I think he was waiting to check the tire pressure until right before we leave. It's the little things I think we'll forget that might be annoying; like toothpaste or aluminum foil or matches to start a fire," Merri said.

"What all is involved with getting the RV ready?" Tess asked curiously. She had never really been in one before.

"I had a crash course, but he said he'll show me more when we have our first stop with full hookups. Do you want to come with me to double-check it? I can show you the inside."

"Sure," Tess agreed.

The silver oval-shaped RV was sitting in the driveway, already hooked up to Gawain's SUV. She popped the car's door locks to drop her backpack off in the back seat before walking to the Airstream. Reaching up, she unlocked the door before pulling the steps out from underneath the body of the RV.

"Let me open the blinds. I don't want to turn the lights on and drain the battery," Merri said.

"I didn't even think of that," Tess replied. "So, there's a battery?"

"Yup. The battery is if you're not connected to electric, but once it's dead you need to hook the RV to electric or to a generator. The front has propane tanks for the furnace and water heater. The fridge runs on electric, so Gawain said he uses a Yeti cooler with ice if he's going someplace without electricity. I guess some RV refrigerators can also run on propane."

Raising the blinds, the space filled with light. Merri looked around, taking in the small kitchen, dining and living area. It looked like everything was put away.

"This is your whole living space?" Tess asked, amazed.

"Yeah. It may be an adjustment. It was just Gawain living here, so it will be interesting to see how we get along in such a small space. It's a twenty-five-foot travel trailer; there's not a whole lot of room, but it's laid out very smartly. He just upgraded a couple years ago to add solar for when he's boon-docking and not hooked up to electricity."

Walking to the dining table, she pointed out how it could turn into an extra bed. There was built-in storage underneath the bench seats as well. On the side opposite the door, there was a workstation where they would be able to use their laptops. It was nice because it could be raised and used as a standing desk. There were cabinets scattered all over, the designers making the most out of the space. Some of the larger-sized food items were stored under the bench seats in airtight containers. Gawain had told her that once they got into bear country, they needed to be careful with how they stored their food. He had seen other campers get raided by a bear before.

"How are you going to cook in here?" Tess asked.

"He has the bare minimum that he needs for cooking, and for plates and utensils, but he says it works. The stovetop has three burners, that's a combo microwave and convection oven, and we have a fridge. It's not a residential size, but it should work great for just the two of us. If we keep our papers and computers at the desk, it frees up the table to use as an extra kitchen prep area. Plus, there's a TV," she pointed out.

Walking toward the back, she pointed out the bathroom and shower. The toilet and sink were located on one side of the hallway and the shower on the other. It was rather minimal in here as well, with two hand towels and three bath towels. The towels were thinner and not as fluffy as regular towels; Gawain had switched to Turkish towels years ago since they dried so much faster than regular ones. He swore they worked just as well, if not better at absorbing water. And then finally their bedroom. The bedroom had a queen-sized bed, which did not leave a lot of room on the sides. But it had a small space to charge a phone on either side. There was storage in cabinets along the back wall, one of the side walls, as well as under the bed. Both the bedroom and the hallway to the bathroom were able to be closed off with an accordion door.

"Do you have enough room for your stuff and any treasures Gawain might find?" Tess asked.

"I have about a week's worth of clothes, a few cold-weather items just in case, my gym shoes, a pair of hiking boots, flip flops in case we go to a campground with a pool and showers, pair of pajamas, a sweatshirt, a light coat, and rainboots. I'm bringing only the magic items I think I'll need, but they fit in one box that can sit in the back seat area of the SUV. The first aid kit can stay in the car too. My laptop and phone don't take up much space. I think all of my stuff will fit in my side of the cabinets. He's using the under the bed storage for any items he finds. He had already upgraded all the locks and there are spells on the RV to keep it and the contents of it safe."

"Berkley and I looked over the spells last night and they seem solid. Are the upgraded locks magical?" Tess asked.

"No," Merri shook her head. "Apparently a lot of RV locks use the same keys, so he changed out the door and compartment locks."

"Really?" Tess asked incredulously.

"Yup," Merri replied.

"Huh. Okay, so I got to ask. What about poop?"

"There are storage tanks underneath: a fresh water tank, the gray tank that collects from the shower and the sinks, and the black tank which collects from the toilet. There's a connection on the outside of the RV that connects to the campground or dump station's sewer via a special hose. Gawain says you empty black first, close that tank valve, and then open the gray to help flush the hose out. After the black tank is empty, you get it ready for the next usage by adding some water and a chemical to help breakdown the waste. If you don't add the water, it can get stuck to the bottom of the tank and cause problems. Apparently, something called poop pyramids form? I don't know, it sounded really gross. I guess we can only use single-ply toilet paper too, so it breaks down faster."

"What about when you're boondocking? What do you do then?"

"Drive to a dump station or some places have a honey wagon that comes around and will empty your tanks for a fee. Or try not to go to the bathroom in the RV," Merri said with a laugh.

"You'll have to send us pictures and updates of your adventures. I'd love to see what you're working on. Doc says he's going to keep looking at the maps to find where the other locations might have been. He said it's been a while since he tried to find any of the first stops, but he's going to keep working on it. He also wanted me to give you this flashlight and these water bottles. It's super high lumens and can be charged by battery, USB, or by hand crank. He said he forgot to give it to you guys this morning when he said goodbye. He said to watch out for snakes and to wear your boots when you're walking around; that area has rattlesnakes. The heat can be dry, which can be deceiving, and the altitude also can affect you, so drink water. These have a special filter; if you run out of clean water, you could fill it at a stream or pond and safely drink. Not that you won't have your magic, but they're good to have if you're tired or need to pass as human."

"We'll be fine, I promise," Merri told her sister. Tess was the youngest, but Merri was starting to feel a little mothered. "Unless you or Emma saw something?" Both of them had premonitions and visions. It had been useful several times already.

"I think this is more of a worrying because you've never really done a trip like this before. You tend to stay close to home," Tess admitted. Tess had always been the adventurer between the two of them. Their other siblings mostly took vacations to see places but had a home base in their childhood neighborhood. Of course, it was a neighborhood that was made up of all family members who were witches, so it was a safe place to call home.

"Gawain's done this a ton of times. We have the solar panels, extra batteries, battery banks for the phones, a cell phone signal booster, extra food and water, an extra tire for both the RV and the SUV, I have my magic supplies, and you guys are just a call away. Shaye was able to heal Ian from across the ocean; I'm pretty sure she can help us if we get into any trouble while we're in the same country," Merri pointed out.

"I know," Tess replied. "Just check in sometimes so I don't worry, please. Even a hello over the Clan link would work."

"I will," Merri promised. She led the way back out to the outside, making sure things were closed and locked up. When your whole house moved, you had to make sure things wouldn't slide around or fall. Gawain had trained her over the past few days, but it seemed different when it was going to be put into practice.

When they got outside, Gawain was there holding his notebook.

"Found it, thank you," he said, giving Merri a quick kiss.

Rolf came out the front door. Everyone else was at work, but they had all said goodbye this morning.

"Have a great trip. Do you have a route planned or are you just winging it?" Rolf asked.

"I have it mapped out this time," Gawain replied with a smile. He did tend to just wing it when it was just him. Rolf had been with him on a trip many years ago and it had driven him nuts. Rolf was a planner. "I wanted to take Merri to a few stops along the way. We're also meeting up with Rob in South Dakota so I can see what he has. I may reach out to Doc if it does look like a legitimate site. I know he said they had stopped somewhere in the area of what are now the Dakotas, but he wasn't sure exactly where, he had been pretty young. I mean I don't even remember if or what I ate for breakfast, so I don't expect him to remember all the places they stopped while he was a kid. Especially since it was so long ago. I'll take pictures of whatever Rob has and I'll send them back."

"Gage said to reach out if you run into any problems as well. I sent his cell phone number to your phone, so make sure you save it from your texts. There are other Wardens out there he can send if you need help. You both have your pendants?" Rolf asked. He was excited for them; it would be nice to get away and he knew Gawain was eager to get in the dirt again. However, after the attack on Ian and Berkley, he wanted to make sure they were safe.

"Yup. I think we have everything we need. We'll send a text when we get to our first stop. There's a couple of casinos, or there's always Welcome Center parking lots. We'll text where we end up stopping. I'm hoping to get a good distance done today. Once we're out of areas with lots of traffic, maybe I can talk Merri into learning how to drive it," Gawain said, smirking at his mate out of the corner of his eye. She had been pretty adamant that he would be the one driving. She had only driven an SUV and had never towed anything before. She was nervous about running into something. He knew she could do it, plus it would be helpful to have a second driver for when he was tired. Or if he got hurt.

Gawain and Merri climbed into the SUV, waving to their family. Gawain plugged his phone into the car so they would have directions. As he pulled out of the driveway, he couldn't stop the grin from coming. He loved having adventures and now he was having one with his mate by his side.

6

erri glanced around, looking for the Arch. They had already been driving about eight hours and stopped a couple times for gas, bathroom breaks, and to walk around. It always felt nice to be able to stretch your legs and move after sitting in a car for hours. They were passing through St. Louis and were hoping to be able to make it to a casino that allowed overnight parking. There were only semi-truck-sized parking spots, no water, sewer, or electric hookups. There was a restaurant in the casino that they could get dinner at, if they got there early enough. Otherwise, they had a box of snacks, bread, and peanut butter in the back seat. Not the most glamorous dinner, but it was silly to try to set up the camp stove to cook something for one night.

Merri was hoping she would be able to see the Gateway Arch from the car windows. It was something she wanted to see, but not necessarily take a ride in the arch itself. As they drove over the bridge, she was able to see it in the distance. She snapped a quick picture with her phone to send to the group back home.

"Are you good with trying to reach the casino in Iowa tonight? There are some places we can overnight park around here if you don't want to keep going," Gawain said, glancing over at her.

"I'm good to keep going," Merri replied. It would be nice to get further away from the city. They had already been cut off in traffic twice. It was making her rethink her own driving. She didn't think she had cut off semi-trucks or RVs, but it was something she would make sure didn't happen in the future.

"Good. I think you'll like the restaurant there. They have poutine and a dessert I'm going to get for you. I'm going to leave it as a surprise, but I'm pretty sure you'll like it," Gawain said.

The rest of the drive went relatively smoothly. There was a brief pop-up shower, but the rain didn't last long. It did make visibility challenging for a few miles, everyone slowing down to see through the sudden downpour. She was ready for another break by the time they approached the casino. The sun was setting, giving off gorgeous yellows and oranges to the sky. Gawain pulled into the overnight parking, finding a spot with room on either side so they felt like they had a little more privacy. There were a couple of semi-trucks in the lot already. Merri had thought the SUV towing an RV was large, but they looked tiny compared to the eighteen-wheelers.

Getting out of the car, she grabbed her wallet and phone before bending down in a stretch. Feeling a light smack to her butt, she turned around quickly to find her smirking mate.

"What?" Gawain asked innocently. "You have a nice butt."

She shook her head at him. "Now you definitely owe me dessert," she replied. As they walked in, she slid her hand into his back pocket, squeezing his own grabbable butt.

Once they were seated, she looked over the options. "I need to use the restroom. If the waitress or waiter comes by while I'm gone, will you order me a sweet tea? I'd like the salad with chicken added if you know what you want when they come over."

"Yeah, go ahead. I'll order and I'll get the dessert too. I'll get it boxed up and we can take it back to the RV to eat and maybe coffee or tea to go?"

"That sounds perfect," Merri said. Dinner out would be great, but it would also be nice to sit with just the two of them and have dessert before bed. "Okay, I'll be right back," she said, getting up, squeezing his shoulder before finding the bathrooms. It wasn't a horrible first day of travel, she thought. She was glad Gawain was driving though, dealing with the traffic in the city would have given her heart palpitations. Maybe, maybe when they were out in the country she would learn to drive. Gawain deserved a chance to look around and see the scenery too. The driver never got to see as much of the sights on a trip.

Walking back to the table, she saw the waitress dropping off their drinks.

"Perfect timing," Gawain said. "I just ordered. You okay if I run to the bathroom?"

Merri nodded. "Go. I'll let everyone know we're stopped for the night."

Gawain leaned down and gave her a quick kiss before walking away. Merri pulled out her phone, sending a group text letting everyone know they made it safely to their first stop and where they were. She should get a picture of the RV in between the semi-trucks if there was enough light when they went back. Maybe she could get it in the morning; she knew they were leaving early again to make it to another casino. This one had a swimming pool they could use and full hookups, meaning water, sewer, and electric. Merri had packed bath wipes for boondocking or overnight stops but was looking forward to having a shower. Even if she would then need to put into practice how to empty the gray and black tanks.

Her salad was delightful, and she could have eaten the poutine all by herself, but she shared. Gawain seemed happy with his fish tacos. After paying, their waitress handed them two boxes and two to-go cups. It was a little too dark to take a picture when they went back outside, so she would try in the morning. Gawain turned on the battery-operated lanterns to give them light in the RV. He opened the windows and pulled out the battery-operated fan from storage, placing it in front of a window to pull in a breeze. Sitting at the table, he gave Merri her drink and placed the boxes in front of him.

"I got you a chamomile. They didn't have a lot of options, but I thought before bed that one might be better," Gawain said. "Are you ready for dessert, or did you want to wait?"

"I always have room for dessert. It's a separate stomach, you know," Merri replied with a grin.

"Okay, so I got chocolate chunk cookies. I figured if we didn't eat them tonight, we could eat them on the drive tomorrow. Now, this is the dessert I wanted you to try," he said, flipping the lid open. It was facing away from her, so she couldn't see what it was yet. "This is called a Zephyr," he said, spinning the box to face her.

Merri looked down at the dessert. Oh, this would do nicely. It was a glazed donut, split in the middle and filled with what looked like cream puff or mousse type of filling, topped with a glaze of sugar and chopped nuts. It looked delicious.

Gawain pulled out a knife and cut it in half. "The chef here created these desserts and I stop to get one whenever I drive by here. They're amazing. They sometimes offer different flavors as well, but I think this one is the original."

Merri took a bite, the creamy filling making it a bit messy as she bit down. Hmm, these were good. Go mate. As she finished her last bite, Gawain leaned over to suck her fingers into his mouth, his tongue curling around them to get every last bit of the cream off.

"Do you want a cookie, or can I interest you in something else for dessert?" he asked huskily.

Merri stood, holding out a hand for him to take, leading

him back to the bedroom. She was glad there wasn't a neighbor on either side of them, she thought as she pulled the blinds closed and started to pull off her shirt.

Merri stretched, waking to a sliver of sunlight trying to peep through the blinds. They had gotten up early yesterday morning to get on the road again. She had used the bath wipes before they left the parking lot and while they helped her body not feel skuzzy, she didn't have anything for her hair. She had never used dry shampoo, but it seemed like something that would be useful if they were going to be boondocking a lot. Gawain said he normally found a river, creek, or pond and used an eco-friendly soap when he was out. That didn't sound quite as fun as a shower. She grabbed her phone and added dry shampoo to a new list.

Yesterday she had also peed in the RV for the first time. Gawain had already prepped the black tank for use before they left home. Gawain told her there was a water pump they could use if they had a full fresh water tank that ran off of the battery, but in general he didn't travel full of water. He waited until he got closer to his destination to fill up. It made sense, extra weight would cost more money in gas and added weight to climb up and down hills while driving. For now, they used a bottle of water to flush things down. She had brushed her teeth using another bottle of water to get her toothbrush wet and to rinse out.

Today they were at the second casino, but this one had a campground attached. They even had a cable hookup, but since they were only staying one night, they didn't bother attaching the cord. She was really looking forward to getting a shower.

Jumping up, she grabbed out clean clothes and told Gawain she was getting a shower. She leaned into the shower, turning the fan on before stepping across the hall to the sink/toilet bathroom. Brushing her teeth, she set her clothes off to the side of the sink and walked to turn the shower on. Stepping inside, she shut the door, washing her hair first. Gawain had told her it wasn't like a house shower, there was limited hot water and limited tank storage. You apparently didn't keep the gray tank open all the time because you needed it to flush the sewer hose out, but you would also get the smells from the sewer coming up through your hose and into the RV. No one wanted to smell that. Finishing her hair, she grabbed her loofa and started washing the rest of her body. She still was covered in soap when she noticed it wasn't draining anymore. She hurriedly shut the water off, not wanting it to overflow into the RV.

"Gawain!" she shouted. "I think something's wrong!"

She stood there shivering, covered in soap bubbles. The door opened.

"What's wrong?" Gawain asked, looking around. "Oh. Yeah, you took too long in the shower with the water running. Let me go empty it and you can finish rinsing off. Be right back."

She closed the door. She could hear him on the outside of the RV, and suddenly the water started draining again. She quickly turned the water back on and rinsed, shrieking in surprise when it turned cold. Guess she wasn't shaving in the shower.

Merri shivered as she turned off the water and dashed out wearing a towel.

"Did it turn cold?" Gawain asked, a faint hint of laughter in his voice.

"Yes! What the heck? I was hurrying, I wasn't in there that long," Merri said, drying off and getting dressed.

"I'm sorry; I forgot you aren't used to an RV and didn't tell you about the shower head. The shower nozzle has a pause button on the handheld part. When I get a shower, I get in, get wet get my washcloth wet and soapy, and then I hit the pause button. I shampoo and wash myself, then I hit the pause button again to turn the water back on and rinse off. I've never shaved in the shower, but I've read that most people shave at the sink or use an electronic razor. I'm part of a bunch of RV groups online and I can give you the logins so you can go in and ask any showering questions to the ladies in the group.

"It takes a while to get used to. There are some campgrounds that have nice individual showers and bathrooms. Others have a shower room, where there are multiple ones all in a row with curtains. It's always a nice treat to have the individual ones; they always seem a little nicer. Some are pay showers, but I generally don't run into them too often. I've never really understood that either; if you're paying a campground fee, I think it should be included. But campground showers are an option too if you hate the RV shower. I just like not to have to lug everything to the bathhouse and back," Gawain added.

"I can see that. If I wanted to buy an electric razor, can we get it in town, or can I buy it online?"

"There is a decent-sized grocery store close by. We can stop and pick one up on our way out of town if you want. Their parking lot is big enough that I can park in the back and have enough room," Gawain said. "If they don't have any, we can try to buy one online. Some campgrounds accept mail for campers and others don't. It depends on where we are. There are pickup lockers in a lot of cities as well. I've used those for Amazon orders when the campground won't accept mail."

"That sounds perfect, thank you," Merri said, giving him a kiss on the cheek.

"Are you ready to pack up and get on the road?" Gawain asked.

"Yup, I have my checklist ready. Let me finish getting

dressed and I'll close up the bedroom and get some waters and snacks in the car."

"Okay. I'll work on the bathroom. Do you need to use it anymore, or are you finished?"

"I'm done," Merri replied.

"Let me grab a quick shower and then I'll close it up."

Merri got dressed, making the bed, and ensuring that everything loose that could fall was packed away. She pulled the blinds down, tucking the accordion door away and securing it. Gawain was incredibly fast in the shower and when she peeked into the stall, she noticed there were now two rubber-bottomed baskets. One held all their soaps, shampoos, and loofas from the shower. The other looked like it held their things from the bathroom: deodorant, Gawain's razor and shaving cream, toothpaste and toothbrushes. The bathroom looked empty, having only the soap container in the sink and the towel, which it looked like Gawain single knotted to the bar. She ducked back into the shower, making sure the fan was shut off and was closed and locked down.

In the kitchen, Gawain was pulling out some collapsible baskets and was packing up their plates, cups, anything from the upper cabinets that could fall out. He grabbed the under the sink items as well.

"Won't those stay in the cabinets?" Merri asked.

"Most of the time they will, but one time I must not have shut the cabinet right and opened the front door to find dishes shattered everywhere. Since then, I've moved them out of the cabinets to be on the safe side. I have Corelle plates and bowls, and they hold up extremely well, but they can still break under the right conditions. Some of the places I go to are pretty remote and replacing things can be a challenge. These baskets are perfect because they collapse and don't take a lot of room when they're not in use."

They worked together to finish packing up the rest of the

kitchen and living room area. Gawain showed her how to turn off the water heater and where the furnace and air conditioner switches were. "Can you run inside and open the sink faucets?"

After turning on the water, she followed Gawain outside, bringing their small garbage bag.

"Let me grab the storage bins and things we need from the back of the SUV, and I'll show you how I get the outside ready," he said.

Gawain turned off the water at the source and then disconnected the hose first from the RV and then from the spigot, making sure to drain any water that was still sitting in the hose.

"Why do you have a water filter out here?" Merri asked, wondering about the metal tube attached to the end of the hose.

"Water quality varies hugely depending on where you are. I always have this filter at the stand, so at least I know the water coming in is okay to use to brush my teeth and that kind of thing. I really like having the stand filter on the counter since it filters out a lot more things. I know some people who put in an entire filter system in their RV, but so far this has been working for me," he said with a shrug.

Merri had never even considered needing to worry about water quality. The things you learned, she thought.

"I have disposable gloves for when I disconnect the sewer hose," he said, handing her a pair. He grabbed a storage bin and a plastic U-shaped piece. She wasn't sure what that was for. He had hooked up the sewer while she had been inside the RV yesterday.

Merri stood next to Gawain and watched as he walked her through it. The sewer hose was sitting on top of a plastic ramp.

"First, I'll empty the black tank. Once that's empty, I'll close it and empty the grey tank, which will wash the hose out. When that one looks finished, I'll shut the valve and disconnect the hose from the RV side," he explained.

Merri watched as he twisted the sewer hose off the RV. Gawain held it up with one hand, slowly lifting the hose and walking toward the sewer. She could see a few things coming out in the clear elbow where it connected to the sewer pipe. That was a little gross. When Gawain couldn't see anything else coming through, he put a cap on the open end before moving down to the ground part. He twisted to disconnect the hose from the elbow, putting a cap on and placing the hose in the storage bin before taking the elbow out of the ground.

"Can you gather up the hose support?" he asked, pointing at the ramp type of thing the sewer hose had been resting on. "It's accordion-like, it just folds back together and then you use this piece to hold it together," he said, holding out the U-shaped piece.

Gawain stood, removing his gloves, and dropping them in the garbage bag. "I'll either have a small container of soap and wash my hands at the water hookup or I'll use hand sanitizer when I'm done." He pulled out a regular hose from another bin. "I use this one to flush out or fill the black tank. I don't like using the same hose for drinking water and the black tank. If I'm going to a new site and will be using the bathroom again, I'll let this run for thirty to forty-five seconds so that there is a couple of gallons of water in the black tank." Once he was done with that, he packed up the hose and put the bins in the back of the SUV.

Walking to the front of the Airstream, he made sure the propane tanks were off. Back inside, Merri closed the sinks when she saw they were done draining. Gawain went to the bathroom and pressed the toilet's foot pedal to open the drain and showed her how to add a scoop of Happy Camper, a couple squirts of blue Dawn dishwashing detergent, and a cap of Calgon fabric softener. "This will get the toilet ready to use. The Calgon helps things not stick. The Dawn does as well but can also help clean it. Every couple of moves, I'll dump a bag of ice down there as well. The ice moving while I drive helps break up any poop pyramids that may be stuck to the bottom." He turned the lights off and gave one last look around. They finished up by putting the stairs away and locking the door. Gawain turned the power off at the post, before disconnecting the specialized RV surge protector and unplugging the electric cord. The last thing he checked was the tire pressure for each tire.

Walking to the right side of the Airstream, he showed her how to bring up the stabilizers. "You want to get these up before you attach the RV to the car because you need to adjust the height of the front jack to have enough room for the ball of the hitch to sit under this cup, the receiver of the RV side of the hitch hookup. If you don't, you can bend the stabilizer bars," he added. "Before I remove anything else, I hook up the RV to the car." Merri watched as Gawain unlocked the hitch lock and used the front jack to lift the hitch to the right height. He climbed into the car and slowly backed up, lining up the ball of the car hitch to the receiver on the RV.

He walked her through lowering the jack so that the receiver attached to the ball. Once it was hooked on properly, he added a lock and plugged the electrical plug into the car. Gawain then hooked the RV chains and sway bars to the trailer hitch on the car.

"What was the wire you just attached? It's only held on by a carabiner to the trailer hitch," Merri said, looking at the very thin wire.

"It's the breakaway cable. It's in case the RV would become disconnected from the car. It activates the trailer's brakes."

Once everything was connected, he showed Merri how to remove the X-chocks between the wheels, and the wheel chocks that sat on the ground to keep the wheels from moving. They got it all packed into the back of the SUV. Gawain started the car while Merri moved behind the RV. She watched as he tested the turn signals, emergency hazard and brake lights. It all was working correctly, and she gave him a thumbs-up before walking around the site to make sure they didn't forget anything.

Climbing into the front seat, she smiled to see he had already put a granola bar and a bottle of tea at her seat. She was eager to get to their next stop in South Dakota.

7

"We're almost to our first stop," Gawain said with a grin.

"I thought we had a few more hours of driving," Merri said, confused. She was pretty sure Mount Rushmore wasn't this close.

"Nope, I have two small stops planned for today. They're a rite of passage kind of stops," he said, putting his turn signal on to exit the highway. He drove through a town, pulling into a parking lot with a few other RVs already in it.

"Come on, let's go!"

Merri climbed out, not seeing anything stop worthy yet. As they walked down the street, she saw that the concrete bases to the light posts had corn stamped on them. Literally corn on the cob, with the husks peeled halfway down to show the kernels.

"Tada!" Gawain said excitedly, pointing to a building across the street.

Merri stared at the building, trying to see what was special about it. It was large with three rounded globes on top of the roof, one in the middle over the entrance doors and one on either side. There were two pillar type of things on both sides of the front door as well. It was eye-catching, but she still had no idea what the "World's Only Corn Palace" was about.

Gawain took her hand, and they crossed the street. From here she could see that the artwork on the sides of the building wasn't painted on, but it was actually made of corn. Corn cobs, corn husks, they were all different sizes and colors, placed together to form images.

"What in the world?" she asked Gawain, wanting to touch to see if it was real.

"It's the Corn Palace! Every year, artists get together and come up with new designs. It started in 1892, but this building was built in 1921. They use corn, grasses, and other grains to make the murals. They have a museum, tours, snacks, and even a festival.

"We can't stay too long, our next stop will need more time, but I thought you'd like to see it. We can go inside and look around if you want?"

"Yes, please!" Merri replied.

They walked around, reading about the history of the Corn Palace. It was amazing to see what people were able to do with dried corn.

"Okay, on to the next stop!" Gawain said.

There wasn't a lot out here, Merri thought as they got back on the road. It was a lot of green land, some farms, some cattle, but they went hundreds of miles and didn't see much. Other than the Wall Drug billboards. There had to be hundreds of them. They were a mix of simple text and decorated signs. The ones with images had dinosaurs, a chapel, a cowboy, a burger, and everything in between. Some looked like they had been there years, but they broke up the landscape and kept the name Wall Drug in your brain.

"Are we going to Wall Drug?" Merri asked. It had to be that, there were so many signs.

"Yup. It's a crazy place. I love the story behind it, it's the epitome of being an entrepreneur. Mr. Hustead had a family and was trying to make his way as a pharmacist, buying Wall Drug in 1931. Wall, South Dakota was often missed by tourists and the small town was suffering during the Great Depression. But Mr. and Mrs. Hustead had an idea of advertising free ice water to draw people in. And it worked! You've seen how empty everything is out here, and then add in that cars didn't have air conditioning, so it must have been very hot in the summer. He put up signs along the highway, I'd imagine similar to what we drove past today, advertising his free water and it drew people in. It's really expanded from the small store. I think you could easily spend a couple of hours there. They still offer free water."

They pulled into Wall, South Dakota. It was still a small town and the gas stations near the highway were busy. The gas stations were smaller, and Merri was grateful that their RV wasn't extremely large. They still had plenty of fuel, but she imagined it would be challenging, if not impossible if you had a large RV. They found a place to park and walked to Wall Drug. It seemed like that was the one thing everyone was there for. It was packed.

There was a small chapel, bookstores, camping supplies, ice cream, souvenirs of anything you could imagine, a roaring T-Rex head surrounded by fake trees. They walked to the open area outside and saw a large jackalope. The gray rabbit had large brown antlers. It was both ridiculous and adorable. People were lined up to sit on its back for pictures. Gawain stood with her in line, and she climbed the steps to sit in the saddle. She wondered if there were any actual jackalope shifters. There were so many legends and tales, especially in this area of the country. What was the expression? Everything has a grain of truth in it?

They found the free ice water in the outdoor courtyard; it was a water fountain with small cups. It was cool, maybe not ice cold, but still refreshing. Merri grabbed Gawain's hand, pulling him into a souvenir store, buying postcards, a small jackalope statue, and a jackalope baseball hat. It was gray with small ears and antlers sticking out of the sides, a bunny face on the front, and a poofy gray tail in the back. She had no idea who would wear it, but she couldn't pass it up. Oh! The triplets would like it, they were the right age. She bought a couple more to mail back home to her nieces and nephew. They had passed a post office on their walk in, and she was hoping they would get a chance to stop and mail them.

"Let's get a snack," Gawain suggested.

They stopped in the café, trying the advertised five-cent coffee. Well, Gawain tried the coffee, although she had a sip and was surprised how good it was. She liked that they kept the tradition of free water and the low-cost coffee even though they clearly were successful now. They bought a slice of cherry pie and some donuts. It was a nice break from driving, and she enjoyed the treats. Gawain was right that they could explore for several hours. There were so many stores in the complex. She sent a picture of her on the jacka-lope to the family, both the Clan and her mom and siblings.

Using the bathroom before they left, Merri was eager to set up and relax at their new campground. Gawain said it was close to Sylvan Lake and was in Custer State Park.

It was getting close to dusk by the time they arrived. Merri climbed out, stretching. She double-checked the ground of the campsite, making sure there wasn't anything dangerous on the ground before Gawain pulled in. Gawain had told her that once he had accidentally run over a nail someone had dropped and gotten a flat tire. She moved the picnic table a little further out, giving Gawain as much room as she could. Gawain backed the Airstream into the site. There were some tall pine trees surrounding them, giving them some shade. It would be nice to sit outside and eat. They couldn't see the lake from here, but it wasn't far away. They had electric hookups but not sewer or water.

"There's a shower and bathhouse, as well as a water

source. We picked up the gallons of water before we came, so we should be okay water-wise, but we'll be able to fill them up if we need to. I heard they renovated the bathhouse since I was last here, so it should be pretty nice," Gawain said as he climbed out of the car. "Plus, you won't have to worry about water backing up on you," he said with a grin.

"Shut up," Merri shot back, shaking her head at him.

They put the wheel chocks in, and Gawain lowered the front jack before he unhooked the RV and pulled the car further out. When he came out, he looked at the spot, tilting his head and staring at the RV.

"What's wrong?" Merri asked, not seeing whatever he was looking at.

"I think I need to level the RV; the left side looks a little lower," he responded as he popped the back of the car open to pull out a square bag and a level.

"How can you tell?"

"At this point, just by looking. My eyesight comes in handy for that. There are systems you can buy that will tell you where it's too low or too high, but I've always just used a level and played around with it. Sometimes it's hard to tell, but when I walk through the inside, I can feel a difference. You don't want to fall asleep with your head lower than your feet, I can tell you that from experience." Gawain used the level to find the low spot and took a few orange plastic squares from the bag. "These are leveling blocks; they stack together so you can get the height you need. They're amazing; I've used them to level the RV, keep the stabilizers from sinking in mud, and for when my steps needed help too."

"How do they work?"

"I try to judge how much adjustment I need to make to the RV level. Each of these blocks that look like a Lego is about one inch high, these flat, smooth ones are about a half an inch. I don't think I need much here, maybe one block under the tires on the left side. I'm going to reattach the car and pull the

RV forward. Put one block behind each tire under the left side and then back away. I'll back it back into place and then we'll check the level again. If it's good, then we'll just put the wheel chocks back and keep setting up."

Gawain pulled forward about a foot, and Merri lined up the leveling blocks and stepped out of the way so he could back up. He managed to stop exactly on the brick. She would have been going back and forth for ages before finally giving up and placing the bricks down in a straight line and then picking up the ones that weren't needed.

They put the chocks down on the ground before they detached the car and checked the level. It looked good, so they put the X-Chocks between the wheels. Gawain set up the electricity while she went inside and started to unpack so they would be able to make dinner.

"How do you feel about campfire packets for dinner?" Gawain asked, looking through the screen door.

"Sure? What are those?"

"Super easy dinner, not a lot of cleanup. You can use a grill or a firepit. You basically wrap everything in aluminum foil and cook by the fire. If there's a grill over the pit, I use that. If there's no grill, then you can cook on the outskirts of the fire or in the ashes when it's burned down. I like to use onions, potatoes, and chicken with a little butter, so it doesn't stick, but I've cooked meatballs and burgers in them too, and any other vegetables that sound good. I'll grab some firewood from the office and get a fire started."

"I'll chop things up while you work on the fire," Merri replied.

She walked to the fridge, pulling out chicken and a stick of butter. They had stopped at a grocery store before they came to the park. To keep things cold until they got to the campground, and then of course until the fridge cooled down, which could take a while, they had bought frozen vegetables and a bag of ice. The ice was sitting on a baking sheet to contain any leakage or drips. They had some carrots and onions, maybe some Cajun seasoning.

Lining the table with pieces of aluminum foil, she stood at the table armed with a cutting board and a knife. She placed a couple pats of butter down on each foil sheet before slicing the onions. She tried to keep them all thin and about the same size. Merri grabbed the baby carrots, quartering them lengthwise and distributing them across the sheets. Cutting the chicken breasts into bite-sized pieces, she laid them on top of the vegetables. Sprinkling salt, pepper, and a little Cajun seasoning over everything, she closed the packets, wrapping each one in a secondary piece. It should be an easy dinner; she would have to watch how Gawain set them on the fire pit.

Walking outside, she saw he already had a decent fire going. It looked like their firepit had the grill piece to it, which would make cooking these easier. Gawain had set up their folding chairs and there was a bottle of water waiting for her in her chair.

"I had a question on the packets. Wouldn't it be easier to make on a sheet pan in the oven? I love finding new ways to do things, so I do want to cook them out here. I was just wondering why," Merri asked.

"When I'm boondocking, the oven doesn't work. It's a microwave convection oven combo and is electric. Some RVs do have a propane oven and they could use it when not on electric. I have a small camp oven that is under our bed in storage. It uses propane and I can use it when electric-less. Cooking in the RV can also really heat up the space, even with the air conditioners running, so during hot days it makes more sense to cook outside," Gawain answered.

"That makes sense," Merri said. "Do you want me to bring out the packets now or wait?"

"Let's wait a few minutes, let the flames die down a little bit. Want to sit with me?" he asked.

Merri nodded and walked over to her chair. "Thanks for the water."

Gawain sat next to her, holding out his hand. When she took it, he raised it to his mouth, giving her a kiss. "Thank you for coming with me. I know it's a bit outside your comfort zone."

"It's been fun so far," she replied. "When and where do we meet up with your friend Rob?"

"We'll stay here a couple of days, see the sights. Then we'll head to Rob. He's on some private property north of Belle Fourche, probably about a two-and-a-half to three-hour drive. We could also stop and see the Geographic Center of the United States. It's over that way. There's a monument in the town, but the actual center is just a geographical marker, a round disk in the ground, and is on private property. The owner's a nice guy and lets people come see it."

"The center of the US is in South Dakota? That doesn't seem right."

"It's close to the Wyoming border, about a thirty-five-minute drive. The center changed when Hawaii was added, so this new center accommodates that."

"Huh. Cool; I love learning new things. And Rob is up near there?" Merri asked.

"He is. He'll meet us at the road and show us back. He has special permission to be there, so we are officially part of his crew while we're visiting. I haven't heard if he has the horn results back. Based on the pictures, I wouldn't say it's a narwhal horn, but it's hard to tell from a picture. If it comes back as an actual unicorn horn, I'll have to give Doc a heads-up. The Convocation would get involved at that point and probably send in Wardens and some of their own researchers. We've both had experience with them stepping in and have worked for them before, but it's a headache. If Rob has to get them involved, I would prefer that we leave before they get there. I don't want them even thinking about our trip and the word unicorn in the same sentence. I know they're there to help protect us all, but I don't want anything even remotely unicorn linking back to Doc in any way," Gawain said.

"I agree, but won't they know we were there?"

"Rob won't say anything, and neither will his crew. If they find any trace of us there, the story will be that we decided to stop and say hello while on our honeymoon of sorts. The bonus of sightseeing and being able to show you all kinds of new things on our way is that the paper trail certainly looks like a vacation. That's not why I planned the stops, they're things I thought you would like, but it is a plus," Gawain hurriedly added in explanation, looking worried.

"I know. I can tell through our bond," Merri reassured him.

"We'll have to fill up on gas and probably water before we leave. He's completely off grid where he's at. He normally has a rain catcher for showers and some type of toilet on his digs, but it won't be fancy."

"I still have the bath wipes and I bought some dry shampoo. It will be fine."

"We can put the foil packets on now," Gawain said, poking at the logs. The fire was still going, but the flames had calmed down a bit.

Merri went inside and grabbed them. She wasn't worried about the dig per se, but she was grateful that they were friendly with Gage, the Warden back home. He had helped the family on a couple of occasions, even sending another Warden to help Ian and Berkley when they were attacked in Scotland. Even if they didn't have cell phone service, which was extremely spotty out here, they could still get in contact with the Clan's telepathic link, and someone would then get in contact with Gage. It was nice to have a backup plan and friends and family who were willing to help if they ran into trouble.

8

Merri had just finished making herself a glass of tea. She had made sun tea yesterday, not wanting to turn the stove on to boil water. It was pretty good, although a little strong. The key turned in the door and Gawain came through, still towel-drying his hair.

"I was thinking we could take Needles Highway over to Mount Rushmore, drive over to the Wildlife Loop at Custer State Park, and then head back on the other part of Needles Highway so you can see all the tunnels and crazy turns. It's hit or miss if I see any animals when I go through the park, so if we don't see any today, we can try again tomorrow," Gawain suggested, looking over at her.

"That sounds good," Merri replied. She did want to see the bison and this crazy road she had heard a lot about. She grabbed their day pack, filling it with sunscreen, trail mix, a travel first aid kit, and waters. If there were a lot of animals, she could see taking pictures and video, so she pulled out the battery pack to make sure she could keep her phone charged.

The road through the park was peaceful, she thought. It was quiet and the landscape was pretty. The sky was a bright blue, only a few white clouds drifting along. The hills were covered in fir and pine trees, the landscape dotted with patches of open fields. She saw several birds floating on the air currents, and she looked at Gawain, wondering if his falcon was yearning to fly. It didn't take them long before the road hugged the side of the mountain, the lanes narrowing until it became a single lane through the mountain. Looking down at her map, she thought they were at Hood Tunnel. It wasn't long, she thought as Gawain slowed down, making sure there weren't any cars coming the other way. The opening was uneven, not a perfect arch. She looked out her window as they drove through, the walls craggy and uneven. Soon after they passed the tunnel, Gawain slowed down again for the set of switchbacks in the road. No wonder they closed this in the winter and RVs weren't supposed to drive this. The closer they got to Rushmore, the more the sides of the roads were lined by towering rocky juts of the mountain.

"If you look behind us, on my side, you might be able to see Washington's face. You can see it better going the other way, but it's right there," Gawain pointed out.

Merri turned in her seat, slouching down so she could see out the back windows. She could just see the side of his head as Gawain drove around the bend. The car slowed to a stop as they joined the lines at the gate.

"I thought you had the National Park pass," Merri asked as Gawain pulled out money.

"I do. Technically, admission is free here, even without a pass, but they charge for parking."

It was busy, but they found a parking spot that wasn't too far a walk.

Merri stood, staring at the mountain face. It was hard to believe that someone had the imagination to design and carve four faces into the rock. It was certainly a grand entrance, walking down the pathway lined with flags to see Mount Rushmore at the end. She did laugh though, because while she knew the faces were huge, from back here, they seemed much smaller than you would expect based on the zoomed-in pictures in schoolbooks.

"Come this way," Gawain urged her. "I know a better view."

He took her along the Presidential and Sculptor's Studio trails. It did give some neat views. You were able to get higher and get a closer look at the monument. She could see Roosevelt better from these angles and it was amazing to see he was wearing glasses! They weren't as visible if you just stood on the main walkway and looked at the monument; Roosevelt was kind of tucked in the back. The people who had made this were certainly talented.

They stopped in the Visitor Center to get their passport stamp. Merri had a journal she started for this trip and wanted to collect stamps from any National Park, or even a state park if they offered the stamps, that they visited. Merri grabbed a couple of postcards to send home when they got back to the campsite. She wasn't sure if the campground office sold stamps or accepted outgoing mail, but the nearby town had a post office.

Gawain drove over to Custer State Park. Merri looked at the GPS screen. That road looked crazy. She could see why they called it a pig-tail bridge. The road curled around itself just like a corkscrew. The next tunnel they came to was square shaped and she could see the line marks running horizontally along the walls. It must have been where they chiseled the rock out or inserted dynamite. They kept working their way around the mountain, coming up to the next tunnel. This one was also square shaped, but there was a gap in the middle, the sunshine filling the space, small trees and greenery growing in the rocky areas outside the tunnel. Gawain pulled over to an overlook area.

"It has a great view, we don't need to stay long, but I thought you'd like to see it," he said. They parked and walked the trail for a little bit before Gawain helped her climb up a small rocky area. The view was amazing. There were trees and rocky mountains for as far as her eyes could see. There was so much undeveloped land here, so much green space, you could just breathe. She let the feeling of being surrounded by nature wash over her, the witch in her loving it.

They already had their Custer State Park pass because of staying in the campground, so they drove straight to the wildlife loop in the park. Once they turned onto the loop, Gawain slowed down to see what they could see. There seemed to be more open land in the park, still plenty of trees, but more fields. For the first several minutes, they didn't see anything, but as they pulled around the next curve, they saw a bunch of cars pulled over.

"There must be something up ahead," Gawain said. "You can always tell when there's wildlife when a bunch of cars are stopped."

Getting closer, Gawain slowed the car down to a crawl, letting Merri get a good look out the windows. He pulled over to stop so they could watch the herd of bison on the side of the road, grazing in the grass. There were a few calves, their furry bodies a little gangly as they ran around. Merri watched them in awe, pulling her phone out to take pictures and a short video. After watching them for several minutes, Gawain pulled out to make room for other cars. They didn't get very far before he had to stop to allow the animals to cross the road, the bison coming out from the trees right in front of them. It was breathtaking to see them all, Merri leaned forward in her seat to watch, even leaning over Gawain's lap to take a video out his window. Some were close enough that you could (but shouldn't) touch them. The hillside was covered with the bison, there had to be hundreds of them. The calves were adorable, there were a few running in the distance, and a few that looked like they might get into a fight. Following the road, they saw a few other animals, including the herd of wild donkeys that lived in the park.

"They call them the 'begging burros' because even though they were released into the wild many years ago, they still associate people with food. Tourists still stop to feed them, even though the park tells you not to," Gawain told her.

Merri watched as a mother donkey stopped in the middle of the road to let her baby nurse. The baby looked so fuzzy. The donkeys clearly had no fear of humans, as they were coming up to people to get pets and snacks. Merri didn't think Goldfish was the healthiest thing to feed them, maybe more fruits, or vegetables. She enjoyed watching them graze in the field.

Gawain sat for another minute before continuing to drive through the park. He eventually pulled off onto another side road, crossing a cool-looking stone bridge. He slowed down again and pointed out a pronghorn walking through the tall grasses. The grasses were brown at the tips, helping camouflage the pronghorn. Its coat was a little patchy, still losing its winter fur. As it walked past them, Gawain started driving until he reached an open area. There were small patches of dirt intermixed with the shorter grasses here.

"Watch," he told her with a smile.

Merri looked out the window, not sure what she was supposed to be looking for. Her eye caught a quick movement, but it was gone before she could register what it had been.

"What was that?" she asked.

"Watch the dirt," Gawain told her.

Merri picked the dirt pile closest to her, watching it intently. She gasped as she saw a little head poke out. The prairie dog chittered, causing another head to pop out of a neighboring hole to answer. A few of them ventured out, pausing to stand on their hind legs and call out to each other, heads turning to search for danger. The one closest to their car found a tasty leaf and started nibbling on it, holding it in its front paws, while sitting back on its rear haunches. Oh my lord, they were adorable. They sat for a few more minutes before heading back toward their campground.

"I was thinking we could go to the Lodge for dinner tonight," Gawain suggested. "Have a date night?"

"That sounds perfect," Merri agreed.

9

Merri woke up, stretching her arms above her head. Dinner last night had been perfect, and they had come back to watch a movie before falling asleep. She was excited to see Sylvan Lake today. Leaning over, she gave Gawain a kiss on his cheek.

"I'm going to go grab a shower," she murmured to him.

"Hmhm," he mumbled in response before burrowing his head back into the pillow.

The showers weren't bad here and she didn't have to worry about the water backing up into the shower because the tank got too full. Not that she minded the RV shower, it was nice to have, but showering like normal was delightful. She did a quick shave, happy to have enough space in the shower stall to be able to bend over and shave her legs. The electric razor did alright, but the regular razor just seemed to get a closer shave.

Getting dressed and brushing her teeth, she headed back to the Airstream. She was happy they weren't too far from the bathrooms like some of the spots were. Inside, she got a pot of coffee going, using one of the jugs of water they had brought with them. They would probably need to fill the fresh water tank and buy more gallon jugs before they made it to the dig site. Both sites, actually; Rob's and the one she and Gawain were going to. She took a couple bagels and heated them up, grabbing the cream cheese out of the fridge. They only had a small container and she wanted to use it up before they left since there was no reason to keep extra groceries that they would need to keep cold.

When the bagels were made and the coffee was finished, she started to hear Gawain moving around in the bedroom.

"I have breakfast ready," she called down the hallway.

"Be there in a sec," Gawain called back. "Let me finish getting dressed and I'll be out."

Gawain came out a minute later, bending down to give her a kiss on the forehead. "Thank you for breakfast," he said. "When I'm done, I'll take out the garbage and run to the bathroom, then we can head over to Sylvan Lake. I have a feeling it's going to rain today."

"Sounds good," Merri agreed. She finished eating her bagel and started packing a daypack. They weren't going far, but she liked having one with them. Some waters, nut and trail mix packets, a first aid kit, whistle. Nothing too crazy. She left the bear spray in the bag, even though she didn't think they would need it with how popular the lake was. Snakes were probably more dangerous around the lake area during the day, she thought. Maybe not, so the bear spray would stay.

Gawain cleared his spot and ran to the bathroom with his dopp kit. He had grabbed a shower late last night, so he would skip it this morning. He really did feel like it was going to rain and wanted to make sure that Merri got to see the lake before they had to leave to meet up with Rob. They had seen quite a few sights already: Mount Rushmore, Crazy Horse Memorial, Custer State Park, Rapid City, the world's largest Quarter Pounder at the McDonald's, and had seen quite a few animals. The last big thing to see in the area was the lake. He thought she would love it and it would make for some great pictures. There were a few caves in the area, but his falcon wasn't big on going into enclosed spaces and Merri had said she was fine with skipping them. Maybe they should do a family vacation with the whole group so that if she wanted to go in caves, she wouldn't be by herself.

He rushed back to the camper, making sure the awning was completely retracted and secured. If it got too windy, it could destroy the awning. Folding the chairs, he tucked them under the RV to make sure they wouldn't go flying. Currently there was only a light breeze, but his falcon was telling him a storm was coming. It wanted to fly on the winds. Maybe he could get some flight time in today. There would be plenty of other birds out and since there wasn't hunting in the park, he would be safe. He'd have to remember to talk to Merri about it.

"Ready to go?" he asked as he went inside.

"Yup, just finished packing a few snacks if we want a picnic or get hungry later," Merri replied.

"A picnic would be fun," Gawain agreed. He loved spending time with his mate. Merri was great at pulling him out of his own head, making sure he ate, and getting him to the Sunday dinners at home.

The drive wasn't long, only a few minutes. The parking lots were crowded. They ended up parking at the far end of a lot, but it was nice enough for a walk right now. He grabbed the backpack and threw it over his shoulder, holding out his hand for Merri. Kissing the back of her hand, he started walking to the lake. The sun was currently shining and would make for some amazing pictures. Walking up the path, Gawain paused as they came to the lake. There were pine trees on the left, large rocky outcroppings on the right and backside. The rocks made good climbing and photo opportunities. The layout of the lake was well planned; a nice path all the way around, a fishing pier on the left side of the lake, a swimming beach on the right side. He could see swimmers and kayakers in the water, as well as some people fishing on the pier. Holding Merri's hand, they walked along the lake. The mostly dirt path was well marked, beaten down through hundreds and hundreds of feet traveling over it. There were a few small rocks scattered about, he wasn't sure if it was old gravel, or just naturally occurring rocks. For the most part it was pretty smooth, although there were the occasional larger rocks sticking out of the dirt. They passed the small beach area; a few families had set up chairs and were playing in the water and lounging in the sun. Reaching the rocky outcroppings, Gawain looked at Merri.

"There's a neat view if you climb up. Want to go?" he asked.

Merri nodded, starting to climb up the rocks. Gawain was close behind her in case she slipped. It only took a minute or so to reach the top, as they weren't incredibly tall. It did give a nice view overlooking the lake though. Merri pulled out her phone and took a few pictures, before pulling Gawain in close.

"Selfie time," she said, smiling at the camera. Gawain smiled for a few pictures, then bent down to kiss her cheek. Merri turned her head, pressing her lips to his. She clicked a picture before pulling back as it started to get heated, knowing there wasn't much they could do out here in the open. Licking her lips, she smiled at Gawain, loving how the sunlight highlighted the white strip in his hair. She hoped that at least one of their future kids inherited the Mallen Streak; she thought it was striking and different. They climbed back down the rocks, keeping hold of each other. Toward the end of the lake, they climbed up another rock grouping. These were higher and she loved being able to adventure like this. This trip had been fun so far, experiencing new places and seeing new things.

On the backside of the lake, the trail led behind the rocks

on the lakefront, weaving between some of the large rock formations, making it seem like they were in a valley. They ended up behind the dam that was located on the far side of the lake. Looking up, it was amazing to see what was holding back all the water. You could see streaks along the middle of the structure where water had trickled down the wall, maybe when the water had gotten too high, she thought to herself. Gawain led her through a very narrow passage between the rocks, leading back to the lake. Turning to the left, they used the stones placed in the water to walk over to the top of the dam, looking over the water. There were several kayakers on this end, enjoying the sunny day, although there were a few clouds moving in.

"If we went through the woods to the right, we would eventually get to the lodge where we had dinner," Gawain said.

They climbed back over to the path just as a dark cloud moved overhead.

"I think the rain's finally moving in," Gawain said. "We should head back to the car. We saw a lot of the main path, and if it blows over, we can come back out."

Merri agreed, although she didn't think this was going to pass quickly. The wind had picked up, blowing in several other dark clouds, and then seemed to drop off. The kayakers and canoers were paddling quickly to shore and the swimmers seemed to already be out of the water. Walking quickly, they made it almost halfway back before the skies let loose, releasing a sudden downpour of water. They were quickly soaked, the rain coming in such a stream that it made it hard to see the lake. Merri grabbed Gawain's hand, knowing he had better vision with his falcon helping him than she did. She was very grateful that they would have blankets in the SUV and that their backpack was waterproof. She slipped a few times as the ground became slick with mud, but Gawain held her upright. They finally made it to the end of the trail and started walking toward their car. The rain kept coming down as they got closer to the parking lot, and the trees by the car provided a nice umbrella. Gawain unlocked the car, both of them rushing over. He tossed blankets over the seats to protect them from getting wet. Merri was now a little chilled, her clothes soaking wet, she shivered a little despite the temperature being warm.

Gawain looked over. "Are you ok…" he trailed off. Merri was soaked through, her shirt clinging to her. Her nipples had turned into hard peaks, giving Gawain the urge to speed home. A drop of water ran down her neck, slowly sliding down her chest, over the top swell of her breast before disappearing down her shirt. He leaned forward, tracing the path with his tongue.

"Gawain! Wha—" Merri broke off, moaning as he cupped her breast, his thumb flicking back and forth.

He leaned forward, biting the peak gently, sliding a hand up her legs, teasing her cunt, pressing his thumb firmly where her clit would be, but not rubbing, just holding there to apply pressure. She moaned again, her hips moving against his hand to get friction, pleasure spreading through her body.

The sound of car doors slamming from the other lake visitors brought them back.

"Let's go home," Gawain said, his voice husky with desire.

He threw the car in reverse, careful not to hit anyone, but hurrying to get back to the RV where they could finish what he started. He kept one hand between her legs, teasing her gently through her shorts, knowing the wet fabric would create a delightful friction. Merri spread her legs, sinking down into the seat to give him a little more access. He slid a hand under the wet material, angling his hand just enough to slide a finger into her wet heat. He needed to get home and have a taste; she was so wet. Pulling into their spot, he gently removed his finger, her eyes watching him hungrily as he sucked it into his mouth. Merri threw open her door, grabbing the backpack to get her keys. He raced after her, locking the door behind him before picking her up and carrying her down the hallway, her legs wrapped around his waist, her lips on his.

Merri grabbed his hair, pulling his head back, kissing her way down his neck, stopping at the hot spot by his ear and sucking a mark. It would be gone soon with his shifter healing, but he let out a low moan pulling her tighter against him. When they were in the bedroom, he pulled the curtains closed, pulling his clothes off, tossing them at the laundry hamper. His eyes almost glowed as his animal side came through, his pupils blown in lust. Merri whimpered, desperate to feel him filling her. She ripped her shirt off, the wet material of her shorts getting stuck. Gawain pulled her close, bending to suck on her breast, his tongue and teeth teasing her nipples, as he helped move her shorts down her legs. He tossed her on the bed, spreading her legs with a smirk. He leaned down, drawing in a deep breath, scenting her before spearing his tongue into her depths. Lapping at her juices, he held her lips apart twirling the tip of his tongue around her clit, applying the amount of pressure she loved. As her hips started to chase his tongue, he slid a finger into her channel, gently thrusting.

"Gawain, please. I want you inside me when I come," Merri pleaded.

Standing up, he pulled her body to the end of the bed. She wrapped her legs around his waist pulling him closer. Merri lifted her head, watching as his hard length parted her lips. She gasped, his penis filling her, his girth still stretching her opening even though he had prepped her. She wouldn't have it any other way. Gawain paused, his hand lifting her head up as he bent down to kiss her, his tongue tasting of her, plunging deep into her mouth, dancing around her tongue the way it had just been doing to her clit. She clenched her hands on his back, pulling him into her, needing to feel him move. The rasp of his dick against her walls soon had her climax rushing toward her.

"Almost. Gawain. I need..." Merri gasped. She was so close, his shaft filling her, rubbing her in all the right ways but she couldn't quite get there on her own.

Gawain reached one hand down tilting her hips, while the other hand let go of her head to reach down and press against her clit. His hips powered into her, the bed making noise at the speed of his thrusts.

'Yes! There mate, please, almost there, just a little more,' Merri pleaded over their link, unable to get the words out aloud. She let out a little scream as he hit her G-spot perfectly, her climax ripping through her, tremors of the aftershocks shaking her body even as she felt the warmth of his orgasm fill her.

"Love you, mate," Gawain said softly, leaning down to press a gentle kiss to her forehead.

"Love you too," Merri said, looking into his amber eyes.

They stayed snuggled together until Merri felt his release start to leak out of her. Grabbing a tissue, she quickly cleaned up.

Gawain pulled out some dry clothes for them. He kissed her forehead again as he went into the kitchen, getting the kettle started so he could make her a cup of tea. She would probably still be chilled from the rain. Thunder sounded outside, causing him to open the curtains and sit on the couch so he could watch the storm. Merri came out, snuggling into his side on the couch seat. They could see lightning against the dark clouds, the sun completely hidden at this point.

"Will you go flying later?" she asked.

"Once the rain stops, I might. Wet feathers make it harder to fly. But if the winds are still decent, I will. It would be nice to stretch my wings before we get to Rob's. He's a paranormal, but I forgot to ask if most of his crew this time were also paranormal or human. If they're mostly human, it might be hard to sneak out of the RV and fly. Here, the trees cover a lot and people will probably be inside because of the storm. If you could open the door or a window and let me out and then back in, I can shift in here and have less chance of someone seeing me," Gawain said.

"I can do that. I love watching you fly," Merri replied.

Thunder struck again, close enough that the RV shook a little.

"Will the RV be alright in the storm?" Merri asked. She was a little worried with how close that sounded.

"Yes. There's a lot of protection spells on it, plus there's the surge protector at the electric post as well. Some campgrounds don't have stable electricity, or in storms like this it can fluctuate, which can be bad for RVs. I had one surge protector melt at the plug when there was a big fluctuation in the current. I had to have a new one shipped overnight. But it's better to melt a two-hundred-dollar surge protector than fry the electric system of the RV. That's my thought at least, but there are still lots of people who just plug right into the base."

The kettle whistled, and Gawain got up to make her a cup of tea, grabbing a thin throw blanket on the way back.

"Here, Mer. This will help warm you up," Gawain said, handing her the tea. Sitting down, he draped the blanket over their legs, raising his arm so she could snuggle back in. It was nice listening to the rain drop down on the metal roof and watching the occasional lightning strike. He was glad they had gotten to the lake when they did. Hopefully he could fly tonight and then it would be the perfect end to their stay.

10

Gawain finished getting the RV hooked up to move. Merri had already packed up the inside and helped with the hoses. They had placed all the refrigerated food in the coolers with ice and frozen water bottles. It should be enough to keep things cold for a while. His coolers were rated for seven days of ice, but they could run into town and replace the ice as needed. He had also made sure any open food like crackers or cereal were put in airtight containers to help keep bugs, rodents, and bears out of the RV.

The drive today wouldn't be bad, maybe two to three hours, so pretty quick in terms of an RV trip for him. Now when they went to the site Doc gave them, that would be an eight-hour drive, maybe a little more. They would also be boondocking while they were there. He had a general archeology permit from the Wardens that would change to whatever local permit he would need, but he wanted to keep a low profile while they were digging around. It looked like it was near the Montana and Wyoming border near Yellowstone, so he was planning on taking Merri into the park at least once. Yellowstone was one of his favorite National Parks; it was simply gorgeous, and the scenery had such a wide variety to it. The potential dig site was luckily off a dirt path for part of the time, so he wouldn't need to be forging his own way too much. He was hoping to park the RV, secure it, and then drive to the site each day. It might draw less attention that way. There were primitive camping and boondocking sites nearby, so they would need to be careful.

Rob had sent a text saying he had his sat phone and to call once they reached the nearby town. He would meet them there and they would follow him back. There wasn't much regular cell phone service, so it would be easier to find the site this way. Rob still had not heard back on the test results for the horn. Gawain had separated his research documents and stored the ones that were not safe for anyone else to see under the bed and had the ones that he could share with Rob in a special container. It would protect them from the UV and rain. They were also spelled to return to the RV if lost or stolen. It was a pretty neat spell and he had been grateful for it many times in the past. If they found anything new this trip, he would have to find the witch who had created the spell for him. He wanted to make sure anything unicorn related was protected but was a little hesitant to show it to anyone else, although his source had been extremely trustworthy in the past. Maybe Merri could refresh the spell, he thought to himself. He'd have to ask her and see if she could create a similar protection; he knew witches could have more of an affinity for certain things than others.

"I put in the directions for the town," Merri said, coming up to him. She had been using the bathroom one last time; she didn't want to stop for a two-hour trip. Rob had told Gawain there were toilets on-site but hadn't expanded on what kind. For all she knew, they were a hole in the ground with a pop-up tent around it. She had bought a large container of hand sanitizer when they went to the store. She wanted to be prepared.

"Awesome, you ready to head out?" Gawain asked, eager

to get on the road. He was very excited to see what Rob might have discovered since the last time they talked. The short phone call from yesterday was only about where to meet him in town.

"I am," Merri replied.

Climbing into the SUV, Merri felt a little bit of nerves. She had never met one of Gawain's work colleagues before, much less been on an archeological dig site. She wasn't quite sure what to expect. She had a feeling she would do a lot of standing around and watching. Not that that was a bad thing; she could always take notes for Gawain or write down her own ideas and notes for the museum opening. She was excited to see how the construction would progress. It was due to start in a couple of days. Tess was going to send her pictures as things started to be built, but she might have to wait for a good cell phone signal to receive them. Tess had sent her a text last night saying that she, Berkley, and even Gage had come over and put magical protections on the building already. They were using the same crew that Rolf used at the house, and while they trusted them, there were also a few new seasonal workers on the crew for summer projects. With all the signs of hunters being more active and near their home, they wanted to get protections on before any work started. Just in case a new crew member was actually trying to scout out the town. They would add additional spells as needed once they started moving items into the museum.

She had an idea for a logo and pulled out her journal to jot it down before she forgot. She wanted it to be something that paranormals would recognize, but something that humans wouldn't think was too weird. They still hadn't agreed on a name for it either. Gawain was very literal on this one and was thinking of Paranormal History Museum. Merri wasn't sold on it though; it seemed like the museum would just be a long list of "sightings" and conspiracy theories with that name. Maybe not. She could always ask the family what they thought. It was almost so on the nose that humans might think it was simply a quirky oddity museum, which might be the best thing. If hunters dismissed it because of the name, they were less likely to try to come in. Of course, the protection spells would keep them out, but it would be better to not even be on their radar.

Gawain turned on a playlist and plugged in the phone with the directions. He pulled slowly out of their spot, getting them on the road. It had been a good stop and he was happy he had been able to show Merri some of the monuments. It was always fun to see the bison. The herd moved throughout the park, so you weren't guaranteed a sighting. Hopefully they could see the ones at Yellowstone too. He needed to make sure they took at least a day and went to the park so Merri could see it.

He glanced over to see Merri was sketching something out in her journal. "What are you working on?" he asked.

"An idea for the museum's logo. I wanted it to be something paranormals would recognize and be drawn to, but something humans wouldn't think too strange."

"What is it?" he asked.

"Hmm, I'll show you when it's done, it's not quite right yet," she said with a smile.

"Okay," Gawain said. He was curious now. He didn't have any ideas when it came to a logo or a sign for the museum. Gawain did have a few ideas for what he wanted the inside exhibits to be. He wanted to have a "unicorn" display and have the story behind the use of unicorn horns in health powders, decorations, and thrones. It would be interesting to both humans and paranormals, while at the same time almost debunking the unicorn myth. He thought if he got enough of those types of exhibits, then people who didn't know about the paranormal wouldn't think the real exhibits were, well, real. Those who were paranormals or were mates, they could take the time to explain about the exhibits, the truth versus the myths. That was the part he was looking forward to; sharing and explaining all his knowledge and finds through the years.

The drive to Belle Fourche was easy. There were several small towns they passed, but there was a lot of farmland as well. You could see some hills and forests in the distance. The town itself wasn't large, and from the road they drove in on, they could only see one gas station. At least it was on a corner, it might help him get in and out easier. This was where they were supposed to meet Rob. Gawain had called him when they were twenty minutes away. Luckily, there was no one else there, so hopefully that would make it easier to pull out of the parking lot as it was a bit of a tight squeeze. As soon as he finished pumping, a vehicle pulled into one of the parking spaces in front of the store. Crap, that would make it harder. The driver of the truck got out and started walking toward them.

"Rob! I almost didn't recognize you!" Gawain exclaimed. His friend had grown a beard and his hair was several inches longer than the short, almost buzz cut, he used to wear.

"Gawain! It's good to see you!" Rob grabbed him in a bear hug. "Where's your m—wife?" he asked, looking around.

"In the car," Gawain said, as Merri climbed out.

"Merri, this is my good friend Rob. Rob this is my m—Merri." He almost slipped on the word mate as well. Even though there weren't a lot of people nearby, they still needed to be careful about what they said.

"It's so good to meet you! I was hoping Gawain would find someone to help ground him," Rob said, shaking her hand.

"I don't want to ground him, just make sure he eats every day and spends some time away from work," Merri clarified. She loved Gawain for who he was.

"Perfect answer," Rob said with a grin. "Let's get going so

we can get you set up and I can show you around before dinner. Is your RV still pretty quiet?" he asked, looking intently at Gawain.

"It is," Gawain replied, knowing he was talking about a silencing spell that had been placed on it. He had had several confidential and sensitive conversations about their digs with Rob in the RV. Before they started, he would ask Merri to refresh the spell. "Would you like to see some of the improvements we made?"

"I'd love that! Maybe after dinner?" Rob asked.

"Sounds like a plan. Let me run inside and grab some beer. Then we can really celebrate seeing each other again," Gawain said. "Mer, did you want anything?"

"I'd love a tea, if they have any," she replied.

"Be right back," Gawain said, giving her a kiss on the cheek.

"If you need any funny stories about Gawain, let me know," Rob said, grinning. "We've been on a few digs together and I've got some doozies."

"Thanks," Merri replied, not quite sure what to think of him. He sounded friendly enough. Of course, warming up to people quickly wasn't normally part of her nature, and she didn't have a good enough read on Rob to know if this was friendly teasing or something else. The danger alert pendant Berkley had made all of them wasn't glowing, so she knew he wasn't a real threat to them. It was more that she was worried about him not being as good of a friend as Gawain thought he was.

"I really am glad Gawain found you. I try to make sure he eats at least dinner when we're on digs together, but he really gets sucked into his work and forgets how long he's been at something. I can't even count the number of times I've found him in the same exact spot the next day. I'm glad he now has someone to look after him," Rob said earnestly. "I may tease him a bit, but I do care for him."

"I'm glad he's had a friend like you to look after him," Merri replied. "How has the dig been going?" she asked, trying to keep the conversation going and not have awkward silence.

"Pretty well. It's been interesting for sure," Rob said, before pausing. "There's some things I wanted to run by Gawain tonight, if we could."

Merri nodded. *'Gawain, what's so special about the RV being quiet?'* Merri asked over their link.

'There's a silencing spell on it. I had it put on several years ago so that we could talk about paranormal or confidential things without being overheard. RVs are generally not the most soundproof of places,' he replied. *'I was going to ask you to double-check and refresh it if needed before he came over tonight.'*

'I can do that,' Merri agreed. *'So, wait! I didn't need to be worried about people hearing us in bed?'* she asked. She had been so worried that someone walking by would hear them having sex. She had certainly heard more than she wanted to while taking a walk around the campground.

'No, anyone outside wouldn't have been able to hear you,' he replied.

'That would have been good to know, hun,' she replied. Good grief, she would have been a lot more interested in doing things if she had known no one could hear her. In every other aspect of her life, she tended to be quiet, but during sex she could get quite loud.

'Sorry, I'm just so used to it, and I forgot you haven't been there the whole time,' he replied.

'Anything else I should know?' she asked.

'Most of my items and documents in the RV are spelled to return if lost or stolen. The RV itself has anti-theft and anti-damage protection spells on it. Since I use it to transport and store items when I'm on a dig, I wanted it to be a safe space. I was going to ask if you could look at it and see if you could beef it up at all. I have a feeling we'll find something good on this trip,' he said. There was

something calling to him, the call only getting stronger the closer they had gotten to this area. It still wasn't very strong, so he didn't think he would find it here. He had a feeling it was going to be in Doc's old tribe's location.

'I can do that,' she agreed. She would need to see if she could study what was there. Maybe Tess and Berkley could join in over the Clan link and see what they thought. Berkley had a knack for seeing spells.

"Here's a lemon tea," Gawain said, holding out the bottle to Merri. "It's the only non-sweet one they had."

"Thank you," she replied, giving him a quick kiss.

"Ready to head out?" Rob asked.

Gawain nodded, putting the beer in one of the coolers before climbing into the car. Rob pulled out and luckily no one else came in, giving Gawain room to move the RV a little more easily. The drive out of town was similar to the route they took in; mostly open areas, some farms, a few houses scattered about. Ten or so minutes later they pulled off onto a dirt path. They made it about a mile before they came to a gate. Rob jumped out to open it, pulling off to the side to let Gawain through before shutting the gate behind them. It was rather plain out here, just a few dry-looking shrubs and a dirt path. He wondered how they had found this site; if Rob had found some clues that led him here or if the owner saw something and contacted them. He'd have to ask him when he came over later tonight.

11

Merri looked out the front windshield, drawing in a deep breath. There were about thirty people outside. She could see tents, vans, campers, a few porta-potties scattered off to the side of the drive. There was a large tent straight ahead and a couple of trailers off to the right. Rob had pulled off into a parking area and then walked up to their car. Gawain rolled down the window to see where he wanted them to go.

"Straight ahead is the meal tent. We have a cook this time, although it's mostly grilling type of foods. Breakfast is normally biscuits and eggs. We have coffee, but it's instant. The trailers to the right are the bathhouses. The smaller trailer is the women's. We only have a few on this dig, but it makes it more comfortable for them if they don't have to share shower space with the guys. We have a company that comes and adds fresh water to the tanks and drains them as needed. I know you have one in the RV, but you are more than welcome to use the showers here and save your water.

"Since you're only here for a little bit, I thought I'd have you pull on the outside of the living area setup. That way you don't have to navigate too much around anyone when it's time to leave," Rob added.

"Sounds good," Gawain agreed. "Just show me where."

Rob jumped back into his truck and drove ahead of them. After driving a short distance, he pulled off the path, circling around a couple RVs and vans before pulling through and facing the road. He rolled down his window, leaned out, and pointed. "I think this should work well for you guys. It's pretty level and easy to get out of."

Gawain gave him a thumbs-up and maneuvered into the space. It should be easy to pull out and leave when the time came. They weren't too far from the bathrooms and showers if they chose to use them. He didn't recognize a lot of the workers around, so he would walk with Merri to the facilities. Rob usually vetted his crew pretty well, but Gawain wasn't comfortable with her walking by a bunch of unknown guys on the way to the showers. He'd seen too many fights break out at digs when the heat and repetitiveness got to some of them.

Throwing the brake on, he turned the car off and grabbed his tools, wanting to make sure the Airstream was level before disconnecting from the SUV. Checking multiple spots, Gawain was pleased. Rob had been right, and it was pretty even ground, not enough difference anywhere to need a leveling block. The outside setup was quick. Merri headed inside to open the windows and let any breeze in. They had fans that could run off the solar panels or from battery packs, but they would save those for tonight. No use in running them when they weren't going to be in the RV much. There wasn't any shade, which would be bad for the heat but good for using the solar panels.

Gawain walked out to the car, grabbing a cooler. Rob was heading toward him, having put his truck back in the parking lot.

"Need anything else brought in?" Rob asked.

"Can you grab that other cooler?" Gawain replied.

"Yup," Rob said with a grin, reaching out to grab it and bumping the door closed with his hip. "Once you guys are all set up, I can show you around the site."

Merri held the door open for them. "I think we're pretty good right now. We can always work on it later. I already got the bathroom items and chargers set up," Merri said to Gawain.

He nodded. Without using the bathroom and shower here, and having meals provided if they wanted to eat with the crew, they didn't really have as much to get out. They could just leave all the dishes packed away. He might pull out the coffee pot though since he didn't like most instant coffees. They had filled their fresh water tank before coming here, plus they still had both bottled and jugs of water. The coffee pot didn't take that much energy and he had a kettle and a French press as well. Coffee was one luxury he tried to always have with him, although for this trip he made sure to pack tea bags as well for Merri. Grabbing his hat, he handed Merri hers. It was quite sunny, and it was easy to get dehydrated or sunburned out here; the dry heat often meant that people didn't drink enough water because they didn't feel as hot compared to when there was more humidity. There had been people who had passed out on dig sites before. He grabbed a water bottle for both of them, Merri taking them and placing them in her small daypack with a smile. He knew she would have her standard sunscreen, snacks, and a small first aid kit in there as well. Gawain followed the others out of the door, locking it behind him.

It was a nice site; they even had some sun sails set up over the dig area to provide shade. Being close to town certainly helped with supplies and it was a nice treat to have a company provide and service the bathrooms and showers. He had been on sites before where he took showers from collected rainwater or rinsed off in streams or lakes. This would be a great place to learn about archeology, he thought, seeing a few younger-looking people he assumed were students. Rob always tried to reach out to the local community and see if anyone had interest in learning and experiencing what they did.

"We have a nice volunteer group this time, about five or so people from the local community and another eight, I think, from schools. We have a mix of high school and college kids," Rob said, pointing out where the volunteers were working under the supervision of Rob's normal crew.

"How did you find this spot?" Gawain asked quietly.

"I had some research that led me here. I had met the owner somewhere many years ago, so at least he was receptive when I reached out to see if I could probe around a little bit and see if there was anything actually here. When I found the remains of what looked like a small village or family group, I cleared it with him to bring in a team," Rob replied.

Rob led them across the ground with scattered clumps of dried grass. "Over there is where I found the narwhal horn. We're still not sure what it was doing so far inland. Maybe it was a family treasure, maybe they traded for it or were going to use it in trading. There hasn't been anything to really indicate why it was here," he told them. "I would think it was unrelated and dropped by someone else, but it seemed to be pretty well integrated with the other items we discovered, found at the same level, other items found below and on top of it."

"Interesting," Gawain replied. He knew Rob was telling him that it belonged here, whether or not it was narwhal or unicorn in nature. He was eager to see the pictures of the dig, maybe get in the dirt and take a look himself, he thought.

"I'll drive you up to his house later so you can meet him. I think you'll have some things in common," Rob added.

Ah, the owner was a paranormal of some sort, Gawain realized.

Merri looked around the site, seeing grid patterns marked off with string. It looked like there were various depths dug out. There were a few heads sticking out of the deeper holes. It was interesting to watch them slowly and carefully unearth something buried, but she much preferred her library research. The library was climate controlled, had less people (generally), and definitely less bugs.

She looked around as Rob walked them deeper into the site, observing people's different techniques and the variety of tools. She had no idea that there were so many different sizes of trowels and that one looked like the tool her dentist used to get plaque off her teeth. There were a wide variety and sizes of brushes as well, most looked like paint and tooth-brushes.

Merri looked down as they came across another grid pattern. This one, Rob jumped down into. Gawain followed him in, but Merri chose to sit on the side.

"This is where I found the horn. There's no evidence of similar items, nothing to suggest why it was here. I dug down quite a bit, trying to find anything else to go with it. I placed a marker on the side over here to mark how far down it was. It's been slightly frustrating not finding anything else like it. There's the normal evidence of someone living here; a few tools, burned wood, fibers, a few animal remains, even evidence there might have been some farming, but nothing that connects to the horn. If it's real, why haven't I found evidence of either human or horse bones? Did they lose it? Cut it off as punishment? Was it stolen? Was the body buried somewhere else?" Rob added in an extremely quiet whisper, "I have a few things to run by you tonight. After dinner."

Gawain nodded. It was very odd that there weren't bones nearby where the horn was found. If the shifter died, he thought the horn would have stayed attached at the skull and the entire skeleton would be here. If for some reason the horn was removed in shifted form before death and then they died as a human, you would think the human remains would be nearby.

'Doc?' Gawain said, reaching out over the Clan link. Cell phone reception was spotty, and he didn't want anyone else to overhear this conversation anyway.

'*Gawain? How are you? Do you need help?*' Doc asked, concern in his voice.

'*No, no. We're fine. We made it to my friend's dig site. He hasn't heard back on the nature of the horn yet, but this is weird. He hasn't been able to find any other bones nearby. If it was stolen and this was a temporary spot for some hunter or human who found the horn, that would make sense, except why leave it behind? I assume that when you die, your horn stays attached?*' Gawain asked.

'*Yes, if we die in shifted form, unicorns keep their horns. It's part of our skeleton. Our old tribe leader never wanted to leave evidence behind, so he would break the horns off and destroy them.*'

'*He broke them off before burial then.*'

Doc hummed. '*For the most part. I remember as a young boy, maybe around five or six years old, there was someone who was dying. They were older, but of course as a child everyone seemed old, so I'm not sure how accurate I am on age. I don't know how or why they were dying, I assumed it was from old age, but the tribe never spoke of it. I have no idea why they were shifted and couldn't shift back to human form. Anyway, the tribe leader wanted to leave. There had been an increase in people traveling near our home and he wanted to find someplace less occupied. He didn't want to wait for this person to die naturally, but killing was not allowed. So, he had this person held down and their horn broken off. Thalia had to be held back from stopping him. She was fierce and as a healer this was an abomination. He wouldn't listen to her pleas to simply let them die on their own time and then remove the horn if he must. I can still remember their screams. Tribe leader took the horn and destroyed it, all the while this poor person was lying there bleeding, in pain. Thalia created a poultice and tried to help, but the leader pulled her away and dragged her off when he declared it was time to move. She was too valuable to the tribe to let her stay behind, is what he said. She would have caught up to us. There is no way that poor person lasted much longer after that trauma. All that to say, yes, if they died as a unicorn, the body would remain unicorn, horn and all, unless it was removed. If they died human, there would be no horn.'*

'Did people just cart around horns?' Gawain asked.

'Back then, and still some today, people believe a unicorn's horn has power. It doesn't. There are a larger percentage of minor healing powers in unicorns compared to other paranormals, but true healers like Shaye are extremely rare, no matter the species. Hunters liked to have it as a trophy. Myth-loving people liked thinking the horns were a source of power or could heal them or keep them from being poisoned. It's not true; you could drink from it, make a powder from it and consume it, try to meld it to your body, none of it will work. The healing came from the person, just like any other paranormal traits or gifts. If the horn is a unicorn horn and is separated from a skeleton, then it was somehow removed. I saw some vicious fights in the tribe and the horns can crack or even break off, just like any other bone. It takes a lot of effort for that though and you would see evidence of damage. If it broke due to trauma, it wouldn't be a smooth base, there would be jagged edges and even fractures running up from the base. If it's smooth, maybe they filed it down, but I think you could still see minor cracks from the break. I would look for saw marks or something like that, something that might show if it was cut off,' Doc replied.

'Rob doesn't have it any longer. He sent it off for testing, but he did take lots of pictures. I'll have to see if I can zoom in and find anything.'

'If it's a narwhal horn, well it's really a tusk, and it is smooth at the base, there is a good chance it was also removed. They can lose them, break them off during their lifetime, and I don't believe they grow back,' Doc added.

'Thanks. It looks like a family or small settlement was here based

on some of the things Rob's crew has found. If it comes back unicorn or we find anything else, I'll let you know,' Gawain said.

'Thanks.'

Well, at least it answered that question, Gawain thought. "I would love to catch up after dinner tonight. Do you want to come over for a beer? We can go over your notes too," he said to Rob.

"Sounds good. I can't wait to hear how you two met," Rob replied.

12

A knock sounded at their door. Gawain moved to open it, smiling when he saw it was Rob.

"Come on in! Merri has some brownies and pretzels for us to snack on, and the beers I bought earlier. They stayed cold."

Rob came in and sat down at the table with a large box. "Thanks. I grabbed everything I thought might be useful."

Merri came out from the bedroom. "Hi Rob. I'll be right with you, go ahead and start eating. I'm just closing up the windows."

Once the windows were closed, she focused on the silencing spell that had been placed on the RV. It was good, but she layered her own version over top of it. Hers was a little beefier, a little stronger. When that was finished, she activated the cooling spell she had made with Tess and Berkley before they had left. The spell wouldn't last long, just a few hours until the candle burned down, but this way they could close the windows for an extra layer of protection.

"Holy cow! Did you upgrade the solar panels to run the air conditioner?" Rob asked, surprised.

"No," Gawain laughed. "I just mated well."

"It won't last long," Merri warned. "Maybe three hours, or

until the candle burns out. I just thought it would be better to have the windows closed for this conversation. The silencing spell should work with them open, but why take the risk."

"You're a witch?" Rob asked.

Merri nodded. "I am. My sister and a friend of ours helped create the cooling spell before we left, so I'm happy it's working."

"How did you guys meet?" Rob questioned, curious. "Gawain almost never goes out unless it's to find new supplies or to do research."

Gawain laughed. Rob wasn't wrong; unless he was on a dig, Gawain tended to be an extreme homebody. Mostly because he was deep into research for a project. "You remember me talking about my friend Rolf?" After Rob nodded, Gawain continued. "He has a large house and some property in Tennessee. Last year, he met his mate. Shaye is great for him. They had some issues with Rolf's dad and ended up calling in friends to help."

"Wait, isn't his dad Vlad?" Rob interrupted.

"Yup. It was a bit of a mess. When Rolf wouldn't join Vlad in his plan to gain more power, he tried to kill Rolf. A couple of times. I was one of the friends that came, along with Shaye's friend Tess. Tess helped a lot with the protections for everyone. Rolf tried to give his dad one last chance, which we all knew the man wouldn't take. Vlad died in the battle, which frankly was best for everyone else."

"Didn't you get into trouble with the Convocation? They generally don't condone larger fights, especially near humans," Rob said.

"Rolf cleared it with the local Warden first. He's also the town Sheriff and didn't want Vlad causing any more problems."

"Knowing a Warden would be helpful," Rob said. "Alright, so you go to Rolf, help defeat a crazy guy. Then what?"

"Tess, Shaye's friend, is Merri's sister. We had a bit of a problem when Sam, her mate, was injured while visiting Tess's family. Merri helped bring him back home to heal. That's when we met." Gawain left out about Shaye's healing ability. It wasn't his secret to tell.

Rob nodded and took a sip from his beer. "It sounds like you guys have been busy."

"A little bit," Gawain agreed. "But I kind of love it. I get to have my research and the freedom to still go on digs, but now I have a home base besides the Airstream. There's a support system now. Well, to be fair, Rolf and them would always have come help me if I needed it, but I don't think I ever really thought about it. We've really become more like a family, a Clan, even though we're a mix of paranormals. Rolf even found a side project to keep me busy when we're not on a dig."

"Oh yeah? What's that?" Rob asked.

Gawain looked at Merri. It wasn't like it was supposed to be a secret, he thought. They were hoping that the museum would be helpful to paranormals, and Rob might have some additional information that would be good to have in it.

Merri nodded, agreeing to tell Rob.

"He bought me a building in town, but it's off one of the side streets. It's kind of a quirky-looking thing. His idea was to create a paranormal museum, but of course it's in a human town, so it would be considered closer to an oddity museum maybe. Shaye was human and pointed out how hard it is to learn everything; as born paranormals or just people who have been paranormals for a long time, we often forget the little things that can be important, we take it for granted, think it's 'common knowledge.' Rolf's idea was to have a history of paranormals, some information and artifacts, but nothing in the main area that would reveal us. Like the unicorn horn, if I could get a narwhal horn, I could add the history about how the Vikings sold narwhal horns to Europeans, claiming they were from unicorns. Humans might think, oh that's neat, that's how a myth got started, but paranormals might ask more questions."

"So how would you get correct information to paranormals? If it's all almost-the-truth information, how is that helping the paranormal community?" Rob asked, genuinely confused.

"We would have a separate section blocked off. This would be the area with more in-depth information and actual history for paranormals. Shaye mentioned having almost like a "So *Now You're A Wolf* or *You Mated A Paranormal, Now What?* type of information, like self-help pamphlets or booklets. We're working on spells to keep ill-intentioned people or regular humans who don't know about paranormals out of the area. We all know simply having a lock won't do much good. I would love to be able to talk about different digs I've been on, or to share my history knowledge. I have some great paranormal history books I could share. I don't think the history gets passed on very much anymore, and it seems to be very species specific when it does. For example, wolf packs tend to teach about wolf history and the bare minimum on other species. It seems to be the common practice, but all paranormal history is important, and it's intertwined."

Rob nodded. "That's true. It's never good to learn just one side as it tends to be biased. I have a bunch of things as well if you need ideas."

"I would love that. The building's being renovated now, and then I'll start digging through my things. Would you be willing to go over my plan, once I make one, to see if I'm missing anything?" Gawain asked.

"Of course. It sounds fun. It's a great idea. You need to make sure you spell everything for anti-theft as well. Or maybe make copies and have those in the museum instead of the originals. I know you have a few things a couple of people in the Convocation would love to get their hands on," Rob advised.

"That's a good idea. Our local librarian might have some ideas for that."

"Marge would be great to ask," Merri agreed. "She's bound to have some ideas after watching over the library for so long."

Rob shook his head. "It sounds like you landed in the perfect spot," he told Gawain. "I'm happy for you." There was a pause as he chewed a brownie and washed it down with a few gulps of his beer.

"Okay, so I wanted to speak privately because there are some weird things that have been happening. Sometimes it was things that were single occurrences, nothing that I thought much about. But then they all started adding up, and I think they're connected. If it's anything like I'm thinking, it's not good either. I found these documents, the ones I sent to Gawain, a few years ago and that got me interested in finding some proof that unicorns had existed. I know we've all read about them in history books or heard stories, but I haven't come across a person yet who has met one. The closest was a story told to someone by their grandfather of a tribe that lived out West.

"I kept hunting though, because it seemed weird that no one knew much about them, where they lived, what happened to them. Gawain could tell you that I fall into conspiracy theories or get paranoid about protecting information," Rob said to Merri. "He's not wrong, but I've had too many run-ins with people in power that keep information for themselves. For example, when Douchebag comes in and confiscates evidence we find at a dig."

"Douchebag?" Merri asked, confused as to who they were talking about. It was definitely a capital D that he used.

"It's what he calls one of the Convocation members we've had issues with. There are a couple we trust, but there are a few that seem to work for their own agenda, not for the good of the whole community. If they come onto a dig, they take over, often destroying things because they don't know the proper techniques to safely remove the items from the ground. They will also take your findings under the excuse that they want to examine them, but you will never get them back. If you file to get them returned at the Convocation offices, you're told they were never there, there's no evidence of them being filed," Gawain told her.

"There's Douchebag, Douchecanoe, and TwatWaffle," Rob grumbled. "The DDT are a pain in my ass. I know they are suppressing information. Anyway, I was in this tiny Greek town trying to hunt down a book. It was getting late, and I was heading back to my hotel when this old guy stumbled into me. It took me a second to realize that he had shoved a bunch of papers into my hands before running off. I chased after him, but it was like he disappeared. They found his body a few days later. The official story is that nothing was missing from his wallet or body, so it wasn't a robbery. Besides being old, he didn't smell of sickness or injury, so I don't think he died of natural causes. The papers ended up leading me to this site, so I'm going on the assumption that it was hunters chasing him.

"I've heard some rumors the hunters are ramping up again and some good friends have had some confirmed sightings. I know for sure of the human variety, but also heard about some paranormals turning on their brethren for cash," Rob said.

"What do you mean?" Gawain asked, trying to get clarification.

"I've heard of a reward being offered for leads on strange occurrences, sightings, or documentation of these things. I'm always careful, you know that, but I found this flyer in town a few weeks ago," Rob said, handing over his phone. The screen showed an image of a poster on a community board.

"Want to earn some extra cash? I'm a writer who loves local legends and myths. I'm working on a new book and would love to include your town. Call or email any local legends or stories on the supernatural, ghosts, monsters, anything weird! Extra payment for any proof!! (pictures, books, drawings, video, sound recordings)," Gawain read.

"I know. It could be innocent enough, right? It's just vague enough to draw people in, wanting their town to be noticed, wanting to get their own five minutes of fame. Maybe some of the paranormals think it would be harmless to give a little information out, nothing that really proves anything. For as long as we live, we still have the same problems as humans. We still need money to exist comfortably. Spells to change our age and name on driver's licenses and property titles aren't cheap. Some might be younger ones that don't really know the danger yet. It's been a while since we had a real hunter problem, they might not even know our history well enough to know such things exist. But I've heard of others who are like Vlad or who are rogues, selling secrets to whoever is sending this flyer out. Because it's not just here. I've seen this in multiple cities and have heard about it in other countries from friends. That doesn't sound like a simple writer. There have been a few cases of paranormals disappearing, and in almost every case, one of these flyers had been placed in the town. It could be a huge coincidence, but I don't think so."

"Can you send us that? I'm going to forward it to our local Sheriff. He's been worried about signs of hunters nearby but hasn't been able to find them in person yet," Merri asked.

Rob nodded, taking his phone from Gawain, and sending a text message.

"I added extra security around my storage areas and have been very careful about who I talk to. For every dig, I check out my core crew group, but when we're getting locals or volunteers, I don't always have a good background check on them. It's why I sent the horn out for testing, even though I really hate getting them involved. I didn't want someone seeing it and selling out the dig. Even if it's just a narwhal horn, it causes problems if people think it's real and come onto the dig site. There are a few of us here that are paranormals and do not want to be found by hunters," Rob said firmly, pulling some documents out of the box.

"Here are the images and measurements from the dig. The horn was about three feet long, a white/ivory color, twisted. It looked smooth on the bottom. I don't know enough about unicorns to know if they shed their horns like antlers or if it's more like a bone that grows large, or even a tusk like an elephant. There's not much information available. Narwhals can lose and break their horns off as well, and without having seen a unicorn horn before, I don't know what differences to look for," Rob added.

Gawain grabbed a magnifying glass and looked over the pictures. It looked like the horn had a smoother base, not jagged or torn like he would expect if it had fallen off in a fight or was damaged some other way. "Do you have any on your phone?" he asked Rob. There were a few possible marks on the base of the horn. Maybe. It was hard to tell if it was scratches on the horn or simply a fuzziness in the printing.

Rob handed over his phone, the images pulled up. Gawain enlarged them, peering closely at the base, looking for marks like Doc had recommended. "I think this was cut," he said. "You can see marks right at the bottom, maybe a saw or something like that. If it was shed like antlers are, I don't think there would be these scratches."

"Let me see." Rob took back his phone. "You're right," he said incredulously after a few minutes, flipping through the images and enlarging them. "I didn't notice those before. So how did it get here? If there was an attack on the unicorn to get the horn, I don't know where the body is. If it's a narwhal horn, I guess they could have cut it off and pretended it was unicorn. After all, that's what some of the Vikings did for money. But this is an awfully long way from the ocean to carry it around and I didn't see anything else to suggest they were a trader. In fact, we haven't found much currency at all, of any kind. There's enough evidence to point to a family or small group living here. Did they keep it as a remembrance of someone who passed, was it a trophy, did they have no idea what it was?"

Gawain shrugged. He was worried about the test results. If it was a unicorn horn, he was sure nothing good would come of it. Even if it was something like Doc's story of his tribe, why hadn't the horn been destroyed?

13

Merri opened the door, eager to go find a snack. She was tired and didn't feel like making breakfast in the RV. She had gone to bed last night and had fallen asleep waiting for Gawain to finish "the last of his notes" on a few things that Rob had shared with him. When she had woken up about four in the morning to an empty bed, she had found Gawain sitting at the table, still going through the documents. Merri had to drag him back to bed. She thought he would still be there if she hadn't woken up.

Nothing was sounding great from what they had stocked in the cabinet, and she decided to make a run to the food tent when she remembered that there was supposed to be a delivery of fresh fruit this morning. Stepping down onto the last step, she froze when she saw the dirt in front of her move. Hearing the unmistakable warning rattle, her heart sped up, fear rushing through her. She could heal a lot more quickly now that she had mated Gawain, but she was still essentially human in nature. Witches could still be injured or get diseases like a cold, the flu, cancer. A bite from this prairie rattlesnake would not only be painful but could put her health in jeopardy. They weren't too far from town, where she would imagine there was either a doctor or emergency services that would have anti-venom. Merri forced herself to take a slow breath, reminding herself that Shaye was only a thought away and could help heal her. Doc had shared his immortality with the Clan, so it wouldn't kill her.

'Gawain,' Merri reached out, not willing to make noise from speaking.

'Did you find something you liked in the mess hall?' he asked. He sounded distracted. He had been about to go through some of the pictures and documents Rob had left for him last night.

'Didn't make it there. I need some help,' she started to say.

'Oh! Can you grab me an apple or banana?' he asked, absently.

'Gawain! I need help outside. Don't make noise. There's a rattlesnake by the stairs. It's already shaking its tail and it's coiled up. Should I try to move slowly back inside? Or stay put?' Merri asked. Luckily, she had put her boots on this morning. Gawain had warned her to always wear her boots outside. She didn't think she would actually come across a snake; she had gotten spoiled at the Nightwood Clan house. While the local area of the Smoky Mountains did have timber rattlesnakes and copperheads, the wards on the property kept them from coming into their space. She could run around barefoot and not have any problems. Not so much here. She kept an eye on the snake, the grayish-tan body curling up, the darker blotches scattered around its body, narrowing to form rings at the tail. The triangular head was pulled back, its tongue scenting the air. The head shape, vertical pupils, and the rattles on the tail were a dead giveaway that this was a venomous snake.

'Stay put. I'm going to help,' Gawain replied firmly.

'Merri?' a voice asked hesitantly.

'Hi, Shaye,' she responded.

'Are you okay? I got a sudden sense of fear from you,' Shaye said.

'There's a rattlesnake close by the RV. I'm pretending to be a statue until Gawain can help,' Merri replied.

'Oh crap! Did it bite you?' Shaye asked, concerned.

'No. I'm hoping it goes away,' Merri said. She kept an eye on it, while listening for Gawain. She knew he could move quietly, but he should have been here already. The RV wasn't that big. Her foot was starting to tremble from holding it up in the air, as she had been about to step down on the dirt when she heard the snake. Sweat was starting to form on her forehead from the sun and the strain of maintaining this position. She had been hoping that the snake would go away if she didn't move, but it clearly was enjoying the sun in this spot.

She heard a little whisper of a sound, and then she saw Gawain's falcon fly out of the RV, luckily on the side facing away from camp. Taking her eyes off the snake, she watched as her mate flew higher in the air. She knew he needed the height to gain speed for his dive. Her leg trembled a little, causing the stairs to make a small sound, so small you probably wouldn't even notice it unless you were hyperaware of your surroundings, a bead of her sweat hit the ground. Her head jerked back to the snake, seeing it coil tighter in front of her. She gasped as it suddenly lunged for her, its mouth open to strike. Merri scrambled back, trying to get out of striking distance, but she fell back against the stairs in her panic. The snake was inches from her leg when Gawain screeched and dove toward them. The snake was so focused on her, that it didn't have time to stop Gawain from grabbing its head in his talons. He flew away from Merri, the snake's body twisting to get free. She wasn't sure how he could let go without getting bit himself. Gawain landed in the grasses, and she couldn't see what was happening, her heart still pounding in fear. She breathed again when she saw

Gawain's falcon fly back over to her, coming to land on the railing.

"Are you alright?" she asked quietly, leaning close to look him over.

He gently nuzzled his head against her arm, careful not to rub any blood on her.

'Merri, are you alright?' Shaye asked.

'Yes, thank you. Gawain took care of it,' Merri replied, opening the door so Gawain could go inside and shift forms.

'Thank goodness. Let me know if you guys need anything,' Shaye said before leaving the Clan link.

Merri followed Gawain's bird inside, shutting the door after quickly looking around. She drew the blinds down, letting Gawain shift without the chance of being seen.

"Thank you," she said, hugging him tight. "I was so scared when it lunged. I haven't seen one that close before."

"I'm not going to let anyone hurt you," Gawain said, pulling her close, nuzzling into her hair. He had been terrified when he saw the snake ready itself to strike and he had let his falcon take over, knowing its instincts would be better than his human ones. His bird was still on alert, keeping watch over their mate even though they had taken care of the threat. He held her for a few minutes before pressing a kiss to her forehead. "Are you still hungry? Let me brush my teeth and I'll walk with you to the tent. My falcon will keep an eye out for danger, but I don't think there will be another snake today."

"Yes, please. I could use a cup of tea too," she admitted. A nice cup of chamomile, she thought. They had hot water available at the meal tent, so she would just bring a tea bag with her. Grabbing a bag, she let Gawain go down the stairs first and stayed close by him as they walked. He slid an arm around her waist, pulling her close to him and pressing a kiss to the top of her head.

They opened the door flap, stepping inside the tent, their

eyes adjusting to the slightly dimmer light. Gawain led them over to a table, pulling out a bench seat for Merri.

"I'll grab your hot water and some food," he said.

Merri sat down, watching as Gawain collected a variety of fruits and some easy to eat pastries.

'Are you alright?' Tess suddenly asked. 'Shaye said there was a rattlesnake close by.'

'I'm okay,' Merri replied. 'Gawain shifted and grabbed it. I was surprised to see one so close to the RV, but it must have just liked the sunny spot. We're at the food tent now. Gawain's getting me some tea and something to eat.'

'That's good. Everything else okay?' Tess asked.

'Yes. Did you get the bison and prairie dog pictures I sent?' Merri questioned, not wanting to talk about the snake any longer.

'I did! That was so cool. The prairie dogs are adorable. I have to go; my next patient is here. Let us know if you need anything! Love you!' Tess replied.

Gawain placed a plate of pastries and a mug of hot water in front of her. "I'm getting some eggs cooked, they'll just be a minute. Are you feeling better?"

Merri nodded. Her heart rate was back to normal. "I am, thank you," she said, leaning forward to kiss his lips.

Hearing a bell, Gawain jumped back up to grab their eggs. They looked nice and fluffy; the scrambled eggs topped with a smattering of shredded cheese.

Rob came over. "I thought I could take you over to meet the landowner today. Would you guys be interested?"

Gawain looked over at Merri. "Would you be up for that?"

"That sounds good," she agreed. It would be interesting to see who the owner was and what type of paranormal he or she was.

"You might want to warn everyone again about safety," Gawain said to Rob as they walked out to his truck. "There was a rattlesnake sunning itself by our steps this morning."

"You guys okay?" Rob asked, concerned.

"We're fine, didn't get bit," he answered. He didn't want to say much more with so many humans around.

"I thought I heard a falcon," Rob said, a slight question in his tone.

Gawain nodded.

"I'm glad you're both safe. I'll make an announcement before we leave to remind everyone to be aware," Rob replied.

After they ate and Merri finished her tea, they left to meet the mysterious property owner. The drive took several minutes, bumping along the dirt road. This must be a huge property, Merri thought. She had run back to their RV to grab her pendant. She had forgotten to put it on this morning but was thinking she should just leave it on all the time. It may have warned her of the rattlesnake. She should ask Berkley exactly what dangers it warned against. She knew it would work for poisoned foods, since they had added that to it after Rolf's blood supply had been tampered with, so it didn't seem unreasonable to assume it would be for anything that would cause harm to them. She draped it on the outside of her shirt, wanting to easily see if it started glowing. Only members of the Nightwood Clan could see it glow, so she wasn't worried about tipping anyone off if it activated.

The house wasn't quite what she expected. It looked more like an earthship type of house, the color blending into the landscape. There was just a slight slope to the land here, the home using that to its advantage. It was built partially into the ground, which must help keep the temperature inside the house cooler. The outside was covered in a type of stucco, and it looked like they must have used the dirt from around here because the colors matched perfectly. There were a few darker spots, which from farther away resembled the various grasses and shrubs scattered around the land. She could see a wall of windows, although there were shutters to cover them, also in the dirt color. As far as she knew, shutters weren't that common in earthship homes. Solar panels lined the roof. Walking past the windows, she could see it was a greenhouse, tomatoes and other vegetables growing inside. It even looked like there was a mini lemon tree.

"Daryl is a paranormal. He likes to live off-grid as much as possible. The back has a walled-off area to give him a little more privacy. It's a really cool-looking house," Rob said as he knocked on the door.

They were in the middle of nowhere, there were no other houses or roads for miles. How much privacy did he need? Merri wondered.

The door opened, and a shorter gentleman stood there. He had pale sandy blond hair, poofy, almost like a puff ball. His eyes were a pale blue.

"Daryl, these are my friends Gawain and Merri. They stopped by to see the dig," Rob introduced them.

"Come on in," he said, moving back from the doorway. Merri looked down, her pendant dark.

"Can I get you something to eat? I was just eating lunch," Daryl said, leading them to the living area. The walls were decorated in landscape photographs, family photographs, and a few pet pictures. The one dividing wall was made of what looked like concrete and colorful glass bottles. When the sun hit it, it must be amazing, Merri thought. Up by the window, there was a tiny obstacle course.

"What kind of pet do you have?" Merri asked.

"Uh, rabbits," Daryl replied, looking startled. He glanced at the play area. "They're shy around new people."

"I still haven't heard back about the horn, nor have I found anything about why it was there. Gawain found what look to be cut marks, like from a saw, on the base of the horn. I wish I had noticed that before I sent it off. He has a few documents that mention seeing a 'horned horse' run by. We've been comparing notes," Rob said.

Gawain looked at Rob, wondering why he brought that up.

"Do you work for the Convocation?" Daryl asked guardedly.

"No. I work for myself. I've had to work with them on occasion and even been hired to do a few jobs for them, but I'm independent," Gawain answered.

Daryl studied his face before answering. "My family has been here a long time. There's been stories passed on. Stories of a unicorn tribe, stories of other shifters that you don't see anymore. The flyer Rob found isn't the only one. My aunt found one in Illinois, my uncle is a truck driver and has found them scattered all over the country. I tend to agree with Rob and that the hunters are making a comeback."

"My friends had a run-in with them when they visited their family in Scotland. We have some evidence of people camping illegally in the nearby National Park, but our Sheriff hasn't found the people doing it. He's also the Warden for the area, so he's invested in finding them," Gawain told them.

"Where are you from?" Daryl asked.

"Right now, we live in Tennessee," Merri added.

Daryl looked up sharply. "You the Nightwood Clan?" he asked, surprised.

"How do you know about them?" Gawain questioned, hesitant to answer.

"Vlad was trouble. He brought too much attention, was too power hungry and didn't care about anyone but himself. He killed a friend of mine many years ago. I was glad to hear he had died. I kept an ear out to hear what happened afterward and heard that his son formed a Clan of his own. There aren't many Clans near there."

"I'm sorry to hear about your friend," Merri said.

Daryl nodded in acknowledgement.

"That is our Clan. We've all been friends for a while, either of Rolf or of his mate. We're more like a family," Merri said, feeling like Daryl was okay to trust with this much. If he really wanted to know, he could always dig through Convocation records. Clan and Pack creation filings were more or less public record.

"How did you get to be a Clan if you're not all vampires?" Daryl asked.

"Rolf and his mate were both human before they turned. We've been friends a long time. Rolf never put importance on what species someone was, just who they were as a person," Gawain replied.

"What kinds do you have?" Daryl asked.

"Vampire, witch, shifter, Fae," Merri replied vaguely.

"What kind of shifters?"

"That's up to them to tell you," Gawain said firmly. "The others you could sense if you met them but telling you someone's animal isn't something we're comfortable doing. If you ever meet them, they'll have the chance to decide to tell you or not. That's not our decision."

"Good. Then I can trust you to keep quiet for me as well," Daryl said before standing up and taking his shirt off.

Merri looked at Gawain in alarm. She had no clue what was going on, but her pendant was still dark, so at least he wasn't a danger to them.

Daryl stood before them, only in his underwear. There was a burst of air, and he was gone.

"Where did he go?" she asked, worried.

"Just wait," Rob said, amusement in his voice.

The pile of clothes moved, being tossed up in the air.

"Holy shit!" Gawain exclaimed. Merri just stared at the tiny antlers.

A jackalope. An honest to goodness jackalope. Holy shit, she thought.

He hopped over to them, sniffing their hands before nodding his head and hopping around the corner. Rob tossed the clothes in that direction. A human arm reached out and grabbed them, Daryl coming around the corner a few minutes later once again clothed.

"My whole family are jackalopes. We're mostly in the warmer Western states. Years ago, the family took over a few tourist businesses and started promoting the jackalope myths. It helps make us seem like made-up things, something that doesn't exist anymore. Hiding in plain sight and all of that. We avoid the Convocation at all costs if we can. They don't know we're here or what we are. We heard too many rumors about certain members not being necessarily safe for the rarer paranormals."

"What do you mean by that?" Gawain asked, concerned. He knew he had run-ins with a few members that always left his falcon on edge. Those he had been very cautious in what he said near them. He thought it had maybe been just him and Rob being extra paranoid. After a while, you did seem to become more suspicious after being on your own for so long. Now that he thought about it, he didn't think he had ever really talked to the rest of the Clan to get their opinions on the Convocation. It just had never come up.

"There's one member, rumor has it he was friendly with Vlad, no idea how he got on the board. There are an awful lot of rarer type of shifters, or shifters who don't fit in with the natural wildlife, who seem to disappear after they run into him. Doesn't matter if it's a matter of them seeing him in a store, passing him on the street, or it was an official matter. They either disappear or are brought in on trumped-up charges, and then never seen again," Daryl said.

"How do you know the charges aren't real?" Gawain asked, trying to be a voice of reason.

"A lot of us keep to ourselves, you know? We don't want to bring attention to us or the community. My aunt had neighbors, cat shifters, that had charges of public endangerment brought against them. They brought in the whole family, including the young kids. Never saw them again. Now, these were quiet people, they had fenced-in land where they let their cats loose, we never heard them or saw them during their runs. The fences were the tall privacy type, inside the fence was full of trees and brush. Even from the air I think you would have a hard time seeing anything. They were sabretooth. Not something you'd see in real life; the humans would have freaked out. But there were no sightings, no rumors of big cats hunting in the area, no farmers complaining about losing livestock, you know the normal things that might hint that a paranormal wasn't as careful as they should have been. They had been talking to my aunt and uncle just days before, saying they had run into a strange man at the gas station. He claimed to be a Convocation member, had the correct identification, but he was abnormally inter-ested in them, asking where they lived, what they did for work, where the kids went to school. Really intrusive questions.

"Because of their nature and the fact that they were close to shifting age, the kids were homeschooled, and the parents worked from home. There was no one to really notice they were missing except my family. A black van showed up one night and took them away. My aunt called into their work when they didn't come back for a week and was told they had quit. It's easy enough to get into someone's email and send a resignation letter," Daryl said sadly. "I've heard of a few other similar stories. This guy seems to be the main player, but he has a couple of others on the governing board who support him and seem to leak information to him. I don't think they're actively kidnapping people, but I do think they're sending any interesting tidbits they learn or see back to this guy."

"Which member is it?" Merri asked. This was crazy. The Convocation was made to help protect the paranormal community. How did he get away with this? There should have been safeguards in place. The governing board, the

Convocation, were the main ones in charge of the paranormals. They acted like a judicial branch, creating laws, overseeing any large trials. The Wardens acted as the police, many of whom held human police jobs like Gage did in their town. It was to help in areas of large paranormal populations; human cops wouldn't be able to handle a paranormal if they decided to try to break out of jail or resist arrest. Other Wardens traveled as needed, like Marco. The TruthSpeakers were brought in to do the questioning and interrogations. They were able to tell when someone was lying. They also had the authority to cast judgment on smaller, simpler cases, as the Convocation didn't usually sit on all hearings unless they were large-scale events, or for a more infamous person. If Vlad had ever been brought to a trial, the whole Convocation would have been involved. For all other trials, there was a rotation set up, having one or two of the members casting judgment based on the testimony from the TruthSpeaker.

The paranormal judgments ran a little differently than a human court. The accused person was rarely present. The TruthSpeaker instead gave testimony about the interrogation and what they had found. Because of an event in the past, where a TruthSpeaker abused their position for their own gain, there was now a witch brought in from the local community. It was a different one each time. They would cast a truth spell over the group and provided spelled crystals. Each member involved in casting a judgment held one of those crystals, which would glow if they lied. That way, when the TruthSpeaker rendered their statement from a questioning, everyone knew that they were speaking the truth of what the person testified to.

So, if it had really been a Convocation member who arrested the family, there should have been a TruthSpeaker there to interrogate them, see if they had caused exposure of their animal sides to humans. There also should have been a public record of it. After the incident with the TruthSpeaker hiding the truth of a case, exploiting it for money, land, and power, all trials were a matter of public record. You had to request the information, but it was available.

"Barry," Daryl replied.

Merri saw Gawain flinch. That couldn't be good, she thought. *'What was that reaction?'* she asked him.

'Barry is a speciesist asshole. I can totally picture him hanging around Vlad. I always wondered how he got on the board. If he is involved in something like this, I can't say it would surprise me. His other name is Douchebag,' Gawain said.

"Did you look into the records, see if they had been arrested and tried?" Merri asked.

"My aunt had a friend of hers ask and they couldn't find anything," Daryl replied. "We didn't directly ask ourselves because we didn't want to draw attention to us. My aunt's property is spelled to not let their scent or anything else that would betray their species out. If they started asking questions, we didn't want Barry coming back to see who was stirring up trouble."

"I had my friend at the Convocation look into it as well. There's always a paper file kept, even if a lot of the more recent records are electronic. He searched for months, never found anything. He looked under dates, under Barry's files, under special species filings. Nothing. There was no trace of them having entered the official Convocation judicial system. Either someone else was involved and it was a big coincidence that they had run into Barry right before they went missing, or Barry was targeting people for his own use, not official Convocation business," Rob added.

"We may be able to ask Gage about it," Merri suggested. "If there is a Convocation member that is tainted, then there needs to be a plan to get him out of power. He might be able to look into the disappearances, ask Marco if he's heard anything as well."

"Do you trust him?" Daryl asked suspiciously.

"We do. He's helped us with several situations, even one out of the country. Our wards are pretty good at keeping ill-intentioned people out, and they let him through every time," Gawain responded. "We have a few ways of detecting danger and have never gotten a whiff of danger or ill-will from him. I'd like to get some answers, if possible. He might know of something or heard about Barry. What's the best way for us to reach you if he finds anything out?"

"I have a burner phone I use for stuff like this," Daryl said, writing out his number on a scrap of paper. "Rob can get a message to me too, if he's still here."

"We'll see what we can find out and let you know. It might be a while since we don't always have great cell service. But I can always ask someone in the Clan to go talk to him and explain what's been going on. Once we hear back, I'll send you a message," Gawain said.

He was very much afraid that this was all somehow linked. He needed to dig deeper into the history of everything, but there had to be a clue somewhere.

14

Gawain looked up as a shadow came overhead. He had been explaining his technique to Merri and she was going to give it a try. Rob was standing there with an irritated look on his face, his phone in hand.

"What's up," Gawain asked, pausing in his efforts to dig out a shard of pottery.

Rob squatted down next to them to lean in close. "I got a heads-up from a friend in the Convocation. We will have incoming in a few days. The unicorn horn must have been real; we haven't found anything else that screams paranormal on-site," Rob whispered. "I would recommend leaving before they get here, make sure you have all your documents when you leave so they don't 'take a look' at them. I already warned Daryl and he and his family are taking a vacation to visit other relatives out of the area."

'Why would them looking at the documents be a bad thing?' Merri asked Gawain. *'It's not like Rob even knows about the documents we held back because of Doc.'*

'When the Convocation borrows or "takes a look" at your stuff, ninety-nine percent of the time you do not get them back. "For the good of the paranormal community,"' he mocked. *'They do help*

keep everyone in check and set up the Wardens, which do help protect everyone. I think most of them probably mean well, but just like in the human governments they want to have the most power. It helps them train people, educate people, and also keep everyone in line.

'Knowledge is a great power, especially when it comes to paranormals. I'm sure they know the weaknesses of every single type of us. They want to have the upper hand, which I know makes sense when you have people like Vlad around, but it is incredibly frustrating having your work taken away and you never see it again. They could easily duplicate the documents, take pictures, or something, but that leaves it out in the world for everyone else to see. Rob and I lost quite a few documents and items to the Convocation, especially in the beginning before we saw a pattern emerge. There are a couple on the board that I trust, but there are a few that I don't, mainly the DDT. They give off a...vibe, this sense of danger and distrust to my falcon. I'll need to make sure that all our things are packed away. They won't be able to sense or find them in the RV and I want to make sure Doc is protected. Hunters aren't the only ones who would love to be able to find out he exists.'

"Do you have everything you need before we leave? I can help document," Gawain offered quietly. They always documented their sites, but after losing quite a few relics to the governing paranormal board, they had started keeping a duplicate set for themselves. Pictures, rubbings, measurements, anything that might be useful later was duplicated. Of course, having camera phones, small memory cards and thumb drives, not to mention cloud storage, made everything easier now.

"I think I have it all; as soon as I found the horn, I made sure to keep stringent records. If there's anything you might need, make sure you get it. I don't think we're going to be left with a lot by the time they leave," Rob added.

Gawain knew that meant Rob's friend gave him a heads-up on who was coming to visit the site. There were a couple on the Convocation that confiscated any paranormal items, especially if it was new knowledge or dealt with rarer species. They were also the ones that Gawain's falcon didn't trust.

"Do you have somewhere to store your own records?" Gawain asked.

"I do. I have a special section in my van. It's been spelled, so it should be safe. I had a feeling and got a scraping of the horn before I sent it off for testing," Rob replied.

"We'll help with the dig a little longer today and we'll head out tomorrow. Let me know if you need anything before we leave, or even after we go. Why don't you stop by tonight for one last beer?" Gawain suggested.

Rob nodded. "I'll let you get back to it. Thanks for helping us out. I'm glad you got a chance to stop by. I'll see you for that beer later."

Merri waved as Rob walked off. *'Is he going to be okay?'* she asked. The talk yesterday with Daryl had put her on edge. It was awful knowing there were members of the governing paranormal body that they couldn't trust. She had talked to the family yesterday over the Clan's telepathic link and explained what they had learned. Rolf had admitted that he had tried to stay out of the Convocation's business as much as possible with all the trouble his father had caused. He hadn't wanted to be guilty by association, even if he had never been a willing participant in the things his father had done. Berkley said he was going to reach out to his family to see if they had heard any rumblings over in England. His sister-in-law normally had a good ear for paranormal gossip. Sam was going to talk to Gage; he normally stopped in the brewery for lunch or dinner and Sam would take him back to the office so they could talk. Emma said she would reach out to her house-keeper on her farm; Samantha's husband Douglas could reach out and see if there was any news, even if he didn't know of it personally. Gnomes generally had the information grapevine down to a science.

'He's had to deal with them before. Plus, there's too many people here for anyone to cause a scene, too many humans that have camera phones and aren't afraid to use them.' Gawain said. 'I'll make sure to keep checking in on him. Daryl would reach out as well if Rob suddenly left without saying goodbye to him.'

'Do you think it's one of the Convocation members that might be corrupt?' Merri asked.

'Based on what he said, I would guarantee it. We'll know for sure when he comes over tonight. For now, just act normal. We don't want anyone noticing something strange; I'm sure whoever is coming will be asking a lot of questions and we don't want them looking too closely.'

They spent the rest of the morning on their square in the dig. Merri helped Gage catalogue it, filling in some forms as he read out the measurements from the pottery shard and the descriptions. He took pictures of the process, sending them to Rob. He also kept a few to send to Doc later, just in case he recognized anything.

After lunch they headed back to the Airstream, Merri turning the fans on, eager to feel a breeze. They still had an almost full water tank, so they didn't have to stop to fill up unless they wanted to. Rob had mentioned that they could connect to one of the camp's water tanks and fill up. She started cleaning and packing up things they wouldn't need for the rest of the night.

"Let's eat at the meal tent tonight," Gawain said. "We can say goodbye to everybody and won't have to worry about dishes." Even if they only made foil packet dinners, they would still be using a cutting board and a knife. They had plastic knives, but it was almost impossible to really cut anything with them. Other than getting some new ice along the way and a stop for a few groceries, they should be good to go early in the morning. He moved to the bedroom to help put away a few of the things they had lying out. The phone cords would need to wait until the next day, but everything else looked good, he thought as he looked around the room. It was one thing he liked about the Airstream; there weren't any slides to worry about having to pull in and make sure things weren't in the way of them coming back inside the frame.

Walking back out to the main room, he cleaned up their desk station, leaving the laptop out for now. He wasn't sure if they would need it during their talk with Rob tonight. Merri had filled the sink with some of the loose items, including a small cactus she had bought in South Dakota. She said they needed some sort of plant in the RV, and she thought the cactus was probably the smallest and most robust option. Looking around, he saw a calendar she had hung on the fridge. It was a lot of little touches like the plant and the calendar, funny towels, and other simple items that she had added that made the camper feel more like a home. He hadn't even noticed when she put them out, but, looking closely, he could see several touches she had made, and it made him smile.

"What's this for?" she asked as he bent down to kiss her forehead.

"Thank you for coming with me and for making this more of a home," Gawain said, wrapping his arms around her.

She laughed. "I didn't do anything," she protested.

"You did. You add all these tiny touches that make it seem homier. And I don't notice when you're doing them, but I do notice the difference. So, thank you," he said, kissing her gently on the lips.

Merri sighed softly. "How long until Rob gets here?" she asked, her hands sliding down into his back pockets, pulling him in closer.

"We have a couple hours until dinner, Rob's coming over after," he replied, his thumbs sliding under her shirt to rub the soft skin of her back along her waist.

"Hmm, maybe we should take a break?" she said, a mischievous glint in her eye.

"A break sounds good," he agreed, picking her up.

Merri laughed, always amazed at how easily Gawain could lift her. She wrapped her legs around his waist, rubbing against him a little. Gripping his hair in her hands, she pulled his face down to hers, her lips gently kissing him before her tongue slid past his lips to tangle with his tongue. He moaned as she kissed him deeply. Gawain grabbed her tighter, walking them back to their bedroom. Kicking the door shut, he laid her down on the bed, his body following, keeping their lips in contact. From here, he could grind against her a little better, making sure the angle was right to hit her clitoris. He leaned his torso back, keeping his hips pressed against hers. He began to unbutton her shirt, kissing the skin as he went until he finally had to move back. Dropping to his knees, he took her shoes off before sliding down her shorts and underwear. Gawain dropped his head to lie against her inner thigh, drawing in a deep breath to scent her. She had finally gotten over being self-conscious when he did this. Whenever she was sweaty, she had always wanted to wash off before he went down on her, but he loved the enhanced smell of her and the saltiness.

He ran a finger teasingly down her slit, looking up at her. Merri bit her lip but spread her legs a little wider for him. She reached out and unsnapped her bra. He loved that she had worn a frontal clasp bra today. Merri watched him as he bent his head, her clean-shaven mons soft and smooth. Her lips were juicy and plump, calling to him. He gently slid a finger between her folds, finding her wet already. Sliding his fingers inside her channel, he searched for her G-spot, bending his head down to run his tongue over her clit. She didn't have a large clitoral hood, so it was easy for him to access it. Thrusting his fingers slowly, making sure to press against her spot as he went, Gawain licked her clit, firming his tongue so he could rub circles around it, teasing her before finally making direct contact. Merri moaned, her legs coming to wrap around his back, pulling him in closer.

"Harder, please," she begged, her hips chasing after his tongue.

Gawain sped up his hand, adding another finger to her wet heat. She was gripping his fingers, pulling him in and he couldn't wait until his dick was inside her. But first he wanted to make her come. He loved being able to give her multiple orgasms.

"There...don't stop," she demanded, her breath coming faster.

Gawain pressed his tongue flat against her clit, rubbing back and forth before swirling it. His fingers pressed against her G-Spot, causing her hips to arch off the bed as she gave a small whine as her orgasm pushed through her.

"Up here," she said, grabbing at him.

Licking his lips, he climbed up the bed, lying next to her, kissing her softly. His dick was incredibly hard, but he wanted to give her time to enjoy her afterglow.

Merri slid her hands under his shirt, pulling it up and off, tossing it to the floor. She'd pick it up later. Running her hands over his chest, she loved that there wasn't a lot of hair, he was mostly smooth. She slid one hand under the waistband of his shorts, finding him hard already. Gawain adjusted his legs, and she looked down as she heard a thump. He had kicked his boots off. Looking into his amber-colored eyes, she smiled at him before pressing a kiss to his lips. It was her turn to wiggle down the bed, pulling his shorts and boxer briefs off. His cock sprang up to smack himself in the stomach, causing her to giggle. She loved his dick, he was thick and long, stretching her to feel completely full but not passing into being painful. Bending her head, she licked his head, precum coating her tongue, his top a darker red from his arousal. Opening her mouth wider, she licked a path from his balls up to the tip before swallowing his shaft. Holding him in her mouth, she made sure to rub her tongue around his shaft, her hand reaching down to cup his balls.

"Yeah, lick it, just like that," Gawain grunted, his hands buried in the bedsheets.

She took him in deep until she hit her gag reflex and pulled back to lick along his slit, plunging back down his shaft. Turning her hand slightly, she kept his balls cupped in the palm of her hand but used her thumb and forefinger to grip the base of his penis. Her head bobbed up and down his shaft, her fingers making smaller matching movements.

"Ah, god, yeah, just like that. Lick a little harder," Gawain moaned out.

His hand came to cup her cheek, as her tongue swirled around his base.

"Stop," he grunted, pulling at her shoulder. "I don't want to come yet."

Merri pulled off, giving the tip a quick kiss. She climbed up and straddled him, holding his shaft in her hand, she rubbed the tip between her folds, coating it in her juices.

"Ah. Yes! Just like that. I love that," Gawain groaned, his hands gripping her hips.

She loved it too, she thought as the tip of his dick brushed against her clit. Leaning forward a little bit, she held his shaft steady as she slid her body down to encase it. She felt the stretch as he slid into her, her body welcoming his. As he bottomed out, she ground her hips, slowly dragging his shaft through her channel, tightening to feel him even more strongly. Gawain groaned under her. Reaching behind, she teased her fingertips against the skin of his balls, lightly touching before placing her hand next to his head. She leaned down and gave him a kiss, her hips still moving, thrusting against his hardness. His pubic hair was a little rough against her clit, but it felt amazing. As she moved her hips forward, she made sure to drop her butt and tuck in toward the end, knowing he loved how it felt at the head of his shaft. As his fingers gripped harder against her hips, she gave him one last deep kiss before pulling back. Pausing her motion, she moved her feet up underneath her, causing her to squat over his body, plunging her hips back down, she braced her hands on his chest, looking down into those amber eyes that had come to mean everything to her. Her pussy clenched around his dick, she could feel her own orgasm quickly approaching.

"Almost there," she panted, her nails digging little half-moons into his skin. Her head slammed back as Gawain reached between them, teasing her clit with his fingertip. *'Yes, there…no a little more to the left,'* she told him, screaming as he thrust hard up into her body and pressed down firmly on her clitoris. Her orgasm barreled through her, and she vaguely registered feeling the warmth of his cum filling her up.

Collapsing on top of him, she drew in a few shuddering breaths, her chest heaving against his. She could hear his heart racing.

'Love you,' Gawain said, tracing his fingers down her back.

'Love you too,' she replied.

15

Gawain's phone alarm went off, waking them in time for dinner. They never quite made it back to packing up for tomorrow, instead taking a nap after their afternoon break. Luckily, there wasn't a lot left to do.

Merri stretched as she climbed out of bed, her breasts perky and delightful looking. Gawain watched her hungrily, despite having come not that long ago.

"Nope," she laughed at him. "The plan was to go to dinner, make it seem like we're leaving to go to the next part of the honeymoon, not rushing out before the Convocation gets here. Then hang out with Rob, finish packing up, grab a shower and go to bed. Come on, let's go," she said as she pulled on her clothes.

Gawain heaved a large sigh but climbed out of bed and got dressed. He was looking forward to seeing everyone one last time; it was a good group on this dig, at least as far as the ones he had met. Rob was already in the meal tent when they got there, sitting at a table with a plate full of food. It looked like Mexican tonight, Gawain thought happily as his stomach grumbled. He loved tacos, burritos, and fajitas.

Rob saw them and waved them over. "I asked Chef to

have Mexican night since it's your favorite. Grab some food and enjoy! I have some beer I'll bring over tonight after dinner."

"Sounds good," Gawain said with a nod. He took Merri's hand and led her over to the buffet-style line. They had all the fixings to make hard tacos, burritos, or fajitas. He held Merri's plate as she fixed her burrito, and then he made his own plate, creating one of each. There was a platter of rice, guacamole, refried beans, Pico de Gallo, shredded cheese, and sour cream, with tortilla chips in a side bowl. He created a plate of nachos for them to share at the table as well.

"I got these to share," he said, setting it in the middle of the table before sitting down with his plate. "I'll have to tell Chef thanks. This looks delicious."

"It's a nice treat before it gets crazy around here," Rob said quietly.

"I made a copy of my notes from this afternoon, I can give it to you tonight for your records. I already sent the pictures. It's been fun getting in the dirt again," Gawain said. It had been fun catching up and being part of a dig with other people again. His intuition didn't jump out and yell there was something amazing to find here, but it was still a lot of fun.

Dinner was enjoyable, chatting about the dig, with a few other team members coming over to say hello. Gawain threw away his and Merri's garbage before making a stop to thank Chef for a wonderful dinner. As he sat back down at their table, Rob stood up, blowing a sharp whistle to get everyone's attention.

"Thank you," he said as it quieted down. "I wanted to say a few things before everyone started heading out. First, thanks to Chef for an amazing meal. It was delicious and a nice treat. Thanks to Merri and Gawain for stopping by to see us. It was nice to see new faces around here. It's been a few years since we were able to work together, so I'm glad we got this chance. I am so honored and pleased to have met the woman who finally got Gawain to look up out of the dirt," Rob teased. "Thank you for making a stop to see me while on your honeymoon and introducing me to Merri. I hope the rest of your trip is amazing and delightful," he added, raising his cup in a toast. "To the newlyweds!"

The tent was full of cheers and congratulations. It took a little longer than expected to be able to leave the tent, everyone stopping by to offer their goodbyes and congratulations. It was sweet though, Merri thought with a smile. It was a warm group of people here.

Getting back to the RV, Rob followed them in and set down the beer he had brought. He had been telling Merri funny stories about Gawain during dinner, but they had been very human-friendly stories.

Now though, he sat down and had a smirk on his face.

"Did he ever tell you about the dig we were at in Florida?"

Gawain groaned, placing his head down on the table.

"No, I don't think he has," Merri said, looking down at her mate, who wouldn't look at her.

"This dig was near some swampy areas, and we'd been warned about the wildlife. We had some fencing put up and work lights, but it clearly wasn't going to keep anything out that was determined to get in. There were alligators and all kinds of snakes nearby, including those Burmese Pythons that have been causing issues. Those things can get big. All our tents were on raised platforms, with a little ledge all the way around, tent sitting in the middle, to try to keep animals out. Anyway, this guy," he says pointing at Gawain, "decides he has to go to the bathroom at two in the morning. He walks out of his tent and while standing on the edge, he starts his stream. My tent is next door and I hear an angry hiss, I run out and I see Gawain peeing. I think he's still mostly asleep because he looks down and doesn't seem to register that he's pissing on an alligator's head. He just keeps going, shakes off, and puts himself away."

Merri is staring at her mate, her eyes wide. Gawain still has his head down on the table, slowly shaking it back and forth. Rob is laughing so hard at this point, he can barely get his words out.

"All of a sudden, the alligator changes into Randy, one of the guys on the crew. We didn't know he was an alligator. I guess he wanted to stretch his animal side without having to deal with the actual alligators. He didn't want to get in a fight with them. He starts yelling at Gawain on how to look before he just pees everywhere. Gawain must have only been asleep for an hour or two before he got up and was having a hard time getting fully awake. Half the camp is now up at this point. Gawain was mortified when he finally realized what he had done," Rob said, still laughing.

"Really?" Merri asked. She would have died of embarrassment. "Holy shit, Gawain. You peed on a coworker!"

"I didn't know it was him!" Gawain protested. "I didn't even know there was an alligator there. I mean who changes into their huge-assed predator form, one we've all been warned about, and then skulks near the living areas of the camp? There were guns in camp in case we needed them for protection."

Rob shook his head. "They eventually made up, but it was the joke of the camp for the rest of the dig. Both of them were left yellow water bottles; it was apple juice, but it certainly looked like something else."

"I definitely look where I'm peeing now," Gawain said.

Rob sighed. "I guess we better get to business. It's getting late and I know you still have some packing to do. I'm going to send you copies of things I think you might find useful," Rob said, pulling out his phone. Gawain got an incoming message; a brief glance showed it had pictures of the horn and images of other artifacts that had been found in the area. "I have everything sent to cloud storage and have a thumb drive in my van, but it never hurts to have it in another trusted spot."

"Who's coming?" Gawain asked.

"Barry," Rob replied, his mouth turning down in a frown.

"Crap. You're going to have your hands full. Are you sure your van storage spot will be safe?" Gawain asked.

"Yeah. It's a good spell and the storage area itself isn't easily noticeable. You have to know it's there to be able to even spot it. I made sure it would be secure. Even if they confiscated my van, they wouldn't be able to get into it. I have a backup plan in place for that as well," Rob added. "I made the speech tonight, so there wouldn't be any questions in people's minds about why you were here and why you left after just a few days. Most people know you are an archeologist, and I didn't want them wondering why you left so early and accidentally saying something near Barry and causing more suspicion."

"I don't like that he's coming here," Gawain admitted. "You still have that satellite phone?"

Rob nodded, pulling it out of his pocket to show him.

"Keep it charged and on you. I'm going to give you Merri's number and Rolf's number back home. You already have mine. If there's trouble and you can't reach me or Merri, call Rolf and he can help. I'll let him know I gave it to you. I want you to keep in contact with me and check in every day Barry is here. Even just a text to let us know you're safe. Our next campsite should be close enough to town that we get a signal with the booster."

"I will, thanks. My guess is that they're going to take over, probably kicking out the humans on the crew at the very least. I'm going to have a lot of pissed-off people and it's going to raise questions with the locals. I don't want to say anything in advance though because I'm not supposed to know they're coming," he said, frustrated.

"Barry likes to use the government angle to take over an

area, so most people out here are going to be suspicious of them, not you. However, if he doesn't know this land is owned by a paranormal, he actually has no authority here. The horn was found on private land, so Daryl owns it according to the United States government. What is Daryl going to do?" Gawain asked.

"Huh. I actually forgot about that; I just assumed we would be working under paranormal law. Let me give him a call," Rob said, pulling out his phone.

"Daryl? This is Rob, I'm going to put you on speaker phone with Gawain and Merri," Rob said, before clicking a button and placing the phone in the middle of the table.

"Hi, Daryl. I just had a thought that I'm not sure will help or not. Barry has a magic permit as well, just like Rob and I do. Now, we use ours if the human authorities come around and it changes to show we have permission to be there under either the city, state, or federal government, depending on what we need. Otherwise, it looks like a paranormal permit. He uses his primarily to take over dig sites and remove people, especially if they're human. He normally has his change to show he's from the human US government. Now, you own this land, so if he tries that, he can be removed from your property. In the United States, any dinosaur bones found on private property is the property of the landowner, not the government. That's not the case for all countries, but here it is. So, if he came in, didn't know that this is property owned by a paranormal, he actually has no authority here. I know you said you aren't registered as paranormals, but how is the land registered? Do you own all the rights to it? Is there someone local you trust to act on your behalf to tell him he isn't welcome?" Gawain asked.

"I do have all the rights to it. It's been paid off many generations ago and I hold the deed. I'm friends with the local Sheriff. He's human but has paranormals in his family. His family is very protective of their human members and has placed multiple types of protections on them. He has a warding around him that makes him invulnerable to any mind control or mind-reading gifts, so if a TruthSpeaker was there, he would be able to protect my secret. He's never asked me to confirm if I am a paranormal or not, so if they got through his shield, he wouldn't really be able to confirm with a yes. Now, I know what he thinks, but he has never wanted to know for sure. I could let him know what's going on and see if he'll be available to 'drop in' every day to check on things."

"I would still leave on vacation," Gawain advised. "Barry might not back down quickly. I'll also see what Gage, our local Warden, recommends. I'll call him tonight and have Rob get back to you if he has any ideas. I know he was still looking into the other things we talked about, but I haven't heard anything yet."

"Daryl, will Barry be able to detect there are paranormals around your house or property?" Merri asked suddenly.

"The house and property are warded, but I've never had someone notice it. It's been so long since it's been done that it's just now part of the property, pretty much undetectable. If he goes searching through property records, he'll eventually find the one time where Uncle Eustace registered the property under his real name and with the paranormal community. He married in and was a wolf, so nothing unusual in terms of shifters. Story goes that he had the property registered so that if anyone would detect the wards, it would be assumed that he had them put in place and then never bothered to remove them after he sold the land to a 'human.' The human was the mate of his niece-in-law, who was my great-grandma, a jacka-lope. We register as rabbits to most people, and there are plenty of jackrabbits around here, so I would think he would assume he was sensing them," Daryl replied.

"Good," Gawain said. "I'll see what I can find and pass it on to Rob, who can then let you know. Stay safe."

Rob said goodbye as well and hung up the phone.

"Do you really think your Warden can help?" Rob asked.

"I don't know, but it's worth a shot. Are you familiar with the Sheriff here? I know Daryl thinks he can be trusted, but what about you?" Gawain asked.

"I've met him a few times and he's always seemed honest. It would be great to have a way to make Barry leave us alone this time."

"Could he try under Eminent Domain?" Merri asked.

"I don't think so, there was nothing big historic documented here, Daryl's house isn't considered a historic landmark, and he could object to it becoming one if they tried. Although it's not that old, so I'm not sure how they would go about it. I tried researching local events to see if I could trace the horn and found nothing. There is no reason they would build a road or highway through his property, or hotels, or anything else that might fall under Eminent Domain," Rob said. "The locals would throw a fit about that anyway."

Gawain borrowed Rob's sat phone to call the Sheriff's office back home.

"Gage? This is Gawain. We may have a problem connected to the issue we talked about earlier. Can you talk to Rolf about it? I don't want to talk about it over the phone right now. Rolf will have the phone number for my friend Rob, who is here at the dig site. If you have an answer after you talk to Rolf, can you give Rob a call? I know that was as clear as mud," Gawain apologized. Gage agreed to stop in to see Rolf after work.

"How are you going to let Rolf know if you aren't going to call him?" Rob asked, confused.

"Merri's going to reach out to Tess. They have a special bond," Gawain replied. He didn't like keeping the Clan link hidden from Rob, but it was an oddity of their Clan that some of the Convocation members, especially Barry, would not like.

A bond between siblings was common enough that it wouldn't raise any flags.

"Thanks for all of this," Rob said. "I didn't mean to drag you into anything. I had no idea how crazy it would get," he apologized.

"We have to look out for each other," Gawain said firmly.

16

Gawain finished getting the Airstream hooked up to the SUV. They had already checked the tire pressure, and everything was good to go. They were just waiting for Rob to come over, as he said he would come say goodbye this morning. The sun was just barely cresting over the horizon, hints of pinks, orange, and yellow reaching across the sky. It looked like a good travel day, no bad weather anywhere along the route. Today would be a much longer drive, probably closer to eight hours. The next campsite was more primitive. There were vault toilets and a dump station nearby, but that was about it. He planned on parking the RV there and driving to the site. It would draw less attention with just an SUV, than having the whole setup. Plenty of people parked and then went hiking.

Gawain stood by the driver's side door as he saw Rob walk toward them. "Thanks for having us out," he said. "It was great catching up."

Rob pulled him into a hug. "Be careful," he whispered. "Let me know if you hear anything or need help. I wish we could have spent more time catching up, but a quick stop here makes it more believable if anyone asks anyway."

Patting Gawain's back, Rob stepped back. "Have fun on the rest of your honeymoon," he said in a normal voice. "Make sure it's more fun for her than this dusty archeology site," he teased.

Gawain laughed. "I will. I think we're going to head toward the Grand Tetons and Yellowstone, get a couple more of the National Parks crossed off her list. We saw Rushmore and Custer State Park; she loved seeing all the bison and prairie dogs, so hopefully we can see some more out there."

"Well, I hope you have a great trip. She's great. I'm glad I got to meet her. Stay safe," he said, stepping back to let Gawain get in the car.

"Keep in touch and let me know how it's going," Gawain said with a pointed look.

"I will," Rob promised.

The drive was starting to get monotonous, Gawain thought. Even though the weather said it was supposed to be clear today, it had started raining, so he dropped his speed and made sure to stay in the slow lane. What most people didn't understand was that RVs, just like semi-trucks, although not as bad, needed more time and space to stop. Slamming on the brakes didn't always mean stopping right away. He had made a few of what he had coined 'honk buddies.' It kept him from getting mad as he drove. He always made sure to drive the speed limit, maybe going a little over but not more than ten. Years ago in Colorado, he had been driving in heavy traffic. He maintained his lane, keeping to the slow lane and keeping up with traffic, although he left a couple car lengths between him and the car in front of him. Because his rig, even though it wasn't as big as some, still took longer to slow down and stop. A car came zipping around behind him, after riding his ass for a mile, and cut in front of him, giving him the middle finger and a loud horn honk. He had been lucky that as soon as he saw it zip out from behind him, he had dropped his speed, or he didn't know if he would have been able to miss hitting them. He had thought to himself sarcastically, 'oh look, they're waving at me, they want to be buddies.' And so, Honk Buddies was created. He had made a few Honk Buddies in his lifetime.

"There's a Welcome Center not too far from here. I thought we could get out, use the bathroom, maybe stretch our legs if the rain lets up," he suggested.

"That sounds good. I could use a break," Merri admitted. It wasn't hard sitting and being the passenger, especially since Gawain knew where he was going and she didn't have to help navigate, but it did get to be uncomfortable sitting for so long. They had stopped for gas, but she hadn't wanted to use the bathroom there, so she had been holding it since then. There just had been no way she was going to go into the creepy station.

It took about another hour before they reached it, but at least it looked clean. Gawain pulled into the truck parking side, pulling into one of the long open spots. Merri grabbed her bag and jumped out, eager to find the restrooms at this point. Walking in, there were only a few other people, but she didn't have to wait for a stall. She gave a sigh of relief when she was done. After washing her hands, she headed out to wait for Gawain. There were a few vending machines, state maps, a few local-ish tourist brochures, but not much else.

Walking over to the vending machine, she bought a PayDay for Gawain and some chocolate for her.

Gawain walked out. "Do you want to risk getting rained on and take a quick walk? It looks like it stopped for the moment."

"Yeah, let's do that. We can rush back if it starts to rain. How much longer do you think we have?"

"Probably a few more hours," Gawain admitted. "We

should get there in time to set up before dark. I was thinking we could drive into town and grab more ice, maybe something for dinner, and some firewood. There'll probably be some downed trees in the woods we can use, but it will be good to have some backup in case everything is wet. We can make foil packet dinners for a lot of our meals, change it up between beef and chicken. I've been wanting to try one with soy sauce and see if I can make a stir-fry version."

"Sounds fun. Maybe some graham crackers and things to make s'mores?" Merri added.

"I'm always down for a good s'more," Gawain said, smiling.

They managed to get one lap around the walking path before the rain started back up. Merri really hoped it stopped before they got to the campsite. Setting up in the rain didn't sound like fun.

Unfortunately, it was still raining when they pulled off onto a dirt and gravel road nestled amongst the trees. She would have completely missed the turnoff, as there was only a small, faded wood sign.

Gawain dropped the SUV into lower gear, seeing a few extremely muddy spots and puddles. He was hoping they wouldn't get stuck. They were going to need to put the pads down under the front jack and the stabilizers to keep them from sinking into the mud.

Driving to the back, he found a spot. He had used this campground before and never realized how close it was to such a potentially life-changing find. His intuition was telling him that there was something close by. It almost made him angry that it hadn't kicked in before, but then he thought about why he was here and realized that just maybe Fate hadn't wanted him to find it yet. It certainly could have made Doc's life a little more stressful, having his old home found. Plus, who knew if he would have met Merri when he did. If he was distracted by another dig, he might not have stayed when Rolf called for help and wouldn't have been there when Merri arrived after Thanksgiving.

The ground here was still wet, but there was a better layer of gravel and the large trees overhead had kept some of the rain from reaching them. Setup went quickly since they didn't have any hookups. Merri stood on the mat by the door and grabbed a rag for someplace to place wet and muddy shoes.

"What do you want to do now?" she asked. "Did you want to run into town or go see the site?"

"Let's go into town. We can find something to eat, grab a few things of ice and some groceries. Let me grab one of the empty coolers and we'll use that for the ice. I'm going to set up the weBoost to help with the phone signals. It looks like we have a bar or two already and this should help us get more." Gawain pulled out the equipment from the cabinet and went outside to set up the outside antennae. He had a pole attachment that he used and set up each trip. It was clamped to the RV, so maybe not the best, but he hadn't wanted to drill any holes in the body of the RV to install a permanent mount. It seemed to work just fine for him though. He moved the interior antennae to the opposite end of the camper, making sure they didn't interfere with each other. Looking down at his phone, he was happy to see that he had three to four bars now instead of one. The signal booster ran off the solar, so hopefully they got some sun in the next couple of days. The batteries should be fully charged after the panels had sun for so long at Rob's dig, but with Merri here he wanted to make sure they would have enough power for what they would need. He wanted camping to be a positive experience, although he knew they would run into rough patches sometimes.

He grabbed his phone, sending off a group text back home to let them know they had made it. He also wanted to check the speed of his internet and texting capability.

GAWAIN: We made it to the next campground. Bit rainy here, planning to hunt for things to see tomorrow. Any news?

That should be vague enough that no one else would know what he was talking about, but enough that his family would know he was talking about finding the settlement site and asking about Rob.

ROLF: Glad you made it safely. Got Rob's number and reached out to say hi. Seems like a nice guy. He was busy so we didn't get to talk much. Gage is hanging out at the house tonight after work, having a grill-out. Everything pretty calm here, although tourist season is going strong, so busy but relatively calm.

Huh. He wondered if the Convocation member had shown up early or if Rob was busy with getting the local Sheriff to help him protect Daryl's property. If Gage was coming over tonight, it must be a briefing on what he had found.

GAWAIN: Cool. Let me know how the grill-out goes.

He got a thumbs-up emoji back.

ROLF: Will reach out tonight.

Now he would be thinking about that all day. Not much he could do about it though, he would just need to wait and see what they said. He sent another text to Rob, letting him know that they had a decent signal where they were parked. Rob sent back their signal for everything was fine.

"How do you feel about burgers and fries for dinner?" he asked Merri. "There's a restaurant in town that overlooks the river. The food is pretty good and the views are great."

"Sounds perfect," Merri agreed with a smile. She would love getting some water views in. She had always liked watching rivers flow and seeing what wildlife came down to drink. She bet they had all kinds of animals coming to the water around here.

"Great," Gawain replied, taking her hand to kiss the palm. "Grab your bag and make sure you pack the bear spray. We are definitely in bear country now, so we need to be aware when we're hiking, keep the bear spray with us, and keep food contained. I'll show you how to use the bear-proof garbage bins they have around; they can be tricky to use the first time."

"Are there really that many bears?" Merri asked. She would love to see a bear, but maybe from the safety of her car.

"There are a bunch of wildlife and shifters around here; bears, wolves, coyotes, all kinds of birds. I've had a bear sniffing around the RV before when I accidentally dropped a hotdog in the firepit and forgot about it when I cleaned up for the night. That was quite the surprise when I opened the door, but at least he ran off when I startled him with the noise. It was so quick that I didn't even think to check if it was a natural bear or a shifter."

"Huh. I'll make sure to have it with me every time we leave," Merri promised.

Gawain gave her a quick kiss before opening the door. Locking the RV, he realized she probably hadn't had huckleberry ice cream before either. He'd have to see if they had it in stock from last season as it wasn't quite time to pick them yet. July would generally be the earliest, and he thought they'd be back home by then. He wanted to make this dig as quick as he could so he didn't draw attention to them.

Gawain opened the car door for Merri, holding a hand to help her in. If they were going on a date, he wanted it to feel like a date. The drive into town wasn't long. It wasn't a large town, but it was near the North Entrance to Yellowstone National Park, so it got a lot of visitors during the summer. He was hoping that the town had recovered quickly after the huge flood. The historic five-hundred-year type of event had wiped out roads and shut the town off from anyone coming or leaving. The park also suffered road losses, which considering there were only a few roads, meant that this entrance had been closed for a while. He was eager to buy things in town, get the local economy going again. He had lots of post-cards and souvenirs he could buy, huckleberry jams and candies to bring back home.

The grocery store was small but had most necessities. Bozeman was a couple hours' drive away and had the larger box stores. He didn't think they would need to go there though, but they'd see. He wanted to pick up some firewood for camp as well. They weren't under a fire ban yet, but it wasn't uncommon for them to happen. The last time he was here, there had been a fire ban, but he had been able to use the propane tanks and his camp stove to make food.

They were early enough in the season that they didn't have to wait long for a table to open up on the outside patio. Their table was on the far side, overlooking the river. The river was back to its normal size, flowing nicely. He would try to let his falcon out later, head to the river to fish. He was sure Merri could use a break to just sit and read as well. Looking over the menu, he decided to get the bison burger with an ear of corn and fries.

"Do you know what you want?" Merri asked, biting her lip as she looked over the menu.

"I'm getting a bison burger, fries, corn," Gawain replied. "What about you?"

"I'm debating between a burger and a BBQ sandwich."

"You should try the huckleberry margarita," he suggested.

"What's a huckleberry?" Merri asked curiously.

"It's a berry, similar to a blueberry, but it only grows in mountainous areas. I think it's in five states and Canada, if I remember correctly. For some reason, it hasn't been able to be cultivated. There's a big rush to find them in the forests when they come ripe, around July to early fall. There's huckleberry candy, jams and jellies, drinks, ice cream."

"Are they that good?"

"Well, the locals and the bears think so," Gawain said with a smile. The wild animals like the deer and the bears were big fans of the sweetness of the berries. "No, they're pretty good. I was thinking we could get some jams and candies to either mail back home or bring home with us, depending on how long we're going to be here. After dinner, I thought we could take a walk and see if the ice cream stand has huckleberry ice cream in stock for you to try."

"That sounds delicious. I wonder if we could get frozen berries sent back home to Sam. He loves finding new things for the brewery's restaurant."

"You know, I've never looked. Maybe we can ask some of the local stores," Gawain said. "There's lots of huckleberry items we can bring back, even if we can't get frozen ones."

Their server came over, seeing if they were ready to order. Gawain got what he had planned on, throwing in a local beer to go with it. Merri ordered a regular cheeseburger with a side of coleslaw and fries. She also ordered a small salad and the huckleberry margarita.

Merri watched as a few birds gathered near the river, probably looking for something to eat. She saw movement in the brush and leaned forward to see what it was.

"Gawain! Look!" She grabbed his arm excitedly and pointed. It was an elk, drinking from the river. She grabbed her phone and took pictures. She didn't see any antlers yet, so she couldn't tell if it was female or a young elk. If she remembered correctly, they didn't grow antlers until they were two. Gawain wrapped an arm around her, peering over the ledge. His head popped up and he tapped her arm to get her attention. *Look to your left, in the tall tree by the riverbed,* he told her quietly.

I don't see anything, she admitted after a few seconds of searching.

Gawain moved his arm, pointing his finger in a certain direction. Merri tried to follow his finger path and gasped. Oh! It was a bald eagle. How lovely to be able to see one in person, in the wild. She was so happy their numbers were getting better. "Thank you, mate," she said quietly.

"I'm guessing we'll see some bison on this trip too. There are herds in Yellowstone. We need to make sure to take at least a day so I can show you some of the sights. Yellowstone is an amazing park and I think you're going to love it."

Merri looked over the river, sipping her drink, leaning against Gawain. She watched as a few white-water rafters came floating down the river, the elk ignoring them as it drank and got a snack from the nearby bushes.

17

Merri looked at the time on her phone as the light snuck past the curtains. Six thirty in the morning. She sighed. She grabbed a bottle of water and headed to the bathroom to get ready. She wasn't sure how long they were going to stay here, so she wanted to conserve the water in the tank. She grabbed a pack of bath wipes and used those to clean up this morning, the bottle of water worked for wetting her toothbrush and rinsing her mouth out.

She squeaked as a hand reached in and grabbed her ass. "Gawain! I'm trying to brush my teeth," she said around her toothbrush.

"Morning, dear. Are you excited to go to the site and see what we can see?" Gawain asked.

Merri looked at her mate. He was almost buzzing, he was so excited. "I am. Especially since I know Rob will be safe. I was worried when he told us it was Barry who was going to be the one coming to the site. Gage had a lot of good ideas that should help Rob and Daryl."

"He did. I almost wish I could be there when they tell Barry he has no authority and needs to leave."

"Do you think he will? Does he have to give back the

horn?" Merri asked. She hadn't been clear on that last night, but it was late by the time they were almost done talking and she had been too tired to bring it up.

"I don't think he'll go easily but Rob can now call on Marco, who will come make sure Barry leaves. I'm still not clear on how Warden positions work; I always thought they were appointed, but neither Gage nor Marco seemed worried about Barry lashing out and firing them. I need to remember to ask them," he said thoughtfully. "Since the horn was found on private land, he should be required to give it back. Now if he actually follows through is another story; it could conveniently go missing. With the local Sheriff there, who is human, which should keep Barry's hissy fit in check, and Marco on standby, I think they'll be okay."

"It's nice that the local Sheriff has paranormal connections. It seemed like they were willing to protect Daryl and his land, even against a Convocation member," Merri replied.

"A lot of communities out here are for less government interference, regardless of whether it's the paranormal or human government. That entire dig is on his private land, so I think a lot of people would support Daryl in keeping them away," Gawain said. He was all for science and archeologists finding new discoveries and advancing what they knew about the world, but he didn't think it should come at the cost of people. He had seen too many incidences of the people in power claiming things for their own under the guise of "for the good of the many." Most of the time it was for the good of the person in charge and no one else.

"I packed the bag last night with bear spray, snacks, sunscreen, hats, first aid kit. I wasn't sure what else we should bring," Merri said.

"I have my tools and a brand-new journal to document everything in already in the car," he said gleefully. "We'll need to bring several gallons of water to make sure we stay hydrated. Oh! I almost forgot; hold on a second," he said as he dug around in the storage bin. "Here!"

Merri looked at the black drawstring bag that he handed her. It was small, about the size of her hand, maybe a little bigger. Opening it, she pulled out a purple rubber funnel type of thing. The top opened to an oval shape and there was a definite straw part at the bottom. "What is it?" she asked, looking at him.

"A lady funnel," Gawain said, his cheeks turning a little red. "I thought it might be helpful to have when we're gone all day. It got great reviews online."

"A lady funnel?" she asked, still confused.

Gawain nodded. "It's for when you have to go to the bathroom outside. You put the cup part up against your skin, and then you can pee standing up."

"Oh! I didn't even think of that," Merri said. That would be better than squatting and hoping a snake wasn't nearby. "Thank you," she said, placing it in a Ziplock bag and putting it in her day pack.

As they left the camper, Gawain looked around. He could have sworn he felt someone watching them, but he didn't see anything. He locked the door. *'Merri, can you throw an extra protection spell on without being noticed?'* he asked.

'Yes. Why?' She was already forming the spell in her mind; she just needed to touch the Airstream and say the final word.

'I feel like someone is watching us, but I can't see anyone. I may just be paranoid with the Barry thing but figured it's better to be safe.'

'The original spells and the ones I added will make sure nothing happens to the RV and nothing gets in or out that we don't want to. This new one will just reinforce that even more. We won't even get ants or fruit flies. No matter how small a device or shifter it might be, it's not getting in.'

"I know you said bears are common here, do you think we'll be safe?" Merri said, placing her hand on the side of the

RV, like she was holding herself up while adjusting her shoe with the other hand. The last word of the spell was 'safe,' and she could feel her magic clicking into place, wrapping around the Airstream, making sure all essential parts were protected.

"We'll be okay. Just pay attention to your surroundings, keep the bear spray and air horn with you, and your walking stick for snakes," he advised.

"I forgot about the snakes," Merri admitted.

"It's going to be a beautiful day for a hike! Let's go," Gawain said, reaching out to take her hand. He let his falcon come forward a little more, trying see what had set him off, but he still couldn't pinpoint anything.

I think we should be careful what we say outside of the RV and make sure you're not shifting out in the open or flying out of the camper window. If someone's watching, they could be doing it from farther away or maybe they set up a trail cam nearby, Merri suggested.

That's true. I really wanted to fly down to the river and fish, Gawain said mournfully.

You still can, we just need to be more careful about it. You need to be able to let him out so he can have fun here too, Merri agreed. *Plus, maybe he'll spot something from the air.*

As they climbed into the car, Merri cast another quick spell. This one being protection and concealment. She made it so that if a person tried following them, they would turn away and lose sight of the SUV. If they persisted, the follower would end up driving into town. It was a reasonable place for them to be, so she was hoping it would buy them some time before whoever was watching them caught on to her trick. If it was a human, they probably wouldn't notice, but if it was a paranormal, they may eventually realize that it was a spell.

She kept an eye out behind them as they drove, Gawain pulling over at random pull-offs to look at the local scenery. They didn't see anyone behind them, so they continued to the GPS coordinates they had mapped out with Doc. They were skirting around the National Park's boundaries, and she was hoping that the site wasn't on Yellowstone's property. Gawain had his permit that would change to show he was from the US government on official business if he needed it, but she was still worried.

The landscape was gorgeous. She really could just sit here and stare at it. There was a bright blue sky today with white puffy clouds, and although it was hot, there was a nice breeze. The mountains in the background were a mix of a barren grayish-brown color dotted with sparse trees and shrubs, and parts that were completely covered in fir or pine trees. The Yellowstone River glinted in the sun, and you could see people floating by on rafts, aiming for the white-water peaks for a more thrilling ride. The ground was a mix of colors; there were bright yellow-green plants, the browns of dirt or dead areas, the duller green of the sagebrush. Then there were hints of color from wildflowers.

Gawain slowed down, looking for a turnoff. "We're on this dirt road for a few minutes and then we are going to be off-road, so it's going to get bumpy," he said. He had gone off-roading so often that he wasn't worried. He had run-flat tires and his own satellite phone with him today. He didn't expect to get much, or any, cell phone reception where they were going. There still wasn't anyone else around, so he felt safe driving to the site. "Can you put a concealment spell around the area once we get there? I normally don't bother, but I'm thinking we need to be more careful on this dig, especially since it felt like someone was watching us this morning."

Merri nodded. "I can at least get one started and expand as we need to. Rob's area was roped off in squares. Are we going to be doing that too?" she asked.

"Maybe. It's just us, so it's not like we need to stay out of each other's area. I'm documenting this for our use, not for anyone else. My gut says there's something here, I can feel it getting stronger the closer we get. I've driven down the main road so many times, I'm not sure why I didn't sense anything sooner," he said, a little frustrated.

"You weren't meant to yet, I guess," Merri replied. Gawain said it was intuition or his gut, but she was convinced he had a bit of finder magic in him.

"Maybe," he replied.

Merri held on to the bar over the door as the car bounced across the uneven terrain. They clearly weren't on the road any longer, Gawain using his phone to navigate toward the site. It was close to a creek or river according to Google Maps overview but nestled in between mountain ridges. It certainly wouldn't have been something that would be easy to stumble upon. Although it was near water, it wasn't the main river that people would have been traveling by.

"When we go to Yellowstone, I'll have to take you creeking. There are several spots where you can pull off and park and wade in the river. The cold water feels great on your feet after hiking, although some spots in the river have more geothermal activity and are hot springs. Those were closed a few years ago, so we'll have to see if they're open again," Gawain said.

"That sounds fun. I can't wait to see the Park," Merri replied.

They drove slowly across the rocky ground, Gawain doing his best to avoid running over the plants. One, because he didn't want to damage the landscape. Two, because he didn't want to leave a visible trail. Although with the concealment spell Merri had created, at least they wouldn't be able to track them via the car.

Gawain looked at the phone, seeing that he needed to adjust his course.

"We should be there soon," Gawain said. Up ahead he could see where the mountain-covered forest sloped down to become flatter ground. There must be something soon, his intuition was just about screaming at him now. He slowed the car down to a crawl. He wanted to get close enough to the site that he had his gear within reach, but he also didn't want to accidentally drive over anything and have to move once they got set up. Of course, if it was the settlement site, he was bound to have to move the car since it seemed like a decent-sized village from Doc's description. Slowing the car to a stop, he looked at the cleared area in front of him. The trees sort of came out and formed an arc around an invisible barrier. He would bet money that was where the village had been, although he was surprised the trees hadn't filled in more. Turning the car around so that they could easily grab items out of the back, he put it in park. "I think we're here. Let's walk around first. I'll grab some flags that I'll use to mark places that I think will have something. Remember to wear your hat, bring your bear spray, and watch for snakes."

Merri nodded. She never wanted to see a snake that close again. Hopefully if there were any close by, the arrival of the car scared them away. She grabbed her hat and clipped the bear spray to her belt. Gawain was already at the back, grabbing his flags. Merri could tell they were in the right spot by how excited he was. She could also feel faint traces of magic. It didn't feel harmful, but she would have to see where that would lead her. She knew from speaking to Doc that a lot of unicorns had healing magic, so maybe that was it. Gawain walked over to a spot, putting down a flag. This continued for about ten minutes, ending with ten flags in total, before he went to the car and pulled out a bin and a canvas bag.

"Can you help me throw this over the car?" he asked, pulling a tarp out of the bag. It was printed to look just like the landscape around them.

"If we have the concealment spell and the permit, why the tarp?" Merri asked as she pulled it down to cover the front of the car.

"I like to be careful. Why draw unnecessary attention to

us? Will the concealment spell work with overhead views like planes or helicopters or birds?"

"With the way it was worded, if they were trying to track us, then yes. If it's a tourist helicopter or a shifter out for a flight, then I'm not sure. I think if they were simply out for fun, then they would see us. If they decided to try to find us, it would activate. But I can see why hiding the car would be useful. We'll look more like hikers and stand out less," Merri acknowledged.

"I have smaller tarps to cover the holes when we dig and need to leave. It won't do much if someone is walking by, but if they don't look too closely, they might not notice."

"What are we tackling first?" Merri asked.

"I want to start at this flag. My gut was screaming at this one, so I think it's going to be something good. I want to keep all the dirt close by in a pile so we can fill the holes in when we're done. As much as I'd love to fully explore this site, I think we need to get things that point to unicorns out first and then if we have more time to explore it, we can work it like a normal dig. Normally I would mark where I knew things were but would slowly start excavating the entire area. I don't know if we have that kind of time. There's something else here too, but I can't pinpoint where it is," he said, frustrated.

"There's magic. Old magic, but other than it not being harmful, I haven't gotten a read on it," Merri replied. "I don't think it's something most people could pick up on, so we could work on your sites first," she suggested.

"Sounds like a good plan," he said, pulling out a shovel and other tools from the bin. Gawain pulled out his new journal to document things as well. He had a ruler, a scale, and a few other things he needed in this bin. He grabbed a couple of foam pads to help them be comfortable as they sat or knelt on the ground and walked over to the first flag, which was the one closest to the woods.

It took a couple of hours of slowly scraping the dirt away and occasionally using the shovel when his intuition told him it was safe to do so, but they finally found something buried in the dirt. There were shards of pottery, mixed with what looked to have been dried herbs. Working his way around, he found a few bottles, a mortar and pestle. Merri was taking pictures as he went, placing the rulers when he unearthed a piece so that they had the measurements, and taking notes.

"Gawain. If this is Doc's old home, this might be Thalia's house. He said they had a tree they met at, and she was the village's healer," Merri said quietly, after quickly creating a silencing dome around them.

He looked up, holding a piece of jewelry. "I think you're right. This is similar in design to the bracelet he gave Emma, and I know that belonged to her. How much do you think we should bring back?" he asked. He wasn't sure the best way to move forward. Most of the time, he documented and gave his discoveries to museums or whoever had hired him. He had conducted digs for his own amusement and had his own small collection, which would be going into their museum when it was ready to open. However, this site was different than his previous ones. Doc had known these people, he had traveled with them, eaten with them, grown up with them. Normally it was very distant relatives at best that he was dealing with, not a friend who had been raised by the owner of the artifacts. Gawain wasn't sure if they should keep every little thing, including the dried herbs, or just big things that were still intact and whole.

"I think we keep things he will have remembered, or think are important. Maybe jewelry, the mortar and pestle is probably something she used with him quite frequently, things like that. Once we document it, I'll get two of the empty boxes we brought, and we'll separate as much as we can here, and we'll go over it again later. If it's nothing paranormal in nature, maybe we can donate it to a local museum," Merri said.

Gawain nodded. That seemed like a reasonable answer. It gave him something to go on at least. "We should close up here and start heading back. Headlights this far from a road or parking lot would draw attention. Let's stop at the grocery store and grab a few more jugs of water before heading to camp."

The grocery store was busy, but they grabbed some waters, and a few apples that looked tasty. It would be nice to have those tomorrow at lunch. Merri grabbed a pack of baby wipes as well. They always came in handy for cleaning things, wiping down hands, that kind of thing. She was going to leave a pack in Gawain's car so they would have an easy way to wipe the dirt off their hands before eating.

"Wow! You must have been hiking all day!" the cashier exclaimed.

Merri looked at themselves, they were a little dirty and sweaty.

"We were out all day," Gawain agreed. "It was such a beautiful day."

"Did you get to see any animals?" the woman asked as she bagged their apples.

"Not today, but I did see a pair of elk at the river yesterday," Merri said.

"If you want to see more, you will have a good chance if you drive into the Mammoth Hot Springs area. They love congregating in the grassy area in town there. The hot springs are really neat to see too. You can walk the path that goes around them; there are a lot of stairs in one spot, but it's worth it. My favorite is the Canary Spring. Make sure you follow the path along so you can see the front side of it. I just love how it cascades and if it's quiet you can hear the water."

"We'll have to check that out, thank you!" Merri replied.

18

Gawain groaned as he stood up from the hole in the ground. Merri was working on getting a different area started while he was working on finishing Thalia's site. He thought he was close to finished. He had found a few timbers that had not completely decayed, and it gave him a vague idea of where the building may have sat. He had marked it off with string, taking a picture and sketching it in his journal. He would ask Doc if that was what he remembered it being like once they had cell phone reception. He had the sat phone, but this could wait until he could text it with his regular phone. There were a few more tools that he had found, some needles, what looked like pliers and tweezers, a few jars, and pots. When he moved the jars, he could hear something rattling inside. While Gawain was curious as to what the remnants were, he also hadn't wanted to get too close to the contents. Some things became toxic after time, and he didn't know what the jars contained. He thought maybe he could seal these and bring them back to Doc. They were pretty jars if nothing else. Each one had a slightly different geometric design, so maybe Doc would remember what they were for.

"Gawain! Come here!" Merri shouted. She had found

something in the dirt and she didn't want to disturb it further. It unfortunately looked like a piece of bone, and she didn't think it was animal. This was a little more than what she had been prepared to find and she wanted to leave this one to Gawain. She was not comfortable digging up a body, no matter how old it was.

"What did you find?" he asked, dropping into the site. "Oh. That looks like a finger," he mused. At this point in his career, bones stopped freaking him out. The first time he had seen one though, he had a mild meltdown. This was Merri's first time, he realized.

"Why don't you go start by the other flag," he suggested. "I'll work on this one. I think Thalia's is almost finished."

"We're not...we're not keeping the bones, right?" Merri asked hesitantly.

"No, we're not. I'm going to look for clues to how they died, see if there are any injuries that suggests they were attacked or killed. I'll put all the bones back, say a blessing, and we'll fill this spot back in. I don't like disturbing graves if I don't have to. Unfortunately, since we're trying to find out if Doc's old tribe left or died out here, I need to investigate a little bit. It is rather odd to have a body so close to where there were buildings though," Gawain replied.

Merri nodded and gathered up her tools. She would get the other flag area started and hopefully she wouldn't find another body, she thought to herself. She was just going to ignore what Gawain was doing.

She wasn't finding too much in this section. A few more pieces of pottery or plates, what might be silverware, and a pin. She took notes and pictures like Gawain had shown her. Scraping the dirt away, she came across a few tools. A little while later, she unearthed pieces of wood imbedded into the dirt. She followed the line of the wood remnants and realized it was probably another structure. She marked where the edges were and measured out the length for the notes.

Gawain was a much better artist than her, so she would let him sketch it in the book. There were a few more tools, these looked like gardening type of tools, like a hoe. Merri brushed the loose dirt away, scraping additional layers away until she came across something that looked like fur. She switched techniques, trying to scrape the dirt away from the edges so that she wouldn't hurt whatever this was. Maybe clothing or a blanket? She really hoped it wasn't an animal carcass, although she didn't think it would be preserved this long.

After a few hours, she managed to get the hide uncovered. It looked in pretty good shape, but she worried about it being exposed to the oxygen in the air. She cast a quick preservation spell on it to keep it from degrading. It looked an awful lot like Doc's horse coat when he shifted. The hide looked like it was wrapped around something, the middle was solid when she poked at it. She took pictures from every angle, measured the size while it was still wrapped up. Gently reaching under the edges of the fur, she tried lifting it out, but it was well stuck in the dirt. Using a small plastic tool with a blunt edge, she started digging out underneath the bundle. About halfway through, she was able to finally work it loose. Turning it over, she again took pictures. She set it off to the side and started scraping the dirt underneath where it had been to make sure there wasn't anything more hidden. When she didn't find anything else, Merri turned back to the bundle. Merri slowly started to unwrap the fur, stopping often to make sure she wasn't causing any damage. When she saw there was what looked like a book inside, she placed another preservation spell for the book. That was definitely not going to like being exposed to the sunlight and oxygen after being buried for so long.

A shadow fell over her and she let out a little scream.

"It's just me, Mer." Gawain laughed. "I'm finished with that section and have it documented and filled back in. The body was all bones at this point, so it's hard to tell anything. I didn't see any obvious injuries that would have caused the person to die, so my best guess is natural causes. What did you find?"

She pointed to the bin of the smaller items she found. "Some household-looking things and then this animal skin. It looks like a horse hide," she said. "There's a book of some kind in it."

Gawain squatted down next to her to look. "It does look like horse, which is kind of disturbing if this is Doc's old home."

Merri nodded. That's what she was thinking too. "I put a preservation spell over the hide and the book, so they don't start decaying. I haven't opened it yet."

Gawain grinned. "Let's see what it is!"

Merri laughed at how excited he was but continued to slowly unwrap it. When she took a glance inside the book, it seemed like a journal. She handed it over to Gawain. "You're better with Greek," she said. Standing up, she laid the hide out on the flat ground. It definitely could have been a horse, although the head piece was missing. Which if it turned out to be unicorn hide, then removing the part that contained the horn made sense. It would look weird to have a circle in the middle of a head where a horn would have been.

"Do you think Doc could DNA test this and see if it's horse or unicorn, or is that too weird to have him do?" Merri asked. "I was just thinking we don't want to send it through the Convocation, especially with what happened to Rob."

"We can bring it home and ask. He may be able to tell just by seeing it. The preservation spell might have trapped enough scent for him to know. I'll still put it in an airtight container, but we'll bring it with us since we don't know for sure," Gawain replied.

Merri watched as he scanned the journal. "It sounds like this may have belonged to the tribe leader. It's a lot of venting and anger. Hmm, this is written after Doc left, I think; it references kicking someone out and how the tribe seemed to go downhill afterward. Do you mind if I read a little bit before we leave?"

"No, go ahead. The old tree stump over there is calling to me," Merri replied.

Walking over to the stump, it had clearly been an old tree when it died. There was no evidence of the part that had fallen over, it was either carted off, used, or decomposed over time. The stump still looked in good shape though, which was odd. But the closer she got, she realized the magic traces she had sensed when they first got there, were coming from the stump. Running back to Gawain, she grabbed a shovel and a few other tools.

"There's something under the tree," she said excitedly.

"Really? Let me put this in a container and I'll come help," Gawain said, jumping up.

They dug about three feet down with the shovel before Merri's magic told her to stop and be careful. They switched to smaller tools and found another parcel tangled in the roots of the tree. Another hide, although this one was clearly a deer or something other than a horse. There was a wax type of coating over it. Merri could sense a preservation spell. Pulling it free from the roots, Merri placed her own spell to make sure they didn't do any damage. The original magic was old and fading. Opening the first fold, she found a parchment with a note.

"To the son of my heart. I don't think I'll see you again before I pass. I'm not sure when you'll come back here again, so I'm burying this at our tree. I'm hoping you sense my magic and know to look here. I kept collecting information and treasures for you whenever I had a chance. I hope you have found your family and your mate. I hope you have much love and happiness in your life. I think of you often and treasure the times you come visit. I love you, *yiós*," Gawain read aloud.

"Let's leave it as it is and bring it home. I don't feel right looking through things meant for Doc," Merri said.

"I agree. Did you already spell this one too?" Gawain asked.

"I did," Merri replied, wrapping the fold back over and standing.

"I think we can call it done for today," Gawain said. "We can get the last couple flags tomorrow. Let's put this in the car, and we can go creeking on our way home. There's a couple of spots where the river is close to the road, so we'll be able to keep an eye on the car while cooling off in the water."

19

"What are you doing here?" a voice asked. There was suddenly a young man standing at the edge of the trees. How he got there or was able to see through the containment spell, Gawain had no idea.

"We were hiking," Gawain replied, moving to stand between the stranger and Merri.

'Get in the car please,' he said. *'I don't like this.'*

'Where did he even come from?' Merri asked. They were so far off the normal trails, that it would have been strange to come across anyone else. The man wasn't wearing a backpack, had no walking stick, nothing that indicated he was a hiker or a camper. His clothes were older, dirty and a little tattered, his shoes worn down, his toe almost poking through.

Luckily, they had filled in the holes that they had dug, Merri placing a restoration spell over the spots so that they returned to their previous state. There was one final spot they had been still working at filling in when this man appeared. Merri had a few spell bottles ready that Tess had given her when they left. She had kept one in the camper and a couple in the car. Grabbing one now, she kept an eye on the stranger, ready to jump out of the door and protect her mate.

"Why did you dig a hole then?" the man asked.

It was hard to get a read on him, Gawain thought. His face was blank, there was no emotion there.

"We were eating lunch and I thought it would be fun to try out my new metal detector," Gawain said. He did have one in the car, but they hadn't used it.

"What you find?"

"Eh, we found an old quarter and some pieces of metal. Not sure what they are. Maybe nails. Nothing too exciting, but it's more about the fun of the search, right?" Gawain vaguely answered. They had indeed found a coin, although it was much older than a USA quarter and some nails, along with a few tools.

"Why's your wife in the car?"

"She's not comfortable around strangers," Gawain said firmly. *'Lock the doors please,'* he told Merri. *'Climb across and get in the driver's seat. I'll fly away if I have to, but I want you ready to floor it if needed.'* He could hear Merri start the car and he felt better knowing she could get away.

"That's a bit rude. I want to talk to her too," the man said, almost pouting.

This whole interaction was bizarre and beyond awkward. It was almost like this guy had no social skills, or maybe it was an act to throw him off, but either way Gawain wanted it to end quickly.

"Well, she's not comfortable around strangers, so she's not coming out. I'll tell her you said hello. I have some water and trail mix if you're hungry," Gawain offered.

"I wanted to ask her things too," he replied, ignoring Gawain's offer of food.

"We really need to get back home, so we need to go. I just need to fill this back in first. It was interesting meeting you," Gawain said, grabbing his gloves and the shovel to fill in the hole. It would act as a weapon if needed.

"Have you heard about people living here?" the guy asked.

"We haven't seen anyone on our hikes," Gawain replied, keeping it vague enough that it wouldn't register as a lie if this person was a paranormal of any kind. He let his falcon out a little bit more, hoping that the bird's senses would get a better feel for this guy, but other than danger, he couldn't sense anything.

'Be careful, my pendant is glowing,' Merri warned him.

"Not now, from a long time ago," the man said, shifting on his feet.

"We're not from here, just visiting on vacation, so I'm not very familiar with the local history," Gawain replied.

"There used to be people living here," the man insisted.

"I'm sure some of the native tribes in the area did live here since it's near water and there were probably lots of animals back then. Seems like a nice spot. I wouldn't know though." Gawain finished filling the hole. "Well, we have to get back. Here's one of the pieces of metal we found, if you would like it," Gawain said, rubbing the piece between his gloved fingers to wipe any residue of himself or fingerprints off before tossing it over. He was hoping it would lend credence to their story and it wasn't anything important or anything that would point to people actually living here. It looked more like something the river washed up and it got buried over time.

'I did a cleansing spell on it as soon as you threw it. There won't be any trace of us,' Merri told Gawain. She understood why he did it, but she also didn't want there to be any way for this creepy guy to be able to track them.

"So, you don't know any legends about here? About special horses? Weird people who kept to themselves until one day they were gone?"

The man wouldn't let it go, Gawain realized. "That sounds interesting. I'll have to check the local bookstores and see if they have anything about it." This was also the truth; it was interesting, and he did normally pick up books about local legends and myths.

"There's a guy who will pay for it," the man said, a touch of hero worship in his voice. "Any stories or myths and legends, he'll pay for. He likes weird things; he'll pay extra for evidence and pictures or video."

"Huh," Gawain replied, moving backward slowly to the car.

"Yeah, I told him my grandpa's stories. He heard them from his great-grandpa. I forget how he heard about it. But there used to be weird horses here. Special horses."

"Maybe they were mustangs or stallions, those are pretty horses," Gawain replied.

"No, no. These were horses with extra pieces, horses that turned to people. How crazy is that? Grandpa said they were weird and didn't like people. They kicked one guy out and when the old lady of the village died, some people left. The rest just died. You find any bones?"

"Bones aren't metal, so the metal detector wouldn't find any if they were here," Gawain replied.

"Can I see the rest of what you found? Maybe I can sell it to the guy," the man said, following.

"No, it's just like what I gave you already. Nothing impor-tant, just a few little pieces of metal," Gawain replied angrily, blocking the man from the car. He heard the doors lock, although his falcon picked up on the fact that Merri leaned over and manually unlocked the passenger door for him.

'Roll the window down enough for me to get an arm in and to hold on. If he keeps coming closer, I'm going to just stand on the running board and hold on to the doorframe. You drive. Lock all the doors, please. I don't want to risk opening the door and having him try to get in,' Gawain told Merri. He didn't want the guy anywhere near his mate.

'I threw a concealment spell over the rest of the artifacts in the

ground. If he goes digging, he won't find anything. It's spelled for ill intentions, which he clearly has if he would be doing it for money. If we come back, we would be able to find it again. I don't want him digging up those poor bones and selling them,' Merri said. She had one hand on the wheel, the car in drive and her foot on the brake. Her other hand still held the potion, just in case.

"I'm leaving now. I don't have anything else to give you," Gawain said, continuing to walk backward to the car door. He wanted to keep an eye on this guy, it didn't seem smart to turn his back on him.

"Now see, I think you have something more in that car of yours. Something you don't want to share with me. Sharing is nice and you're not being nice. I need to sell something to the guy, I promised. So, you're going to give it to me," he said, pulling a knife out from behind his back.

Save me from stupid, Gawain thought to himself. *'Start driving, I'll run and jump on,'* he told Merri.

She froze at the sight of the knife.

'Merri! Go!' Gawain yelled.

The fact that he raised his voice at her snapped her out of it and she started driving, slow enough that Gawain could catch up. She made sure the window was all the way down so he would be able to reach in and hold on. Chanting under her breath, she tossed a protection spell at her now running mate. The crazy man was chasing after him. She turned the car slightly so Gawain could run straight at it. As soon as his foot touched the running board and his hand gripped the door, she drove away faster, the car bouncing across the ground. Gawain slid the top of his body through the window, somehow getting all the way inside, still holding on to the small shovel. She heard something break in the back of the SUV.

"The asshole just threw his knife at my car!" Gawain shouted.

"At least it didn't hit you," Merri said, her hands shaking

as she drove away. She put the potion down, not wanting the glass to break. Glancing behind them, she saw a lone figure standing in the distance. She made another spell, cleaning up their tire tracks as they drove, making sure he wouldn't be able to follow their tracks and find where they were going. With one main road, if he could see what direction they went, it would be easy enough for him to track them into town. Of course, it might be easy anyway, as they were staying near the closest town to the dig site.

"I'm sorry it got so crazy," Gawain said. He had been on some insane digs before where things went wrong, but he had dragged his poor mate along this time. She had already seen a rattlesnake up close, gone days without a shower or running water, peed in the woods using a funnel, and now they had a crazy person throwing knives. Well, knife, just the one, not that that made it any better. He'd be lucky if she would be willing to go on another dig with him.

"Let's pull into a hotel," Gawain suggested. There were a couple of hotels nearby, and he would bet that they would have things like toothbrushes and deodorant for sale. If not, the grocery store was within walking distance.

"Why?" Merri asked as she pulled into the first parking lot.

"Let's see if they have a room for tonight. We can buy toothbrushes and toothpaste, deodorant, and cheap phone cords. Let's have a night out of the campground, where you can take a long hot shower and we can get some dinner."

"All our clothes are at the campground," Merri pointed out.

Gawain shook his head. "I started keeping a set of clothes for both of us in the car after we got drenched at the lake. Let me go see if they have a room, if not I'll call the other ones."

Merri nodded. "I'll stay here," she said.

Gawain walked into the lobby. "Hi, I was wondering if you had any rooms available?"

"We just had a cancellation for tonight, but otherwise we're completely booked," the woman said.

"Tonight would be perfect. We've been camping and could use a break from it," Gawain joked.

"It has been rather warm," the woman replied. "How many will be staying with us?"

"Two, just my wife and I."

He could see her trying to peer around the desk to see if Merri was just standing outside.

"She's waiting in the car. Someone just hit the back of our car and she's a little shaken up about it."

"Poor thing. I had that happen to me once and I was jumpy the rest of the day. The water pressure is good here, so a nice hot shower will help. I just need your credit card to book the room."

Gawain pulled out his wallet. "Do you sell deodorant or toothpaste and toothbrushes?"

"We do, there's a small store to the right that should have everything you might need."

"Thanks." Gawain signed the receipt and walked over to the little hotel store.

He grabbed a bottle of tea, a chocolate bar, toothbrushes and toothpaste, and deodorant. The hotel had a dining area as well, so he checked out their menu. It looked decent enough to stay in and eat on-site. He really wanted to give Merri a chance to relax. They had everything they needed from the dig site, his gut telling him they wouldn't find anything more paranormal related. He thought tomorrow they could wander around town and explore Yellowstone.

20

A night with air conditioning and a hot shower could make such a big difference, she realized when she woke up. It was amazing how much better she felt. It was still stupid early, but if they were going into the park today, it was probably better to go early.

"Gawain, wake up! Let's shower and then check out and get breakfast! I want to see the park," Merri said, lightly shaking his shoulder.

"Hmm," Gawain grunted, stretching. "Okay, sounds good. You go get started," he mumbled.

Merri laughed but ran into the shower to get ready. She wouldn't say she luxuriated in the shower, but she took some time to enjoy it. It was back to camping today.

Gawain drove so that Merri could see out the window. The elk were everywhere this morning, along the entrance to the park, in the Mammoth Hot Springs area. They finally found a place to park and walked along the hot springs trail, admiring all the different colors. Gawain wanted to hit all the highlights of Yellowstone today, so they didn't linger too long in one spot. Continuing along the road, he suddenly pulled off to the side.

"Why'd we stop?" Merri asked.

"Look really closely on my side of the road, look in the woods," he said.

Merri peered around, squinting to try to see what he saw. A few branches moved and suddenly there was a bear climbing over some fallen tree limbs. Her breath caught as she watched the wild animal meander along like he didn't have a care in the world.

"That was amazing, thank you," she said as the bear got out of eyesight.

"Let's head toward Old Faithful. It's a must-see when you're here, but then I'll take you to my favorite geyser, Castle Geyser. It's not as reliable, but for some reason I just like it better. We can see Grand Prismatic Spring while we're in the area as well. The colors are amazing."

The parking lot for Old Faithful and the Old Faithful Inn was packed. Gawain finally found a parking space and they hurried over to make sure they caught the explosion. Merri watched as the geyser erupted, amazed by the stream of water shooting over a hundred feet up into the air. When it ended, they walked the path to Castle Geyser, managing to find a spot to wait. They had about ten minutes or so until it was predicted to erupt. It started by gurgling, having little burps of water release from the top before it finally built up enough steam to explode. The stream wasn't quite as high as Old Faithful, but it was still very impressive. Merri turned so that her back was to it and pulled Gawain in for a selfie.

Parking for the Grand Prismatic seemed a little better, although there was still a line of cars in either direction.

"This is the bad part about being close to or in peak season, lots of tourists," Gawain grumbled.

"It's not that bad," she replied, giving him a kiss on the cheek. "Wait! Shouldn't we follow the crowd that way?" she asked, pointing to the right.

"Nope, follow me. This way goes to the overlook; you get

to see more of an overview of the spring. Plus, it normally has less people," Gawain told her.

A short hike later, they stood on the overlook decking. The bold colors really stood out against the sandy brown color of the earth around it, nothing growing close to the spring. Merri took pictures, knowing they wouldn't quite capture the sense of being there. It was breathtaking; the reddish-orange outer ring bleeding into yellow, to a faint green, and then the center was a bright almost neon blue. You could see the steam coming off it, even from here. The boardwalk platforms built around the spring were filled with people, but they looked like ants from where they stood.

Gawain wrapped an arm around Merri, pulling her in to kiss the top of her head. "I have one more spot I want you to see today. I know it's a lot, but I want to make sure you get to see some of my favorite parts of the park."

"Sure, what is it?"

"It's called the Artists' Paintpots. It's another geothermal area, and it's usually less busy than some of the other areas."

Merri watched out the window, loving the scenery. The terrain changed from thick trees and hills, to plateaus full of grasses. The geothermal areas were well marked with steam coming out of the ground, with some of the areas having nothing growing around them. In the barren areas, you could see the remains of tree trunks, the plants no longer able to exist in such an environment.

Gawain was happy to see that the parking lot wasn't full yet. They walked along the wooden boardwalks, passing a stand of bark-less tree trunks standing in an open field, the ground around them steaming. They followed the path, stopping as they reached the top and were able to overlook the entire area. The area was dotted with steam venting from the earth, various little pools of water in different colors scattered about. There was even a small stream of water carving its way through the earth.

Following the trail, Gawain pulled her to another over-look, this one looking over his favorite part in this area. The mud pots. Similar to the hot springs, they were geothermal pools, but were filled with an opaque light grayish-colored mud. As you watched the pool, bubbles formed from escaping gasses. It was fun to watch; bubbles formed before sinking back into the surface, some spots shot out drops of the mud, sometimes a couple of feet in the air. The pool had a gurgling sound, similar to when you boiled water. He really could stand and watch this for hours.

"When it's drier, there's less of the liquid in the pool, and it crusts over. But the sound of these pools is so different than the others. I don't know why, but this is one of my favorite ones."

"I can see why you love this park. There's such a wide variety! You have the animals, the wooded areas, the river, the geothermal areas. There's rafting on the river, hiking, restaurants to eat at. I really do think there's something for everyone to like," Merri said.

As they drove back toward town, Gawain's falcon told him to get ready to stop. As they turned the corner, there was a herd of bison scattered along the green fields near the river. He pulled the car over to the side, letting Merri grab the binoculars to watch them for several minutes.

Reaching town, Gawain stopped at his favorite store. He stopped here every time he was nearby. Rhonda, the owner, was a paranormal herself. The store had just about anything huckleberry that you could think of. Merri had tried some ice cream, but he really wanted to show her all the crazy number of things people made with the berries. Plus, he wanted to see if he could get some sent back home. He agreed with Merri that Sam would have a blast coming up with something to make with them.

Merri looked around the store. There was huckleberry everything! Tea, syrup for pancakes, pancake mix with dried berries in it, chocolate bars with huckleberry, licorice, jam, honey, syrup for drinks, saltwater taffy, popcorn with a candy coating, jellybeans, margarita mix, coffee, hard candy drops, pie filling, barbeque sauce, ice cream, vodka, lotion, soap, candles. Good lord, there was so much. They had a few samples out and Merri eagerly tried a few things. She loved the hard candies; they would be a big hit with Ian and Emma. She grabbed a barbeque sauce for Sam, some tea for her and Emma, jellybeans for Tess, chocolate bars for Shaye.

"What would Rolf like?" she asked Gawain.

"The taffy. He can never pass up taffy," he replied.

Merri grabbed a margarita mix, a vodka, and a coffee as well, knowing they could have fun making drinks when they got back. She grabbed a few postcards to send back home. They had all loved getting them from Ian and Berkley's trip and she wanted to keep that tradition going. The front register also sold stamps and there was a mailbox close by.

Walking past a rotating display of rocks on her way to the cashier, Merri suddenly stopped. There was something there calling out to her. It wasn't often, but sometimes a certain gemstone or rock would be drawn to a specific person. It seemed like one wanted her to have it. She walked to the piles of rocks, holding her hand out to see where it was. Ah! This pile, she thought as her hand warmed when she reached the lower level. Squatting down to see the display, she gently sorted through the rocks until her fingers found a warm stone. She pulled it out, standing to look at it in the light. It held such pure protective energy. It was unique; a clear stone with a few streaks of orangish-red and speckles of black. It very much wanted to go home with her. She cast a quick spell, but the stone was clean, no other spells placed on it.

"Alright," she said quietly to the stone. "I guess you're coming home with me."

She carried the rest of her treasures in the basket, the stone in her hand. Gawain was talking with the shopkeeper.

"That would be great," he said, excitedly. "That's perfect!"

"What's perfect?" Merri asked.

"Rhonda has a supply of huckleberries in the freezer. She can mail them back home for us with overnight shipping. She has a shipping box that's a Styrofoam cooler and uses dry ice."

"Oh, that is perfect! Thank you," Merri told her.

"Are you leaving today then?" Rhonda asked.

"I'm not sure yet." Gawain laughed. "We've been here a few days, but we might try to stay a little longer. I love huckleberries and Merri hasn't had them before, so we wanted to stop in. I know you always have a good selection in stock. We have a friend at the house who will take care of the huckleberries when they arrive. I'm so looking forward to eating them when we get home!"

Rhonda laughed. "You'll have to come back for the harvest one of these times. It gets crazy as everyone rushes to find them in the woods. My brother has a bunch of acres that he leaves wild so that the huckleberries will grow. I'll put my card in here in case you want to order more," she said, putting the business card in the shopping bag with Merri's items. "Oh! I didn't know we even had any Montana Moss," she exclaimed when she got to Merri's stone.

"It was in the rock display." Merri pointed.

"That is so weird, that's for little kids to make their own treasure bags. I can't believe they let this one slip through. Your win though!" she said.

"What is it?" Gawain asked, looking at it.

"Montana Moss Agate," Rhonda told him. "It's an agate that's pretty common around here due to the volcanic type of activity in the area. They're usually clear, but can also have a base color of gray, reddish brown, yellow, or white. The inclusions, the black specks, are thought to be manganese oxide, the reddish-brown color in some of them from iron oxide. I've never had one come in on the rock shipment though, they save them for making jewelry and displays out of. This one must have been meant to be yours," she said with a smile. "I have cage pendants; I'll throw one in for you. You just gently bend the wire and slide the stone in, then bend the wire back, and instant necklace."

"Thank you," Merri said.

Walking down the street, Merri held Gawain's hand. "Thank you for taking me with you on this trip. It's been a lot of fun."

"Even with the crazy guy?" Gawain asked.

"I'd like to skip that part next time, but yes, overall, it has still been fun. I've gotten to see so much," Merri replied.

They stopped in a few more stores, picking up additional souvenirs along the way. On the way back to the car, they were stopped by a voice shouting at them.

"Yoohoo! Hello!" The woman waved. It was the receptionist at the hotel they stayed at yesterday.

"Hi," Gawain replied, stepping closer as she rushed down to them.

"Did that young man find you?" she asked.

"No? What young man?" Gawain asked.

"He said he had damaged your car and left without exchanging information, but he felt horrible and wanted to make it right. I told him you headed into the park, but you had already checked out and were going back to your campsite. He said he would find you, but I didn't give him your information because you're a guest and that's confidential. He wouldn't leave any information either, so I'm not exactly sure how he was going to reach you," she said with a huff.

"Well, thank you for trying to get that for us. We didn't see him," Gawain said. "I'm sure my insurance will cover it when I get home."

Gawain waited until she went back inside, and they were back in their car, before speaking again. "I know we wanted to stay longer, but if he's looking for us, I think we should head out tomorrow. I don't like this at all."

Merri agreed. It was very creepy.

Pulling into the campground, they saw some flashing lights and looked at each other. Gawain let out a sigh as he realized they were coming from the direction of their site.

"Get the phone ready. We may need to call Gage," he told Merri.

"I'll call him right now," Merri said, pulling out her phone. She had a feeling that this was related to the hostile man from the dig site.

The phone rang a few times before a voice answered. "Hello," Gage said, his voice deeper and rough with sleep.

"Gage, I am so sorry to wake you. We had an incident yesterday at the site and we're afraid it followed us to the campground. We just pulled in and we can see lights flashing from the direction of the RV. No one else was camped near us. I wasn't sure how we should proceed. I'm pretty sure the guy from yesterday is in with the hunters, even if it's just selling them information, based on what he said. We have a lot of sensitive things stored in the RV. They're under protection, but that's probably what he was looking for. He was talking about special horses with extra pieces, I think is how he worded it. Horses that changed to people," Merri said.

"You're close to Yellowstone?" Gage asked.

"Yes," Merri confirmed.

"Stay on the line. I'm going to call the Sheriff down there on my other line. He's an old friend; he's human but his family has a few paranormals married in and he's known about us since he was a kid. Kind of like your friend Rob's buddy," Gage said.

Merri waited, hearing a slightly muffled conversation on the other end.

"Rick? It's Gage. I hate to bother you, but I have friends at a campground near you that need help. Yeah, they just pulled into the campground and saw flashing lights coming from the area of their camper. They ran into someone who was causing trouble yesterday and they're afraid that he may have found them again. It's hunter related. I'm not sure, let me ask," Gage said to the other phone.

"Merri, was the guy human or paranormal?" Gage asked her.

"I honestly don't know. He didn't register one way or the other to my senses. He didn't chase after us using any paranormal gifts, but he seemed…off. Like, very little to no social skills, awkward, old clothes. He told Gawain that he had heard the tribe stories from his grandfather who supposedly heard them from his great-grandfather, he wasn't sure how Great-Grandpa had heard it. My pendant was glowing for danger, but I couldn't get a good read on him, neither could Gawain."

"Rick, the guy seemed off but neither of them could get a good read on whether he was human or paranormal. I'll reach out to Marco and see if he can stop by. If the guy is spouting about paranormals, normal jail probably isn't a good idea. The hunters will just get him out if they hear about it… Yeah, okay. I'll let them know. Thanks," Gage said before clicking off the other phone call.

"Okay. Merri, Rick is going to call his people and let him know to hold the guy there, that he's wanted for something federal and that he is coming in to help and has let the authorities know. He wants you to head to the site, but stay in the car, hopefully out of sight from the suspect. He's also letting his people know that you're incoming and he's going to take care of statements. Just keep it vague enough that there's truth but leave out any archeology-type references if the deputy asks questions. I'm going to send Marco in to help."

"We had one hole that wasn't filled in all the way when he arrived," Gawain told him. "I said we were trying a new metal detector and only found a quarter and some tiny pieces of metal. I gave him one of the pieces, it was cleansed by Merri first, and there was nothing paranormal about it."

"If he starts shouting about that near the deputy, explain that you were just trying out a new toy. Have those pieces to show if you still have any," Gage said. "Rick's fine to know the truth, but the official paperwork he'll have to submit, and his deputy need the cleaned-up version."

Merri climbed into the back seat, leaning over to root through the boxes. They had kept the small pieces of metal simply because the man had interrupted them. They had been going to toss the fragments back as they didn't match anything else at the site and seemed more like river debris than anything else. Climbing back into the front, she dropped them into the cup holder.

"Got them," Merri said.

"Good. You have an alibi for yesterday and today?" Gage asked.

"After he threw the knife at the car, we went into town and stayed at a hotel. We ate dinner there as well. I know the receptionist, Angie, would remember us because she flagged us down in town to tell us the man who had hit our car was trying to find us to fix the problem. She mentioned we were staying at a campground. We went to the park, so my America the Beautiful pass was scanned when we entered. There are probably cameras at the entrance and around Mammoth Hot Springs that might have seen us. We came back in town, did some shopping. We have receipts and we talked with a couple shopkeepers."

"Great, just want to make sure all our bases are covered. It sounds like a crazy story. Tell Marco everything and I'll catch up when you guys get home. I know you're probably having fun, except for this, but I want you guys where I can protect you better. If hunters are in the area and this guy blabbed about you at all, I want you home," Gage replied. "Okay, head to your site, Rick should be there soon. That should have been enough time for him to get in contact with whoever responded to the call."

"Thanks, Gage. When we heard he was looking for us, we had already been talking about coming back," Gawain said.

"Be safe," Gage said before ending the call.

Gawain reached over and took Merri's hand. "It will all be fine," he promised. He knew the warding spells on the Airstream would have protected it, but he still wasn't sure what they would find when they got there.

Driving slowly down the road, they both gasped as they came up to their site. There was debris everywhere, small fires were being put out with an extinguisher. The headlights glinted off pieces of glass, so they stopped the car. They waited until the policeman noticed them. Glancing over, he held up his hand in the universal signal for wait as he focused on the flames. Gawain looked around, seeing the head of someone in the back of the police car. There looked to be a sledgehammer and an ax lying on the ground. Their camp chairs were mangled pieces of fabric and metal, their propane tanks disconnected and thrown off to the side. He was glad they had made sure to turn everything off before they left each day.

Just as the final small fire was put out, another set of flashing lights pulled up behind them. Merri's phone dinged with a text.

GAGE: Rick should be there any minute. Here's a picture so you can make sure it's the right guy. Marco will be there as soon as the other officer leaves. He's dropping in.

MERRI: Thank you!

"Gage sent a picture of Rick, the Sheriff he sent. Marco will be here once the deputy leaves," Merri said, showing Gawain the picture.

Gawain looked in his rearview mirror, watching as a man climbed out of the other police car. "That looks like him."

Rick walked by the driver's side door and Gawain rolled his window down.

"Wait here for now. I'm going to talk to my deputy and have him help me get the suspect into my car and then I'll send him back to the station. I'll go over what happened yesterday and today once he's gone," Rick said.

Gawain nodded and left his window cracked open so his falcon could hear the outside conversation better.

"Thanks for responding so quickly," Rick said as he approached his deputy.

"I think this guy is going to need the psych ward. There's something not right about him. Keeps going on about people horses and getting money. Man's been reading too many centaur books or something."

"I found some flyers for someone paying for local legends and proof of 'weirdness,' whatever that means. I pulled them down, but that may be what he's talking about in terms of getting money. If you see any more flyers, let me know. We need to make sure that people know we're not welcoming of this type of behavior," Rick said, his voice hard and uncompromising.

The deputy nodded. "I'll keep an eye out."

"Did you already read him his rights?" Rick asked.

"Yes," the deputy replied.

"Help me move him into my car and then you can head back to the station. I don't think we need the two of us here. The fed should be here soon," Rick said.

"Are you sure you don't want me to stay? At least until the other officer gets here?"

"Nah, I'll be fine. He's in cuffs and will be locked in my car. The RV owners are friends of a friend, so I can trust them," Rick assured his deputy as they walked to the car.

As soon as they opened the back door, even Merri could hear the man screaming about how he needed to get what they had, he had to sell it to the man, they were stopping him for no good reason.

"Sir, you are not the owner of this site, campground, or RV. You were found attempting to damage and break into someone else's home, and you admitted to being here to steal from them. We have plenty of reasons to arrest you," Rick said dryly as he helped place the resisting man in the back seat. Shutting the door, he locked the vehicle.

"Thanks for the help," Rick told the deputy. "Be safe driving back." He patted him on the back and watched until the other man had driven away.

"You can come out now," he said to Gawain and Merri. "Watch your step, there's garbage and glass everywhere."

As they climbed out of the car, Gawain grabbed a couple of flashlights. He was glad they had their boots on, the ground close to the Airstream was littered with glass. Based on the fact there had also been fires, he was guessing Molotov cocktails. Rick walked around, taking several pictures of the damage when Marco appeared.

"Who did you piss off?" he asked, looking around.

Gawain huffed out a laugh, knowing that Marco was here to help. The wording still ruffled his feathers a little bit, so to speak. "Gage said it's okay to say everything," he said quietly, a slight question in his voice, subtly nodding toward Rick.

Marco nodded as Rick came over to stand with them. Merri quickly cast a silencing spell over their group. Marco glanced at her but didn't say anything, so Gawain continued.

"We've been looking for an old village site that may have ties to paranormals. I found a few documents that had pointed to it being around this area. We've had some issues with a few members of the Convocation, so we were trying to keep the dig quiet. We already let Gage know about that," Gawain added to Marco.

"Which members?" Rick asked.

Gawain paused, glancing at Marco from the corner of his

eye. There was a tiny nod in return, so Gawain continued. "Barry is the main one. I've had run-ins with him in the past and I recently learned he has quite the history of harassing others as well. There are a lot of coincidences adding up that seem extremely suspicious, including people disappearing after speaking with him. He's always been an ass, but it seems like it goes deeper than that. A lot deeper."

"Yeah. He's come here before. Likes to take over and damn everyone else," Rick said. "He always seemed slimy to me."

"Stuff relating to the rarer paranormals, seem to go missing when he's involved," Gawain added.

"So this site is potentially for a rarer paranormal?" Rick asked. "And the suspect is going on about horse people. Alright. I don't need to know specifics, but generally tell me what happened."

"We had been at a friend's dig site before coming here. We had recently been talking about tracking down proof that a certain type of paranormal had existed. He told me that he may have found an artifact from what might be an extinct species, so we decided to make a stop to see him on our trip. After being there a couple of days, he received a tip-off from a friend, saying he was going to have a surprise visit from a Convocation member. It was Barry. We decided to leave, not wanting to draw Barry's attention to this site. We came here, set up, ate dinner in town. The next morning, it felt like someone was watching us. I couldn't sense anyone close, but I couldn't shake the feeling. Merri put extra protection on the RV and a concealment spell over the car so they couldn't track us. If they tried, they would be led into town.

"The next few days went fine. We would get there super early and leave before dark, since we didn't want the headlights giving the location away. We found little things here and there. We only took the items that were paranormal in nature or indicated paranormals. There were a couple of designs on the pottery for example, a journal of some sort that clearly was talking about shifters. There is also at least one body buried there. No sign of obvious mortal injuries on the bones, so my best guess was death by natural causes. We reburied the bones and the other things left behind. Merri put a protection spell over the area after we met this guy.

"It was our last day at the dig, and we had one small area left to fill in; everything else had been restored. All of a sudden, this guy is standing there. It was bizarre; I have no idea where he came from or how he saw us through the concealment spell. His interactions were strange. It was like he had no social skills. He kept creeping closer to me, not maintaining normal personal space. I told Merri to get in the car. The guy and I talked; he wanted to know what we were doing. I said we had been hiking and then I tried out my new metal detector, to explain the hole in the ground. When he asked if we found anything, I told him we had found a quarter and some metal pieces. It was junk metal, probably washed in by the river because nothing else on-site matched it. He wanted to know if we had found anything else, including bones. I said no. He mentioned there was a guy paying for local legends and proof of weirdness. He wanted to look in our car and see what we had found. I told him that was all we had and tossed one of the metal shards to him. Merri used a cleansing spell before he took it. I tried to leave, and he pulled a knife. I told Merri to start driving. I jumped on and climbed in through the window. The asshole threw his knife and it hit the back of the car. If you look at the rear passenger light, you can see it's broken. I have tape over it now until we get home, and I can get it to the mechanic.

"Merri was understandably upset. We stayed at a hotel last night. The woman at the front desk will remember us. We ate dinner at the hotel. This morning we went to breakfast and then explored Yellowstone. I scanned my park pass when we entered. We went to Mammoth Hot Springs, Old Faithful,

Grand Prismatic, and the Paintpots. We have pictures on our phones, plus I'm sure any cameras at those areas may have picked us up. Next, we went shopping in town. Angie flagged us down saying there was a man looking for us; he told her he damaged our car and wanted to make it right. He wouldn't leave a name or number. She told him we had checked out and were camping in the area but said she didn't give him any other information. We came back here, already thinking of leaving since he was still trying to find us and saw the lights. Merri called Gage, who called all of you. That's it. Nothing really crazy. He was angry I wouldn't let him go through our car," Gawain finished. "I have no idea how he knew it was this campground though, much less that this was our RV. Unless it ties into the feeling of being watched earlier, because the spell Merri put on the car means he couldn't have tracked us that way."

Rick took a few notes and a picture of their rear taillight.

"Marco, is he human or paranormal?" Rick asked when he came back.

Marco hummed, peering over to look at the prisoner in the back of the police car. "It's an odd one, that's for sure. I don't know if he has a blocker on or what, but I'll figure it out eventually. I'm going to send him to a paranormal jail. Barry doesn't know about this one, so I don't think he'll hear about this incident. I'll stop at the dig site and finish the restoration, make sure there's nothing remaining that could point at you.

"Whatever spells you had on the RV worked great; it doesn't look like there is any damage. I'm going to put a concealment spell on both the RV and the SUV. I know you have one on the car already but mine will be a little stronger," Marco said.

Rick nodded. "The guy was very frustrated by the time my deputy arrived. Nothing he had tried did any damage or let him inside. He had Molotov's, the ax, and was swinging the sledgehammer at the windows when the deputy arrived.

I'm going to keep an eye out for any more of these flyers he saw. I already threw a couple out. If I find out who is putting them out, I'll let you know," he said to Marco. "I'm going to make it clear we don't want or accept the flyers around here. Because another camper called this in, there has to be an official report. It's going to be simple; you were out hiking, trying out your metal detector, and were harassed by the suspect. Suspect damaged your car in anger, followed you back to town, and tried to burn your RV. I'll put in that he seemed in need of a psychiatrist and that he was taken into federal custody."

Marco nodded. "The federal warrant will show up in the system, if anyone goes looking for it." Marco held his hand out to Rick. "Gage said to take this. Wear it all the time. It'll protect you from paranormals. This one goes in your house, and these can be worn by your family. We don't want you getting any blowback from helping us, so make sure you call at the first hint of something wrong and wear that all the time."

Rick nodded, slipping the bracelet on and the other items in his shirt pocket. "Will do. Thanks. It was nice meeting you; I wish it was under better circumstances and that this wasn't chasing you away. It's a beautiful area."

Merri spoke up. "It's one of my favorite places now," she said. "We'll be back, there's so much I didn't get to see yet. Thank you for your help."

Rick tipped his hat before walking to his car.

"Hey, Marco! You going to take out the trash?" he yelled.

"Yes, dear," Marco replied sarcastically, but a second later, the head disappeared from the back of the police cruiser.

"Thanks," Rick said as he climbed in and drove off.

Marco turned back to face them. "Drive home safely but try to get there as quickly as you can. Gage and I still can't track down the people who were camping in the park back home. Which means they have help and are using concealers somehow. There's safety in numbers and with Gage being in town, I'll feel better once you're home. My gut is telling me that Barry is involved somehow, but I'm not sure if we're looking at a single group or two groups with similar goals.

"Good job on the protection spells," he told Merri. "Call me if anything seems fishy on your way home. I just sent you my number. Don't worry about your campsite, I've got it cleaned up," he said with a small smile before disappearing.

Merri looked around and all evidence of the evening had disappeared. The glass was cleaned up, the propane tanks back on the RV, the ax and sledgehammer gone. Their chairs fixed and back to normal. The picnic table was even placed back where it belonged. "That was helpful," she said quietly.

"Let's get the inside ready, take a shower and go to bed. The spells will keep us safe, and we'll leave early in the morning," Gawain suggested.

'Merri! Are you alright?' Tess suddenly burst into her head.

'We're fine. We had an incident yesterday and tonight, but we called Gage and he sent Marco to help. We're safe, but the hunters have been distributing the flyers here too,' Merri replied. Exhaustion swept over her, and she really just wanted to go to bed. It had been such an amazing day before they came back here.

'He told us about it. I just wanted to make sure you guys were alright. Be safe coming home. Check in with me on your way back, okay? I want to know you're safe. Get some sleep, I bet you're tired. Love you,' Tess said.

'I will. Love you too,' Merri replied.

"That was Tess. Gage told them at least a little bit about what happened, and she was checking in," Merri told Gawain, letting him know why she had been quiet.

Gawain leaned down to give Merri a kiss. "Go get a shower, I'll pack up the chairs and check the tire pressure, and get the SUV lined up for a quicker hookup in the morning."

"I'll make sure to leave you enough water to get a shower

too," Merri replied, giving Gawain a quick hug before heading inside.

Letting out a long sigh, Gawain looked around their site. It would be easy enough to leave in the morning. They didn't have any hookups here, but they would need to stop at a dump station and empty their tanks before they left town. He would push hard to get home as quickly as possible, but they would need to stop to sleep at least a couple times along the way. They still had plenty of snacks for the car trip, but they might need to stop for food other than peanut butter and jelly sandwiches for dinner.

He was really disappointed their trip was ending so soon. He was hoping to be able to share more of Yellowstone with Merri, maybe even take a day trip down to see the Grand Tetons. Merri had seemed to love Yellowstone; he would need to make sure he brought her back, for a vacation-only trip. He was glad that she had at least gotten to see some of the wildlife as they drove around the park yesterday. They never made it to the petrified tree or some of the other geyser areas.

'Mate. It's fine. I'm disappointed it got cut short as well, but we'll come back,' she reassured him. *'It's not your fault. Come inside and stop pouting. I'm just getting out of the shower, why don't you come get cleaned up. I'll work on putting stuff away and we can snuggle in bed.'*

'Snuggle?' Gawain asked.

'Hmhm. Maybe even naked snuggles,' Merri hinted.

'I'll hurry up,' Gawain said with a grin. He took the fastest shower of his life after coming inside and seeing Merri putting things away wearing only a towel wrapped around her body.

21

M erri couldn't help the sigh of relief that escaped as they saw the signs for the town limits. It had been a long three days of driving. They had run into one rainstorm, but thankfully it had passed over them quickly. Gawain had tried to push as much driving into one day as possible, but she told him twelve hours was the limit. She didn't think it was safe to drive that far each day, especially with the lack of sleep they both were suffering from. Marco had put a concealment over their vehicles, but the threat of hunters still made their nights restless. Add in a couple of hot nights, and their sleep cycle was screwed. Last night she had used the last of the cooling spell candles so that they could close the windows and block out most of the road noise. They had left the shower fan cracked open to let fresh air in, but it had been the best night's sleep they had since the RV had been attacked. Gawain had made one last stop at a dump station to empty and flush out the black tank so it would be ready to go back into storage.

"Do you want to drive by the museum first or head home?" Gawain asked.

"Let's go home. I really want a shower, to sit on the couch, eat real food, and catch up with everyone. I'm sure they can sense we're close and will want to make sure we're okay," Merri said. "Tomorrow we can unpack the RV and go see what's new in the museum. I'm sure they'll update us tonight with the progress anyway."

"Sounds good," Gawain replied. He was eager to sleep in their bed and have a little more space to move. Normally he was content in the RV, but this trip had a lot more upheavals than he had expected, and he wanted to surround himself with his family and feel safe. He knew the spells that Marco and Merri had put on the Airstream and the car were strong, but after being so close to someone connected to the hunters and hearing Rob and Daryl's stories, it made him want the security of his Clan. He also wanted his mate to feel safe; he could tell the attack on the RV had really shaken her. She would feel better being near her sister and the comfort of her routine at the library. Gawain was grateful she had been willing to step out of her comfort zone and follow him onto a dig site, but he needed to be careful to make sure she got what she needed to recharge as well.

Pulling up to the estate's gates, he saw they had been opened for them. He felt a grin come over his face when he saw the whole family waiting, including Emma's wolfdog Rockefeller. He had never had someone, much less a family, to come home to before, at least not since he was a child. Even on dig sites, he had been in his own tent or in the RV. Rolf, Sam, and Berkley had always made it a point to call him at least once a month and if he was anywhere in the area, he knew he always had a standing invitation to come stay. However, knowing that this was his home and that they had the Clan bond joining them together in addition to their friendship, made him feel even more accepted and connected. He finally had a place to nest for good, and no matter how many adventures he went on, this would always be his home.

"It's about time, you got here!" Sam shouted. "Hurry up,

Emma made dinner and it smells delicious! You'll have to tell us all your stories. Gage said he was going to try to slip away early and join us, but not to wait, so let's go!"

Merri laughed, grabbing her bag and the case of goodies that they had brought home to give out to everyone. "I think they might have missed us," she said, opening the car door.

Gawain grinned. He put the emergency brake on the car, planning on leaving the RV connected for now. Walking to the back, he grabbed his laptop and bag before taking a set of wheel chocks out. Rolf grabbed them out of his hands, setting them in place for him.

"It's good to have you home," he said, bumping his shoulder into Gawain's. "I have a lot to tell you about the museum. They got the framing in for all the rooms, the electric run, and the bathroom installed upstairs. I think you'll be happy with how it looks. Berkley, Tess, Marge, and Gage have all been over there to put additional protections on it."

"I can't wait to see it," Gawain said. "It'll be nice to be home and work on that for a while. Rob said he might send some things for it as well."

"You got a package with his return address on it while you were gone. We left it in your office. Berkley did a magical scan of it, but we didn't open it."

"Did the berries arrive for Sam?" Gawain asked, walking up the steps to the house.

"He got the package and put it in the freezer like the instructions said, but he didn't open it yet. I think he wanted to wait until you got home. He loves hearing the story that goes with treasure finds," Rolf said, good-naturedly rolling his eyes with a smile. He honestly loved that about Sam but liked to give him a hard time about it sometimes.

"I think he'll get a kick out of coming up with new recipes using them. We don't get them here, so the brewery menu could have a new specialized item. I know he's always looking for things to change it up." Gawain stopped before going inside the house where he could hear laughter and the sound of his family's voices all melding together.

"I don't know if I ever told you this, but thank you," Gawain said.

Rolf looked at him quizzically. "For what?"

"Being my friend, welcoming me into your house, making it possible for all of us to find our mates, giving me a museum to help keep me active and happy," Gawain replied. He found it amusing that he could see a faint pinkening of Rolf's face.

"I didn't do that," he protested. "Fate brought us our mates. You've been a great friend as well, coming to help when Vlad became a problem. I have this big house, it made sense to open it up for you guys if you wanted to stay. You're the perfect person for the museum, and I think it could help a lot of people," Rolf said.

"Fate did bring us our mates, but if you hadn't been who you are, we wouldn't have come to help. You're an amazing friend, and I want to say thank you. I know I'm not the easiest to deal with sometimes," Gawain replied. He knew Rolf didn't want to hear about what a great guy he was, he always downplayed it as simply being a good friend. Gawain knew that not everyone had the same patience or willingness to accept people for who they were without trying to change them a little bit. That's what made this Clan so special in his opinion; everyone had their own personalities, they all had different strengths and weaknesses, different hobbies and interests, but they came together and supported each other and loved each other for who they were. It seemed to be an increasingly hard thing to find in this world.

Rolf shook his head. "You're passionate about what you do. There's nothing wrong with that. You make a point to be there when it's important. Come on, let's go eat. Emma wouldn't let us sneak any cookies until you guys were home," Rolf said, changing the subject and urging him inside.

The rest of the family was gathered in the kitchen, the

wolfdog curled up on one of his beds chewing on a treat. There was a feast laid out on the counters, pulled beef and pulled chicken keeping warm in the slow cookers, the smell of freshly baked bread lingered in the air, and he could see a basket full of rolls, a large salad, grilled corn on the cob, cut up watermelon, and a tray of cookies. Oh, there were lemon cookies. Yum. He couldn't wait to try them.

"It looks delicious, Emma. Thank you," Gawain said, setting his laptop down.

"I'm sure you guys must be hungry, you and Merri go first," Emma said with a smile.

After everyone got their food, they sat at the large table. They had left a plate out in case Gage made it in time to eat. Gawain knew Emma would set aside a container full of food for him to take home if he didn't make it to dinner. They had been eating about ten minutes when there was a knock on the door. Ian jumped up to get it, coming back into the room with Gage.

Merri noticed that Gage's magic was strong, almost agitated at the moment. Normally she could feel it, but not this strongly unless she was at the Sheriff's office. There it seemed to have seeped into the very bricks of the building. Out of the corner of her eye, she saw Emma shiver and shrink back in her seat a little bit, Doc wrapping an arm around his mate. It hadn't been that long ago that Emma had been uncomfortable being around their local Sheriff. He was an imposing figure, extremely tall, broad shoulders, large muscles, a few scars visible on his skin, short buzz cut hair. His magic was the strongest she had ever felt, and she still wondered if that was from being a Warden or it was just his innate abilities. However, he had proved to be a caring person and a good friend.

"Sorry, Emma," Gage's deep voice rumbled when he saw her reaction.

Merri watched as Gage took a deep breath and drew his

magic back in, dampening it to his normal levels. Well, at least the normal level he let them feel.

"It's okay," Emma replied softly. "It just took me by surprise. Sit down, let me get you a plate." Merri knew it was Emma's way of apologizing. Not that she had anything to apologize for; her life hadn't been made easy by a larger, stronger man, and they all knew her story. Gage had helped them in that situation as well.

"Thank you," Gage said, sitting down in the open chair.

"How was your day?" Berkley asked. Gage had just recently started hanging out with them a little more, so the dynamics and interactions weren't quite easy yet, but they were getting there. He thought Gage needed the friendship and he was hoping the Sheriff would relax enough around them to let this connection and friendship grow. He imagined being a Warden was a lonely job, but he had a feeling that Gage was meant to be part of their group.

"It was alright. Nothing too exciting in town. One tourist said they were pickpocketed, but we found out they had dropped their wallet in the bathroom. It was turned in at the hostess stand and nothing was missing. I found some more garbage in the woods. It looked like people were camping there again but I still can't get a sense of what they are. It's starting to really tick me off. Marco's the best tracker I know and he's going to come take another look," Gage replied.

Berkley looked at Merri and Gawain. "Gage helped us finalize the concealment spell for the pendants. I think we finally have it worded so that it would conceal that we're paranormals from human hunters, but not other paranormals. We tried a few different variations, but this one seems to be spot on. Marco brought the hunter's pendant over to test it and it didn't light up, but he could still sense what we were," he said.

"Why not just word it to conceal our paranormal status from all ill intentions?" Gawain asked curiously.

"Originally that was what we were going to do, but when we heard that there might be Convocation members involved, we rethought it. For example, Barry has access to the Clan paperwork, knows who and what we all are. If we spell it to conceal our paranormal status from ill intentions, it would look incredibly suspicious if he met us in person and couldn't sense that we were paranormals. It would be a huge give-away that we had a concealment or protection spell on us and could potentially cause more harm by taking away the element of surprise from the protection spell."

"Huh, I didn't think of it that way, but that makes sense. But you figured out how to have it conceal us from human hunters?"

"Yes, and it will still provide protection against evil intentions with the original spells I had placed on them, so it will protect us against paranormals as well," Berkley said.

Gage nodded. "I'm glad we finally figured it out. This is delicious as always, Emma. Thank you."

"Tell us all about your trip. What was your favorite part?" Tess asked.

"The baby bison were so cute!" Merri said. "I really want to go back to Yellowstone and explore it some more. It has such a wide variety in its landscape. We did see a bear as we were driving, some bison, and a lot of elk." Merri pulled out her phone and opened the photos of the trip, passing it over to her sister. Sam looked over Tess's shoulder and when they were done, they passed it on.

"Oh! They are adorable!" Shaye exclaimed. "What was the favorite thing you ate?"

"The huckleberry ice cream, I think. Or the Zephyr," Merri replied. She had enjoyed trying a few new foods, but the huckleberry was nice because it was in so many different dishes.

"I know you sent a picture of the Zephyr, but what's a huckleberry?" Shaye asked.

"I hadn't heard of it either until we were in Montana. They're similar to blueberries, but they only grow in certain areas, usually mountainous areas and they only grow in the wild. We brought some huckleberry stuff home for you guys," Merri said, jumping up from the table to grab their bin of goodies to pass out.

"Sam, that was what was in the frozen package. It's a bunch of huckleberries. We thought you'd like them for the brewery. They're harvested July through September, so if you want more, Rhonda, the store owner, sent her card. Her brother has land where huckleberries grow and she harvests them each year. She does have to fight her brother for them sometimes though since they're bear shifters," Gawain said.

"I'd love to try some new recipes," Sam said excitedly.

Merri passed out their goodies. Handing a jar of jam to Gage, she smiled at the look of shock on his face.

"You didn't have to. Thank you," Gage said quietly, while cradling the jar in his hands. When was the last time someone had given him anything, Merri wondered.

"Well, you've been adopted in, so that means you get gifts too," Merri replied softly, patting him gently on the back.

They all moved into the living room, bringing cookies, tea, and coffee to sit and talk. Merri and Gawain told them about the rest of their trip, the crazy man who had chased after them, and the cleanup Marco had helped with at the campsite. Gage added in what he knew and told them Marco had been sure the man had been human, although there might have been a little paranormal in his family history. He was working on getting a description of the man who had paid him for his stories. There hadn't been any more flyers found in the area, so Rick was hoping that they had moved on, but would let Gage know if they were in the area again.

Before Doc and Emma left the room to go to bed, Gawain called out to them. "Doc, wait a minute!"

Gawain ran outside to grab the container for Doc from the

car and brought it into the living room. "We found this under an old tree stump. The stump was still well-preserved, although the rest of the tree was gone. Other than the magic protecting it, we didn't sense anything. I don't know if you want to get Berkley or someone who's a little stronger than Merri and I are in sensing spells to give it a once-over. It was wrapped up like this and as soon as we saw your mentor's name in the note, we wrapped it back up. Thalia left you one last thing," he said gently, handing it over to Doc. "We didn't look inside."

Doc held it tightly. "Thank you," he said quietly.

Berkley came over and squeezed Doc's shoulder. "It seems all clear from what I can sense. Your pendant will alert you if there's any danger, if you want to open it in your room." He figured this was a personal gift from the woman who had helped raise Doc. He would probably want to open it in private.

"I think I'll take it upstairs," Doc agreed. Emma followed after him, wrapping an arm around his waist, leaning her head against his arm.

"You don't have any idea what was in it?" Ian asked.

Merri shook her head. "It was a note from Thalia. It just mentioned she had kept collecting treasures and information for him. And that she hoped he had found his family and mate."

"Get some sleep, I'm sure you guys are exhausted. I have another surprise for you tomorrow," Rolf said with a smile.

"Can I get a clue?" Gawain asked.

Rolf laughed. "Nope. You'll see it tomorrow and then we can go check out the progress on the museum. Sleep tight," he said as he walked upstairs.

"I wonder what the surprise is?" Merri asked.

"I don't know, but the last one was a good one," Gawain said, pulling her in for a kiss.

EPILOGUE

Merri was checking the cash register and making sure the credit card machine was connecting to the internet when she heard the bell over the front door chime as it opened. Looking up, she smiled at the person that walked in.

"Hi, Marge! Welcome to our museum." They weren't officially open yet, but they had started putting some of the displays up and had sticky notes all over the walls of where things were going to go.

"Hi, it looks great. I'll take a look around in a bit. I can't wait to see it when it's finished. Do you have a minute to talk? Is everyone here? I had an idea I wanted to run by you all," Marge replied.

"Not all of us, no," Rolf answered as he came down the stairs. "We have about half here? But we can get together in a couple of hours, or do a quick conference call? Sam's at the brewery, Ian and Berkley at the store, Doc's finishing up at the clinic."

"It's not an emergency; a call would work, or you can just run my idea by them and then let me know what you all think later," Marge replied.

"Yeah, we can do that," he agreed.

Merri, Rolf, Shaye, Tess, and Marge gathered inside the store, where they could see if someone walked in.

"When Merri first started at the library, she made a comment about making my own book to appeal to paranormals. I think she suggested *Cat in the Card Catalog* for the title. Since then, it's been brewing in the back of my mind. There are not a lot of children's books written specifically for paranormal kids. I wanted to see if you guys would be interested in joining forces, so to speak," Marge said.

Tess looked around the group, confused as to what Marge was asking. "Joining forces?"

Marge laughed. "Sorry! It helps if I explain it all out loud, doesn't it? I had it all planned out in my head, but you clearly can't just know what I'm thinking. If you would like to help me write some children's books. We can stock them in the library and sell them in the museum," Marge added.

"I don't think it would have to be limited to little kids' books either," Merri said thoughtfully. "Have you read the dinosaurs have manners books? Maybe something like *No Shifting In The Stacks* to teach paranormal kids how to interact with the human world. It's getting so much harder to distance ourselves from humans, and I think the groups that have managed to stay more remote will have a hard time reintegrating since so much has changed in the world so quickly. We could make a few different versions of basically the same content for babies and toddlers, kids, teens, and adults.

"I was thinking of having something, even if it's only a list, of new inventions, technology, and history that has occurred in the last two hundred years. I had one gentleman show up at my last library that had been a hermit for the last sixty years. He had no idea about the wars that had happened, the use of computers or cell phones. I caught him trying to shift into his bear form in the back parking lot and had to stop him. I had to explain indecency laws and the fact that pretty much everyone now carried a camera in their pocket. Heck, even buildings now have cameras on them. He ended up moving back to the woods. All the changes were too overwhelming."

"I can see where that would be helpful," Marge agreed. "I made some mock-ups of the self-help and beginner pamphlets too," she added, handing over a stack of papers.

"Oh, these are wonderful," Shaye exclaimed as she looked through them. "This is just what I was talking about."

"I think we can all agree that we would love to help you make some children's books," Rolf said. "I like the idea of helping bring something into creation that one day our children might read. How cool would that be?"

NOTE FROM THE AUTHOR

Thank you for reading *Linked In History*! If you enjoyed the story, please consider leaving a review. Reviews, no matter how short, are invaluable to independent authors.

Keep reading for a sneak peek into *Hoarded Secrets*, book six of the Nightwood Clan series.

If you keep flipping through after the Sneak Peek, you'll find the list of characters.

The word *yiós*, found in Thalia's letter to Doc means 'son' in Greek.

Merri pulled on the library door, but it was still locked. That was strange. On days like this, when they were going to be working before it was officially open, they had started the tradition of eating breakfast together. Today was Merri's day to bring in goodies. Marge normally had the back door unlocked already and would be waiting in their little breakroom slash office. Balancing the cups of tea in one hand, Merri pulled out her keys and opened the heavy wood door.

"Marge? I brought tea and some muffins for breakfast. Are we still working on cataloguing the new items in the back room this morning?" Merri called out as she walked in.

The lights were still out, no sounds of movement or Marge calling back. Merri stopped, setting the drink carrier and bag of food down on the entrance table. Pulling out her phone, she dialed Marge. In the depths of the library, she could hear the phone ringing, no sign of Marge answering.

'Guys, I think I need help at the library. All the lights are off, the doors were locked when I got here, and Marge's phone is ringing somewhere inside but she's not answering,' she said over the Clan link.

'I'll be right there. Merri, are you in the front or the back?' Ian asked.

'Back door to the office,' she replied.

Seconds later, she heard a sound outside.

"Merri, it's me," Ian said through the door.

"I forgot just how fast you are," Merri said with a stressed laugh, as she opened the door. "This isn't like Marge, and I have a bad feeling."

"Never hesitate to call us if something feels wrong. Berkley was going to get Gage to meet us. Let's stay put until they get here. Rolf and Gawain were at the museum, they're on the way too."

'Merri, Emma, Shaye, Doc, and I are at the clinic. We're in with patients right now, but if you need us, we can ask Sherri to reschedule the non-emergency appointments for today,' Tess offered.

'Ian's here and Rolf and Gawain are on their way. Berkley went to get Gage, so I should have enough people here. It's eerie, something is off. Stay with your patients. If anything changes, I'll let you know,' Merri replied.

The door flew open, and Gawain rushed inside.

"Are you okay?" he asked worriedly.

Merri nodded, walking into her mate's arms for a hug. Gage followed him inside, squeezing around them.

"Okay, tell me what's going on. Berkley just told me to get down here. He was locking up the store and will be right down, Rolf's standing outside guarding the door," Gage said, his hand on his gun belt.

"This sounds silly," Merri replied. "When I got here, the doors were locked. I know it's before opening, but we were going to catalogue some new items in the back room before we officially opened. We eat breakfast together on early days and she normally is waiting in here with the door unlocked. I walked in, called out for Marge, and didn't get a response. All the lights were off. I called her phone; I can hear it ringing in the library but there's no answer."

"I got here soon after she called out over the Clan link," Ian added. "I don't sense anyone else in here, and Marge's cat is hard to miss. I do smell something though," he said, looking pointedly at Gage, whose eyes widened slightly when he realized that Ian meant he could smell blood.

The door opened again, and Berkley walked in with Rolf. "What's—" he started. He stopped and immediately started a protection spell.

"What is it?" Rolf asked. He knew that look on Berkley's face, and it wasn't good.

"There was magic thrown around here recently. Not good magic. Everyone stay close to Gage or me until we make sure it's safe. Merri, can you flip on the lights?" Berkley asked.

Gage moved with Merri toward the master light switch panel. Opening the door to the main room, she flipped the lights on and gasped. The library was trashed. There were books on the floor, the lamp on the help desk hanging by its cord, the shade shattered. Merri rushed to the desk, but Gage grabbed her before she got there.

"Just a minute, Merri. Let me go first," he said gently.

She waited, trying to peer over the desk to see what he was looking at.

"Ian, can you come here?" Gage asked.

Merri watched as Ian walked around to the backside of the desk, then seemed to follow a trail. He walked all the way to the paranormal room's door. He jiggled the handle, but it was locked. Pressing an ear to the door, he came back to the desk and shook his head.

"I don't think anyone is in there," he said.

"What did you find?" Merri questioned. "What happened?"

Gage motioned for her to come around. The computer screen was cracked, blood drying on the desk. She saw a few drops on the ground leading away from the door. That must have been what Ian was following.

"Whose is that?" Merri asked, desperately hoping that it wasn't Marge's.

"It smells like Marge and someone else," Ian said quietly. "I don't recognize the other scent."

"There's something here that's familiar," Gage said, his nostrils flaring as he took a deep breath. "I'm going to need to call Marco in. He's a better tracker than I am."

Merri looked around, hoping to find any sign of Marge. Maybe she was hiding, Merri thought desperately. Her eyes caught on something glittering under the desk. Dropping to her knees, she crawled under the desk to get the object barely visible underneath the drawers. All her hope vanished, her heart dropping and a sob escaping as she saw Marge's keys. She never would have left them here unprotected.

'Merri? What happened?' Shaye asked. *'Are you hurt?'*

Merri shook her head, knowing Shaye couldn't see her. She opened the Clan link once more, even though half of them were here, it would be easier to tell the rest of them at once.

'Marge is gone. She's been taken.'

Merri's Family Tree

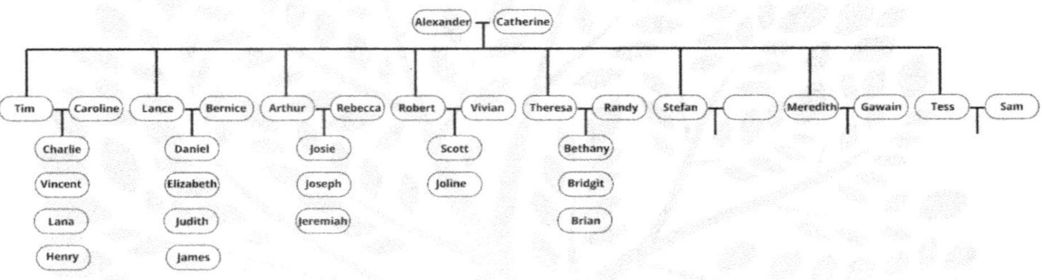

NIGHTWOOD CLAN

LOCATION

The series is mainly set in Rockfort, Tennessee, a fictional town next to the Great Smoky Mountains National Park.

CHARACTERS

Rolfston
Species: Vampire
Mate: Shaye
Job: Investments, day trading, Clan leader
Special Abilities: Telepathy, shielding
Book: Bite Me Again

Shaye
Species: Human/Vampire
Mate: Rolf
Job: Nurse
Special Abilities: Healing
Book: Bite Me Again

Sam

Species: Werewolf
Mate: Tess
Job: Brewer/Chef/Owner, Black Wolf Brewery
Rolf's friend
Book: A Hairy Situation

Tess

Species: Witch
Mate: Sam
Job: Medical coder, nurse
Shaye's friend
Book: A Hairy Situation

Emma (Emmaline)

Species: Vampire
Mate: Doc (Albert)
Job: Landowner/small farm
Special Abilities: Visions/Premonitions
Rolfston's mother
Book: Pointed Love

Doc (Dr. T, Albert)

Species: Alicorn
Mate: Emma
Job: Doctor
Special Abilities: Some healing, visions, magic,
*   immortality*
Book: Pointed Love

Ian
Species: Vampire
Mate: Berkley
Job: Leathersmith, Blacksmith
Special Abilities: Speed
Shaye's friend
Book: Forged In Love

Berkley
Species: Fae
Mate: Ian
Job: Owner/Potter, The Winged Potter
*Special Abilities: Can sense auras and species, slight
    healing ability, senses magic/spells*
Rolf's friend
Book: Forged In Love

Gawain
Species: Falcon shifter
Mate: Merri
Job: Historian/archeologist
Rolf's friend
Book: Linked in History

Merri (Meredith)
Species: Witch
Mate: Gawain
Job: Librarian
Tess's sister
Book: Linked in History

Vlad (Vladimir)

Species: Vampire

Evil father of Rolfston

Note: Appeared in Bite Me Again. *Vlad had been attempting to gain supporters to take over the paranormal world. When Rolf wouldn't join him, he tried to kill him.*

Sheriff (Gage)

Species: Unknown

Mate: none (yet)

Job: Sheriff of Rockfort, Warden

Special Abilities: Very strong magic

Duncan

Species: Dragon

Note: Vlad killed his sister. Assisted in battle in Bite Me Again.

Sherri

Species: Human

Job: Receptionist at Doc's clinic

Marge

Species: Cat shifter, black jaguar

Job: Librarian in Rockfort

Marco

Species: Unknown

Job: Hunter for Wardens

Note: Warden friend of Gage. Helps the Clan in A Hairy Situation, Forged In Love, Linked In History.

Beth
Species: Human
Mate: Josh (witch)
Job: Florist/Owner, Rockfort Blooms

Mary
Species: Human
Mate: Bill
Job: Bakery owner

Bill
Species: Human
Mate: Mary
Job: Bakery owner

Samantha
Species: Brownie
Job: Caretaker for Emma's farm in England, weaves and quilts blankets. Mentioned in Pointed Love

Douglas
Species: Gnome
Job: Ferrier, Sculptor, helps on Emma's farm. Mentioned in Pointed Love

Thalia
Species: Unicorn
Job: Healer
Note: Doc's mentor growing up, deceased. Mentioned in Pointed Love.

Jacob

Species: Human
Mate: Terrance (bear)
Job: Farmhand
Note: Emma's friend, deceased. Mentioned in Pointed Love. *Nickname Hennie Pie.*

Ter (Terrance)

Species: Bear shifter
Mate: Jacob
Note: Deceased. Mate to Emma's friend Jacob (mated in afterlife). Mentioned in Pointed Love.

Charlotte

Species: Human/Vampire
Job: Farmer
Note: Ian's mom. Mentioned in Forged In Love.

James

Species: Human/Vampire
Job: Farmer, Blacksmith
Note: Ian's dad, Mentioned in Forged In Love.

Robert

Species: Vampire
Mate: Aggie (Ian's aunt)
Job: Lord (in England)
Special Abilities: Speed
Note: Ian's uncle in-law. Mentioned in Forged In Love.

Agnes (Aggie)
Species: Human/Vampire
Mate: Robert
Job: Artist (painter)
Note: Ian's aunt. Mentioned in Forged In Love.

MINOR CHARACTERS

George
Species: Vampire
Mate: Matthew
Note: Robert's brother. Robert is Ian's uncle.
Book: Mentioned in Forged in Love.

Matthew
Species: Vampire
Mate: George
Book: Mentioned in Forged in Love.

Clara
Species: Vampire
Mate: n/a
Job: Currently a Broadway actor
Book: Mentioned in Forged In Love. *Ian's cousin.*

George
Species: Human
Book: Mentioned in A Hairy Situation, *Sam's produce supplier.*

Graeme
Species: Human
Job: Blacksmith
Book: Mentioned in Forged In Love, *showed Ian around his workshop, discussed ideas for Ian's own forge.*

Bert
Species: Human
Book: Mentioned in Forged In Love, *part of the hunter group that shot Ian.*

Carly
Species: Human
Book: Mentioned in Forged In Love, *young nosy cashier in Ian's parents' town.*

Dan
Species: Vampire
Book: Mentioned in Bite Me Again, A Hairy Situation, *Vlad minion. Attacked Sam/Tess.*

Roger
Species: Vampire
Book: Mentioned in Bite Me Again, A Hairy Situation, *Vlad minion. Attacked Sam/Tess. Delivered poisoned blood to clinic/Rolf in* Bite Me Again.

Tim
Species: Human
Book: Mentioned in Pointed Love. *Wood carver at winter market. Shelly (wife), Natalie (daughter, just had baby girl), 2 sons.*

Rob

Species: Unknown/Paranormal

Book: Mentioned in Linked In History. *Archeologist, friend of Gawain.*

Daryl

Species: Jackalope

Book: Mentioned in Linked In History. *Rob's dig was on his land.*

Barry

Species: Vampire

Book: Mentioned in Linked In History. *Convocation member.*

Randy

Species: Alligator

Book: Mentioned in Linked In History. *Archeologist.*

Rick

Species: Human

Book: Mentioned in Linked In History. *Sheriff near Yellowstone, friend of Gage. Human but has paranormals in his family.*

Rhonda

Species: Bear shifter

Book: Mentioned in Linked In History. *Shopkeeper in town.*

Angie

Species: Human

Book: Mentioned in Linked In History. *Hotel front desk.*

ABOUT THE AUTHOR

I have loved reading since I was a child. I also enjoy baking, photography, and seeing new things. My favorite books are romances with a happily ever after. The world is a crazy place; sometimes escaping into a great book is the only way I can truly relax. Happily ever after is my favorite type of book, so my stories will end with a HEA, even if the road is a little bumpy getting there. I currently reside in the Midwest with my family.

If you sign up for my newsletter, you will get a free short story! *Christmas with the Nightwood Clan* is a glimpse into the group's first Christmas together and takes place during the Christmas in *A Hairy Situation*.

www.HarperDakota.com
www.HarperDakota.com/newsletter
Harper Dakota's Readers Group

facebook.com/authorharperdakota
instagram.com/harperdakotaauthor